D1383666

She

Waits

Thanks For Reading!

Kate Sweeney

By
Kate Sweeney

SHE WAITS
© 2006 BY KATE SWEENEY

All rights reserved. No part of this book may be reproduced in printed or electronic form without permission. Please do not participate or encourage piracy of copyrighted materials in violation of the author's rights. Purchase only authorized editions.

ISBN 10: 1-933113-40-5
ISBN 13: 978-1-933113-40-1

This is a work of fiction. Names, characters, places, and incidents are the product of the author's imagination or are used fictitiously, and any resemblance to actual persons, living or dead, businesses, companies, events, or locales is entirely coincidental.

CREDITS

EXECUTIVE EDITOR: REESE SZYMANSKI
COVER DESIGN BY SHERI (GRAPHICARTIST2020@HOTMAIL.COM)

Published by
Intaglio Publications
P O Box 794
Walker, LA 70785

Visit us on the web: www.intagliopub.com

Dedication

To my mother—from her paperbacks in the attic
to the adventures in our minds—Thanks, Mom.

Acknowledgements

Many thanks to my editor, Reese Szymanski, who made me believe I could write without an over abundance of adverbs.

To my family who believed from the beginning, and Tracey—my beta, who never seemed to tire of my typos.

Finally, to Kat who took the chance, and Den, whose one e-mail, started this and made all the difference.

CHAPTER ONE

I *swear she came out of nowhere.*
I was up early that morning, on my way to Galena, Illinois for the weekend. Throwing myself together, not an easy task, I added a single lesbian's best companion, my dog Chance. She jumped into her side of the Jeep. Yes, it's *her* side. I'm waiting for the day she'll strap on her own seatbelt.

I was on my way to meet my sister for a long-deserved peaceful weekend. I should have stayed home and done laundry.

A couple of dear friends, Jan and Barb, had told me about this quaint town, just outside Galena. Apparently, a friend who lives there was having a little trouble. They had been visiting this friend last month, and some strange things happened while they were there. Nothing they could put their finger on, but something was wrong with their friend and, naturally, they were worried. Even more so when their friend decided not to go to the police.

With my curiosity piqued, I suggested they call this girl and, if she agreed, I'd take a detour and meet with her on my way to Galena. Of course, the woman declined my help and who could blame her? She didn't know me at all. Apparently, this woman's aunt had voiced her opinion to Jan and Barb stating she thought it was indeed a good idea that someone try to help. Evidently, that opinion was not shared by her niece.

My P.I. instinct reared its forgotten head and got the better of me though, so I decided to drive through anyway. I thought again of my father, who had been a Chicago cop. I'd learned a great deal from him. He used to discuss his cases with my sister Teri and me.

Because he was a homicide detective, the cases were murder, which my poor mother found gruesome. He would lay out all the evidence before me and I would watch in awe as he dissected every bit of information. I would throw my two cents in and together we figured out who done it. He told me I had a knack for figuring out puzzles, while I was just happy to be doing something with my father.

It was because of him that I became a private investigator. Thinking of my father brought me to Bob Whittier and I wondered how he was doing. I hadn't seen him in more than a year. My mind wandered back to when he agreed to my wild idea of starting our P.I. business.

"I'll do all the legwork. We'll even put your name first!" I offered. "Whittier and Ryan."

It obviously wasn't a good incentive. Bob was still not convinced. So a few days later, I was surprised to see him on my doorstep.

"I hate retirement. While I was sitting around, I could hear my arteries harden. I need to get back into it, Kate. I suppose being Dan Ryan's partner for nearly fifteen years wasn't enough. Now, I gotta be partnered with his kid. Who's gonna look after you if I don't? Okay, you win."

"Yes!" I screamed and almost jumped into his arms.

"Let me go, you Amazon. God, you're strong. You will *do all the legwork, young lady."*

Whittier and Ryan Private Investigations lasted for nine years. It's been almost four years since we gave up the business. I ran my fingers over the scar on the back of my neck. I shivered thinking about how Bob and I almost lost our lives.

Yes, Bob and I decided to limp away with whatever body parts we still had intact. We both thought it was a wise decision. Now, I'm back to my first love, photography. It's a nice quiet existence and I'm glad to say taking photos of nature hasn't killed me...yet. I'll leave that to my editor.

I shook myself back to reality and realized I was coming up to the small town nestled comfortably in the middle of the woods. If you blinked, you could have easily missed it. It actually reminded me of the old movie *Brigadoon*, the small village lost in the mist of time.

Smiling to myself, I noticed a sign that read *Cedar Lake, pop 1300*. As I headed into town, it appeared to be mainstream Americana: Everyday people going about their everyday lives.

I would find out much later that nothing could be further from the truth.

It was like something out of a Norman Rockwell painting. Beautiful maple trees lined the streets. The colors were magnificent and the golden leaves fell as the breeze gently shook them from the branches. It was a cool, crisp sunny morning. When I opened my window, the aroma of burning leaves instantly took me back to my childhood, when in autumn that wonderful earthy scent flooded everyone's senses.

God was in His heaven and all was right with the world, until I hit the young woman on the horse. Well, I didn't really hit her. I almost hit her. Actually, I almost hit the horse, or the horse almost ran into my car. I'm still not quite sure. I only know I almost soiled myself.

I had seen her from the corner of my eye, from out of nowhere came this black blur galloping as if she was hell bent on some maniacal steeplechase. At the last minute, I swerved to avoid them. The car skidded as I slammed on the brakes. A maple tree caught my bumper nicely, stopping me from continuing into the peaceful woods.

All at once, I was engulfed in a sea of marshmallow when the air bag slowly deflated. I looked over at poor Chance. She was sprawled on the car floor looking up at me. She quickly jumped back up and barked.

I examined her for injuries. "Hey don't blame me. I told you to put your seatbelt on," I said, as I quickly untangled myself.

The rider was lying still on the side of the road and for a horrifying moment I thought, *Crap, I killed her*. I ran over to her, begging the gods for help. I knelt down beside her and gingerly turned her over, looking for signs of life. The saddle was off the horse and lying in a heap on her left ankle.

She looked young, no more than twenty-two or -three. *Great, I've killed a child.*

I checked her pulse. I checked to see if any bones were broken. I checked for bleeding. I didn't know what else to check. While I was thinking, damn, I *did* kill her I looked down to see that her eyes were wide open and staring at me. I jumped back like a scalded hound. She scared the life out of me.

"Are you all right?" I asked.

She struggled to her feet, waving off my attempts to help. "Am I all right?"

I tried to help her—what a stupid thing to do. She almost knocked me over getting to her horse. She spoke in soothing, sweet low tones to the snorting beast.

After making sure her horse was uninjured, she limped back to me. "Christ, are you crazy?" she bellowed.

I took a step backward. She looked scary, with leaves in her disheveled chestnut hair and her blue eyes glaring. *My, she is short.*

"Well I…"

"What in the hell were you doing?" she interrupted. Her look demanded an answer.

"Well, you—"

"Christ, you could have killed somebody."

"Yes, I realize that." I was trying to get a word in edgewise while backing away.

"Christ, you imbecile!"

That did it. Nobody calls me an imbecile, except my editor. I tried to remain calm. "Look Miss, if you'd let me get a word in, I'd like to apologize."

"Well?" she demanded quickly.

My Irish blood was boiling now. "Well, I apologize. I did not see you galloping as if the hounds of hell were nipping at your heels. I'm sorry I knocked you off your horse, but you don't seem any worse for wear and there is no need to be insulting. Now, why don't you take my card so you can send any doctor bills to me? After that, it seems we have two choices here. Climb up on Ole Dobbin there and chase the hounds back to hell or allow me to give you a lift wherever you like."

Surprising myself that I got that out in one breath, I gave her a challenging look.

She glared at me and I noticed her hands were trembling. Fine. Now, I felt a little sorry for the poor kid.

"Look—" I started, but she interrupted me.

"No, you're right, I'm sorry. I was riding a little fast and not watching where I was going, either."

What a backhanded apology that was. You know, when she wasn't glaring at me, I noticed she had a pleasant-looking face. She was a petite young girl, only five-foot four.

Then I glanced at my car, saw the small dent in the front end and felt a pang of guilt. Chance was poised, awaiting my okay to jump out the window, like that was going to happen. I turned to see the horse, a very big black horse, snorting and staring at me with such wild eyes he looked like Seabiscuit on mescaline.

I was about to say something, when off in the distance, I heard a woman yelling. I looked up and saw an older woman driving our way in, of all things, a golf cart. I was stunned and looked around in all directions. Where the hell did she come from?

Her chariot of death was heading right at us. Like a deer caught in the headlights, I knew she was going to hit me but I froze. As I watched my life pass before me, our gazes locked in horror. She couldn't stop and I couldn't move. I heard the young girl yelling and, at the last minute, I leapt out of the way. The demented cart came to a screeching halt inches from my foot. For one second, we were all silent.

As the woman got out, the cart gave one last gasp of life as it lurched, then died quietly.

"Good heavens, that was close! I still haven't got the hang of this ridiculous contraption." The woman laughed maniacally as she struggled from the cart. Then she looked at the young woman. "Margaret, are you all right?"

They knew each other. That figured.

"And who the devil are you? Do I know you?" she inquired, looking perplexed.

"Well, I..." It was all I could say. I was staring at the golf cart, waiting for it to come back to life like something out of a Stephen King novel.

"Aunt Hannah, I'm fine. I sort of fell off my horse," the woman who was apparently Margaret said.

"Nonsense, you haven't fallen off a horse since you were six years old. What the devil happened, and why are you riding that insane horse after what it did to Bedford?"

I raised my eyebrows, wondering. I leaned over to Aunt Hannah. "What did it do to Bedford?"

"Oh, good gracious, don't you remember last year?"

I saw realization slowly cross her face.

"Young woman, who are you?"

"Unfortunately, I believe I'm responsible for your niece's present condition. See, I was driving and your niece bolted out of nowhere and I—" was interrupted. Again.

"You mean you hit my niece?"

"Well, no. See, I…" I stopped, scratched my head and gave up. "Yes ma'am, I did. I hit her and I'm sorry." I admitted this obediently and raised my hands in defeat.

"Nonsense, you seem far too nice and look far too pretty to be knocking people off horses. Besides, I know how headstrong my niece can be."

She smiled and winked at me and I instantly liked her.

Hannah was about 5' 6" with silver hair and looked like everybody's favorite aunt. She reminded me of the old actress, Mildred Natwick, one of the *Snoop Sisters* from that old TV show. I am horrible at remembering faces so, being an old movie buff, I associate them with a star of the silver screen. Her dress was impeccable, as was her demeanor. She was refined, but not too proper. I liked this woman, chariot-of-death and all.

"Excuse me, but in case anyone is interested, I was knocked off my horse!" Margaret yelled, waving her hands.

"Margaret, you know full well that you were not supposed to be riding that creature at all! And just what were you doing on the main road?"

Inching ever so slightly toward my new friend, the Hollywood icon, I leaned against my car and waited, patiently if not smugly for an answer.

She glared at me then turned to her aunt. "Let's talk about this later. I just want to get home."

I felt a little tension in the air as I watched both women. "Pardon me, I was telling your niece that I would be glad to give her a ride home if needed. I was also going to give her my card in case there were any doctor's bills. I think that would be only right."

I was trying to keep the situation formal, not wanting to get into another caustic conversation with this young woman. I cursed my curiosity and wanted to get on my way.

"Thank you. That's fine with me," Margaret said indifferently.

"Margaret, when I saw that wretched animal gone from the stable, I immediately called Bedford. He's coming with the trailer to take that beast back to the stable and have it shot." She stopped and let out a small laugh. Margaret was not amused which for some odd reason, amused me. "I'm sorry, dear, that was a bad joke. Besides, I do not think that animal will fit in the cart. Now, Miss... Oh, good heavens, I don't know your name, dear."

"Ryan, Kate Ryan." I held out my hand and she shook it, giving me a curious look.

"Ryan? Hmm, well, Miss Ryan, my name is Hannah Winfield and this ungracious young woman is my niece, Margaret Winfield."

I searched the younger Miss Winfield's face. The name seemed familiar somehow. I stuck out my hand. "Margaret Winfield, it's a pleasure," I offered as I gazed down into the blue eyes.

"Miss Ryan, delighted," she said, oozing sarcasm as she took my hand.

I took her small hand in mine and it dawned on me who she was. Jan and Barb had been telling me about this girl. I remembered our conversation distinctly now: "We have a friend we think might be able to use your help, the way you helped Jan last year. She lives in a small town near Galena. Her name is Maggie Winfield..."

Crap...

CHAPTER TWO

I was dumbfounded. What were the odds of meeting her like this?

Hannah broke my thoughts. "Well now, what say we get off the road before we're all run over? How about we take my cart?"

She was serious. She frightened me. "How about we leave the Hannahmobile here and take my car?" I offered hopefully.

We all looked at my car, nestled against the maple tree. I turned to my companions. Hannah grinned evilly.

"The Hannahmobile?" she offered. "I'll let you drive." *Yeah, that was a big incentive.*

As soon as we got into the cart, my daffy dog immediately attacked Hannah's face, slobbering all over her. Hannah laughed and ruffled her ears. Margaret climbed in the back and my fickle canine immediately found her new best friend and laid her head on Margaret's lap. What a colossal traitor.

As I was about to pull away, a truck with a trailer pulled up and an elderly gentleman got out.

Hannah leaned across me, and screeched right in my ear, "Bedford! Bedford, for heaven's sakes!" She looked to me. "It's Bedford, and he's a little hard of hearing." Again, she shrieked, "Bedford, over here!"

"It's Bedford," I said simply to Chance.

I glanced at Margaret. I almost saw a smile.

Bedford made his way over to my side of the car with a terrible limp, and, for some absurd reason, the face of Dracula's insect-eating ghoul, Renfield, flashed through my mind. I tiredly rubbed the back of my neck. I glanced at my watch—much too early for a cocktail.

Bedford leaned so far into the cart that I thought that he was going to climb right in with us. "Good morning, Miss Winfield," he said.

"Good morning, Bedford," came simultaneous replies.

Hannah leaned past me and looked out at Bedford. "Bedford, take the creature back to the stables. Under no circumstance is anyone to ride that beast." She turned and looked at her niece. "And I mean anyone."

I glanced back, Miss Winfield said nothing.

"Yes, ma'am." Bedford went to the horse.

The minute the horse saw him, he snorted and stamped, so it took Bedford several minutes to get him into the trailer. I had no idea how the diminutive Miss Winfield managed to stay on that horse.

"Well now, let's be off," Hannah ordered.

I started the cart and promptly received different directions from each woman.

Hannah was chattering away with her niece as we pulled onto another tree-lined road, which took us deeper into the woods. I was suddenly aware of an anxious feeling sweeping through me. You know that feeling of anticipation one has when starting an adventurous vacation? I could feel my heartbeat quicken as I glanced around the quiet woods. No, this anxious feeling in my gut was not the thrill of an adventure. When the sprawling estate burst into the view, I shivered quickly and found myself glancing nervously around the quiet woods. I glanced at Hannah Winfield. Why did these two women suddenly become quiet?

Hidden back in the woods was a sprawling two-story Georgian brick with an enormous greenhouse attached on the left, and a very large garage on the right, complete with what looked like a small apartment over it.

Radiant burnt-orange ivy covered the front of the house and I could only imagine how many rooms there were. A path led from the house to a stable back on the left about thirty yards away, and then off into the woods.

I pulled up the circular drive and stopped at the front door. When I got out, Chance also jumped out and began running around in circles as if for dear life.

"Don't worry, let her run, poor thing," Hannah said.

I turned to Margaret and saw her struggling to get out of the back of the cart. I went and offered my hand without saying a word. She looked up, said nothing, and took my hand. She started to walk, but couldn't.

Hannah screeched for Bedford again. Like nails on a blackboard, it went right through me.

"Oy," I mumbled as my eyes crossed. I had such a headache.

By her reaction, I could tell Miss Winfield felt the same. "Christ, it's too early in the morning for this. Aunt Hannah, please, I don't need Bedford. I can get in the house fine."

"You say Christ far too much for my liking, young lady. Why in the world do you use that word so much?" Hannah asked.

"I was wondering the same thing myself." I couldn't help myself as I felt the blue eyes glaring.

"Can we just get into the house?" Margaret asked vehemently, slowly limping toward the front door.

"Oh, all right, but once we get inside I'm calling Doc Jenkins," Hannah said.

Once inside, I felt very much at home, but still the anxious feeling nagged. Dark oak gave the foyer a warm, cozy feeling. What you first noticed was the large staircase as you enter the foyer. To the left was what I assumed was a library, or perhaps a den, and to the right, a living room.

So, being totally female, or more correctly, just plain nosy, I craned my neck to see into the living room, wondering what lay beyond. "Which way do we go, Miss Winfield?"

"Let's go into the living room, to the right," she said. She sounded exhausted.

I helped her to the couch and propped her foot up on a pillow. I didn't take her boot off because I remembered a bit of first aid: Never, ever, remove a shoe if you sprain an ankle, because it will blow up like a huge blowfish. I'd just let the doctor do that when he got there so I could blame him.

Hannah appeared wheeling in a small teacart. "Miss Ryan—may I call you Kate?"

"Please, we've been through far too much in one morning to be formal," I said.

"Good, then I shall call you Kate, and you can call me Hannah, or Aunt Hannah if you prefer." She seemed so excited. I could tell she loved having people around. She looked at her niece. "Now, what about you, dear?"

"I would prefer not to be called Aunt Hannah or Kate if you don't mind."

I chuckled at that one. Hannah wasn't that amused, or at least she didn't show it.

"Don't be sarcastic, you know what I mean. Do you want Kate to call you Maggie or Margaret or just plain stubborn?"

"I opt for just plain stubborn," I said.

"Whatever."

"Oh, for heaven's sake." Hannah looked at me and rolled her eyes. "Call her Maggie." She went to Maggie and kissed her on the forehead. "Don't worry, dear, all will work out. I'll call Doc right away."

I sat down in an unbelievably comfortable chair across from Maggie. I took a cup from the tray. "Would you like coffee or tea?" I asked.

"Tea, plain, would be perfect," she said.

As I poured her tea, Hannah announced that the doctor would arrive any minute.

"Aunt Hannah, I'm all right. I'm just tired," Maggie admitted, sounding every bit of it.

"Nonsense, I'll not have my niece splattered all over the road and not have her properly looked after," she said and then saw my horrified look. "No offense Kate."

Maggie offered a smug grin. "You want to see Doc, that's all."

"Why you little... I never heard such drivel! You ought to be ashamed of yourself," Hannah blustered and stalked back toward what I presumed was the kitchen.

We sat drinking our tea in relative silence until Maggie said, "So, what brings you to our little hamlet, besides the urge to knock people off their horses?"

I decided to ignore her accusation. "I heard about your town from a friend of mine. She said she'd driven through a few months ago and said it was quite picturesque. I thought I could get a few good shots this time of year. So, here I am." It was *almost* the whole truth, but I still felt uncomfortable lying to her.

"So, I gather you're some kind of amateur picture taker," she said.

"Amateur? I'll have you know that in my circle, I am much respected."

"Pretty small circle?"

"Small circle?" I replied, feeling like parrot. "Look, do you know how close I came to winning the…" I looked away and shook my head. "Why am I explaining myself to you?"

Hannah came out of the kitchen and poured herself a cup of tea. "I can hear you all the way in the kitchen, what's going on?"

"Aunt Hannah, did you know we were in the company of a great photographer?" Maggie asked.

I looked up at the ceiling, and counted to ten.

"I thought I recognized you! Margaret, dear, this is the photographer I told you about last month," she said, looking at me. "Her photos have been all over. I understand they're in great demand by wildlife and conservation journals across the Midwest. Didn't your photos of that beautiful bird help the conservationists in Wisconsin? I thought I read about that somewhere."

My mouth dropped open. I had no idea anyone would remember that—it was three years ago.

Hannah looked at her niece, who looked as dumbfounded as I. "Yes sweetie, she's *that* Kate Ryan. Now close your mouth and apologize." She turned, took her teacart, and just like that she was gone, again.

We both stared at the door like a couple of idiots then laughed. I offered my hand to Maggie. "Pax?"

She looked surprised. "Pax," she finally agreed, shaking my hand.

I was slightly impressed she knew the Latin term for peace. It's not that unheard of, but I was impressed nonetheless. "I didn't think someone your age would know Latin."

"*My* age?"

The doorbell rang and, like a bat out of hell, Hannah flew out of the kitchen to answer it. For a second I thought she was wearing roller skates.

I couldn't quite make out what was said at the door, but Hannah quickly ushered in a handsome elderly gentleman—and I do mean *gentleman.*

His hair is what struck me first. It was thick, wavy and snow white. He was at least 6'2" with steely blue eyes and an Errol

Flynn-type mustache. He looked at Maggie, then me, then back at Maggie.

"Well young lady, what is it this time?" he asked gruffly.

"She knocked me off my horse," Maggie said, accusingly.

I stood there gaping, not saying a word.

"Really? I heard you were on Thunder," he said then turned to Hannah and me. "Would you two excuse me? I have to examine the patient."

As we walked to the kitchen, I heard Maggie say to the old doctor, "I'm fine, Doc, nothing broken. A mild sprain I'm sure…"

The kitchen was enormous, light and airy with counter space everywhere. An island in the middle was surrounded by four barstools. We sat at a breakfast area in the far corner, in front of a huge picture window that had a lovely view of the surrounding woods.

"I am sorry about all this, Hannah. I feel very responsible," I said.

"Nonsense, you've done nothing. Margaret should never have been on Thunder. He's got a wild streak in him. You were just in the wrong place at the wrong time."

"If I'd been going a little faster, or if your niece was riding a little faster, which is hard to imagine, she could have been seriously hurt. But I have to wonder why she was riding that wild horse so fast, especially on a main road." I stopped and gave Hannah an apologetic look. "I'm sorry, I ask too many questions. Comes from my father, the detective."

She watched me for a long moment then looked out the window. "Do you know that I've lived here my whole life? Nothing stays the same, you know. Everything changes, and not always for the better." She looked directly at me. "Not always for the better."

A shiver ran up my spine at her uneasy tone. I really should have stayed home and done the laundry.

Hannah smiled as we sat at the kitchen table. "I can tell you're intrigued, but I hope it's not a story, or photos, for your magazine that you're after. Kate, my dear, you have an honest face, and I like you."

I felt guilty. I had to tell them I knew more about them than I was letting on. "Hannah, before you go on, I have to tell you. I know two of Maggie's friends. They spoke with me a while ago and told me about Maggie. This morning, when this happened, I swear I had no idea who you were. Then, when it dawned on me, I—"

"Kate, you don't need to explain. I remember talking to those nice girls as well. They told me of a friend of theirs who might help. It's you?"

"Yes, but—"

She put her hand on mine. "I'm going to tell you a little story. I believe I can trust you. It will feel good to tell someone. Where should I start? Six months ago, Maggie's father, my brother, Jonathan Winfield, was killed in a hit-and-run accident in Chicago."

"Hit-and-run? Did they ever find the guy?" I asked.

"No. The driver was never found," Hannah replied, sadly.

"I'm sorry for interrupting."

"That's all right, dear. Now, about two months ago, certain curious things began happening. I suppose I should let Margaret tell you about them. To be honest, I think she needs someone to talk to. Someone objective, like you. She's been so cut off from everyone of late. You're actually the first outsider to come into this house in several months. Maggie's barely gone to visit friends even." She Hannah seemed agitated, looking away from me before saying, "Well, there is Allison, but who actually wants her around anyway?"

I was curious about this last comment especially. However, I said nothing as she continued.

"I worry about her. She needs to join the human race again and see people other than family. Although lately family seems to be all we have. You see our family all live relatively close. My other brother, Nathan, and his wife, Sarah, live about a quarter mile west. This estate is somewhat of a compound, so to speak. I probably shouldn't bother you with our family details, but it does feel good to talk to someone detached from this," she finished with a tired smile.

"Well, I don't want to pry or intrude, but I've been told I lend a pretty good ear. So, I don't mind if you don't," I said. I watched her suddenly weary face as she looked out the window and found myself wanting to comfort her. However, not knowing her at all, I felt like I was trespassing.

"You can ask me anything you like Kate, anything at all."

"Where is Maggie's mother?"

"She died twenty years ago when Margaret was a young girl."

"That's terrible. How did she die?" I asked. Hannah searched my face as I waited.

"Miranda was like a sister to me. I loved her the minute Jonathan brought her home. Everybody did. Miranda was a sweet, wonderful woman who always seemed to be laughing. She was smart, attractive and loved her family. She married someone she thought she loved. *She* was in love, but Jonathan didn't know how to love her back. However, Miranda had a weak side where Jonathan was concerned. He bullied her sometimes. I don't know why. She took it and I don't know why. Then, again, Jonathan was like our father."

I waited for her to continue and when she didn't I felt uneasy. "Uh, was that a bad thing?"

Hannah let out a small snort. "Well, it wasn't good. You see my father Alexander Winfield loved money and loved power, but had no clue how to love people. He was rarely at home, and Jonathan unfortunately, was the same. They were like mirror images. Jonathan started working harder and being at home less. He would spend weeks at a time away on business and come home only long enough to see that all was fine before he was gone again."

"That had to be as hard on Miranda with her husband, as it must have been for you and your father." I was still wondering why she avoided my question of Miranda's death.

"It was. It's no secret my father had a wandering eye, which Mother was tempted, I'm sure, to remove on more than one occasion."

We both laughed as she continued. "Miranda and I spent so much time together in those days that we became like sisters. I made sure she was not alone. We spent a lot of time with Nathan and Sarah. Still, I knew she missed Jon. When she found out she was pregnant, I thought that would bring them closer and bring Jon home more. In fact, after Margaret was born, everything seemed fine for a whole year, but then he went back to his old ways. I remember at a dinner party, even Nathan got angry at Jon, and Nathan rarely got angry at anyone." When she smiled this time, I could see how much she loved her younger brother. "Nathan is a very affable fellow. He's so different from Father and Jonathan; he's more like mother and me. But he's married to a hard woman. Sarah can be tough as nails." I could hear the sadness in her voice.

"I'm sorry, my dear. I didn't mean to go on so. You caught us all at a bad time. Would you like another cup of tea?"

"No, thank you. Please go on."

She got up and poured herself another cup of tea. "Our parents had a great deal of money. My father had a knack for buying up companies and selling them at a great profit. He made millions because he was rather ruthless at it all. When he died, Jonathan fully took over the business he'd been helping Father run for so many years. Jonathan was just as ruthless as Father, and, just like Father, Jonathan knew business, but didn't know people.

"Nathan on the other hand knew a great deal about people, but very little about business. Becoming a doctor was something he always wanted. He and Walt went to the University of Chicago together. Walt was a brilliant student—"

"Sorry, who's Walt?" I asked, feeling the conversation getting away from me.

"Dr. Walt Jenkins. He's the handsome man out there examining my stubborn niece. He's known around town as Doc, but I call him Walt," she said and I heard the affection in her voice. She then blushed and cleared her throat. "Now, where was I? Ah, yes, poor Nathan. Medical school was a little more difficult for him. He struggled, but got through. He has a small practice in Galena, mostly wealthy old women with nothing to do all day but complain," she said and shook her head. "If I ever get like that I hope somebody shoots me."

"I can't imagine you ever being that old," I said smiling. I really liked her. "So tell me, Hannah. Did you go into the family business as well?"

"Good heavens, no. I spend most of my time on the Board of Directors at the clinic, and I love charity work. My father used to tell me I'd give it all away if I could. I suppose he was right. Jon chastised me severely for the very same thing. Sarah was the brains behind getting the clinic up and running. She's also been the fund-raiser from the beginning."

"Which clinic are we talking about?"

"I'm sorry, dear. The Winfield Clinic. My father Alexander started it way back when. Anyway, I was very wise with my share of the inheritance, as was Jonathan, who had controlling interest in both the clinic and Father's business. Nathan wasn't wise at all. He and his wife Sarah spent it like there was no tomorrow. They would travel and spend. Jonathan felt he was making money for the company so Nathan could throw it away. He would tell Nathan he was weak, letting Sarah wear the pants. And make no mistake, she does to this day.

"Now, Nathan's and Sarah's son Charlie is taking up where his father left off. He takes trips abroad, alone, to have his little flings. He's lost, though. He's the wandering son of a weak father. Sarah dotes on him, as she always has. However, I notice tension between all three of them whenever we are together."

"Hannah, what was Charlie like as a kid?"

"God, when he was younger he was full of the devil—a typical boy. He and Maggie never got along. He was quite a bully actually. Sarah spoiled him and Nathan allowed it, I'm afraid. Even Jonathan tried to step in on several occasions but I think he hindered Charlie more than helped him. He should have taken such interest in his own daughter," she said with a wry chuckle. "I personally think Jon never understood or wanted to know about Margaret's lifestyle and the fact that she's gay. He was wrong and I told him so. Don't get me wrong, he loved Margaret, but as I said, he didn't know people. The fact that she is gay happens to be the way God made her. That's very liberal for an old broad, eh? But don't you feel the same way about yourself, Kate?" she asked me directly and smiled broadly.

I was caught completely off guard. I remembered when I told my family. It was a little hard on my father and mother. My father thought he had done something wrong in his parenting—like maybe they should have made me wear a dress more often, and not let me play softball, or climb trees with the boys as much. I explained to him that he did everything right, and he and my mother let me be myself. What more can you do for a child?

My sister Teri, on the other hand, knew all along. She and Mac, my brother-in-law, loved me unconditionally. They all loved me, not in spite of being gay, but because I was Kate.

I looked to see Hannah sporting a contagious smile that made me smile in return. "Boy, you're good," I said. "I'm not even going to ask you how you knew. And to answer your question, yes, I feel the very same way. I have always been comfortable with myself. I like who I am. Being gay is a part of me like my hair or my skin. It's who I am."

I told her of my family, and how they felt about my being gay. "I'm very fortunate to have a family that loves me. Maggie is lucky to have you even if you do drive around in a golf cart. Why in the world do you, by the way?"

"I was in a little accident a few months ago. I was driving Margaret's car and when I tried to stop the brakes gave way. I wasn't going too fast but I slammed into the side of a building and injured my hip. It was hard for me to get in and out of a car and I couldn't stand staying at home so Walt suggested I try a golf cart. I'm fine now, I just like riding around in the little thing. I am sorry I panicked this morning. That was close, wasn't it?"

"You lunatic, you almost ran me over." I was laughing in spite of myself. The woman made me laugh. "So, you sly thing, now we have our cards on the table. Tell me, dear Aunt Hannah, who is Allison?"

She looked at the door to see if anyone was coming. I foolishly looked as well. When she leaned forward, so did I. With a mischievous look in her eye, she said, "Well, I never cared for her. Two years ago when Margaret and she were in London—"

With that, the door banged open and we both jumped— interrupted, yet again.

Doc walked through the door. "You better go and sit with her," he told Hannah. "I can't get the waterworks to stop. Do you have any coffee?"

"Is she all right, Walt?" Hannah asked.

"Hell, she'll be fine. It's just a mild sprain. Good idea not to take that boot off," he said. I gave myself a mental slap on the back and smiled inwardly.

"She's a strong, healthy young woman, Hannah. She'll be right as rain by tomorrow. Keep her off the foot. Why don't you give her your cane? You don't need it. It's been two months. You're not Grandma Moses, yet."

Hannah blushed and ignored his last remark. "Oh, the poor child. Walt, what are you looking for? The coffee is on the stove as usual, you nut."

"That's my girl," he said affectionately.

She patted him on the shoulder as she walked by and out the door.

I got an overwhelming feeling of love. I felt at home and at ease. I turned to see the good doctor scowling at me and I took a step back. Well, so much for love and ease.

I felt like I was going to confession when I was a girl. Not knowing what you did wrong but sure you had to say something, anything.

"It was my idea to keep her boot on," I blurted, then winced. *Good God, Kate.*

He looked down and poured a cup of coffee as he smiled. "Would you like a cup?"

"No, but I'm sure there's a cup of hemlock here somewhere."

Doc laughed. "Don't worry. Maggie told me it was all her fault because she lost control of the horse."

"And was on a horse named Thunder I heard was supposed to be destroyed. What's up with that horse?"

"Nothing special, it trampled Bedford a year ago, and left him lame. The only one who could handle him was Maggie's father. Now, Maggie stubbornly tries to continue where Jonathon left off. Thunder is high-spirited as you can now attest. I guess she doesn't want to part with him," he said. "Hannah bending your ear?"

"No, she has quite a way about her, though. She mentioned Maggie's parents. I am sorry. That's very sad."

Doc hesitated then nodded. "Yes, it is. So Maggie told me you're a photographer—wildlife and such."

Well, I'm not going to get much information out of him. "Yes, and such." I felt like I was on an interview.

"Much money in it?"

"Enough for my lifestyle," I answered, looking right at him.

"Good girl." He drained his coffee cup. "Well, I'm off. If you stick around, make sure Maggie stays off that foot. She could use a friend about now. I know you just met, but perhaps you might keep her company for the day. It might help take her mind off things…"

"And those things would be?" *I'm getting the runaround here.* First, Hannah ignores my question of Miranda. Now, Doc.

Our eyes met and I could see him gauge his next words. "I think you came around at the right time, young lady. As I said, she could use a friend. She doesn't have many. In any event, I'm sure I'll see you again." He held out his hand and gave me a very hearty handshake as he looked over my shoulder. "Whose dog is that digging in the yard?"

"Oh, God!" I said. "It's mine. Excuse me Doctor, won't you?"

I let go of his hand and ran out the back door. Good grief, how embarrassing. I wanted to kill the little cur.

CHAPTER THREE

I got out the back door in time to see my insane dog run away with something in her mouth. It looked like a bag or something—like maybe one of those burlap bags new trees come in. Like a fool, I chased her into the woods. She, of course, thought I was playing and did that dodge thing dogs do. She darted back and forth then stopped and waited for me to move.

"Chance, get over here, now!" I said, doing my best imitation of an owner in control.

Because she listens so well, she charged off into the woods. As I lost sight of her I yelled, "Good, run all the way back home you stupid cur!"

I truly loved my dog but wondered what she had dug up. As I walked back to the house, Maggie and Hannah were watching me from the deck. Maggie was smiling and Hannah looked at me as if I were an escapee from Happy Dale.

"I'm sorry, she dug something up in your yard," I said, feeling like an idiot.

"It's all right, Aunt Hannah's dog used to dig all the time," Maggie said. Her smile was genuine.

"Hey, where is your dog? Chance could have a playmate." I smiled, but it faded when I saw their faces.

"The poor thing died. He was—" Hannah began.

Maggie interrupted quickly. "Aunt Hannah, don't. It's all over."

I looked at Maggie and tried to figure out why she would cut her aunt off like that. "I'm sorry," I said, not knowing quite what to say. After a few moments of awkward silence, I tried to change the topic. "Shouldn't you be off that foot?" *Nice segue, Kate.*

"Yes, she certainly should. Let's all go in. What time is it?" Hannah looked at her watch. "Good heavens it's after noon, time for a cocktail! It's getting cloudy and it'll take the chill out of our bones."

It was getting rather cool. I turned and looked for my crazed canine but she was still nowhere in sight. She'd be back in an hour or so, after she finished snooping and burying whatever she'd found.

Maggie limped into the den and I followed.

"Have a seat, anywhere," she offered, plopping on the couch while I looked around the massive den.

"Your aunt's house is huge."

"This house belongs to me. Aunt Hannah has lived with us since my mother died. Both of my parents are gone now, so it's just the two of us."

"I'm very sorry about your parents—your aunt told me about them earlier."

"I had a feeling she was going to do that. She likes you. You have an honest face. Aunt Hannah is very impressionable."

"We had a very interesting talk, nice but interesting."

Hannah came in with a tray full of glasses and a decanter. "Pour if you will, Kate," she said.

"My pleasure, Hannah."

"You have an engaging personality, Kate. And beautiful green eyes. Doesn't she Margaret?"

"Of sorts."

"Now," said Hannah sitting down with her drink. "Tell us about yourself, Kate. How long have you been a photographer? Are you originally from Illinois?"

As soon as I opened my mouth to speak, the doorbell rang. *I wonder if I can do that again?* I opened my mouth again, and by golly, it worked.

"Hello, is anybody home?" A woman's voice came from the foyer.

I watched Hannah and Maggie stare at each other—neither moved.

"Ladies, someone's at the door." I looked first at Maggie, then at Hannah, watching for any reaction.

Hannah took a long, long sip of her sherry. You could almost call it a swig. Maggie drained the contents of her glass, laid her head back on the arm of the couch, and closed her eyes. *Well, when in Rome.* I drained my glass as well.

"Helloo!"

"We're in here, dear," Hannah called politely.

Maggie lifted her head and glared at her aunt. I remembered that look from earlier that morning. I was grateful I was not the recipient. Hannah rolled her eyes.

In walked the most strikingly beautiful woman I had ever seen. She was 5'9" and all legs. She looked like Ava Gardner and had legs like Cyd Charisse. Okay, I'm a sucker for Hollywood. Her hair was jet black, short and wavy. Her eyes were green and somewhat almond shaped. She had high cheekbones, full red lips and long shapely legs that went "all the way to the floor" as my father used to say. She was wearing a plaid skirt and with those legs who wouldn't and a V-neck sweater with a blazer: very classy.

All at once, I felt like a frumpy bumpkin in my jeans, flannel and loafers. I thought for sure she was going to take out a cigarette and wait for someone to light it. I might have, if I smoked, and if I had a lighter.

This strange, elegant woman looked at Maggie. "God, Mags. Are you all right?"

I'd stood when she entered the room, but she breezed right past me to sit on the edge of the couch. *See if I light your cigarette.*

"I saw Doc, he told me what happened," she said and touched Maggie's forehead. "Are you all right?"

"Allison, there was no need to come over. I'm fine. Really," Maggie said.

My eyes widened as I realized who this woman was. I gave a questioning look to Hannah who had a mischievous smirk on her face.

Allison glanced at Hannah. "I'm sorry, Hannah, I didn't mean to be rude and ignore you."

"That's all right, my dear, you were only rude to our guest. This is Kate Ryan," Hannah said, pointing toward me. "Kate this is Allison Carson, a friend of the family."

I stood and extended my hand. "Nice to meet you."

"The pleasure is mine," Allison said insincerely, taking my hand. I noticed the realization flash across her face.

"Yes," I said, answering her unasked question. "I'm the one who knocked her off her horse."

"Really? And you're sitting here drinking sherry? How nice."

She was beginning to annoy me. "Nothing like a glass of fine sherry after knocking someone on their ass and—"

"Allison, would you like a glass of sherry, dear?" Hannah chimed in, saving the day.

Allison smiled sweetly at Hannah. "No thank you, it's a little early in the day for me." She looked at me. "But you enjoy yourself."

She *so* didn't mean that and I was now truly annoyed.

Allison turned back to Maggie. "You take care, and give me a call if you need anything. Anything at all." She kissed her on the forehead.

She said good-bye to Hannah and came over to me. "It was nice to meet you Miss Ryan. Will you be leaving soon?" She purposefully stood too close to my chair so it would be very awkward if I tried to stand.

I picked up my glass of sherry and crossed my legs. "I couldn't say. But it was a pleasure meeting you. Any friend of the family—"

Hannah shot out of her chair and took Allison by the arm. "Thank you for coming over, dear. Give us a call later, won't you?"

Allison looked over her shoulder as Hannah ushered her out. "I'll call you later, Mags."

"That would be great, Allison," Maggie called into the hallway then glared at me and started to say something.

"You've got lipstick on your forehead Miss Winfield," I said with a smug grin. I leaned over and presented a napkin.

She wrenched the napkin out of my hand.

I heard Hannah saying her good-byes before rejoining us. "Goodness, it is getting dark," Hannah said, sitting back with her sherry. "I think we may have a good storm. Now, where were we?"

"You were asking if Miss Ryan is from Illinois," Maggie said, with her eyes closed.

"Ah, yes." Hannah sat down and picked up her sherry. "Well?"

"Ladies, I have no idea where I'm from or where I'm going, but could someone get the knife out of my back?" I turned to expose my back. At least Hannah and I had a laugh.

"I think I could use a small refill," Maggie said. She struggled to sit up and retrieve her glass.

"I got it," I said absently, rising to get her glass.

"I can get it," she insisted as she struggled.

She couldn't reach it and she knew it. So, I shrugged and watched her flounder for a moment. It was too much; she nearly fell off the couch.

"Man, you're stubborn," I said impatiently and grabbed her glass from her.

"Thank you," she said too sweetly as I handed her the refilled glass.

We sat for a moment in silence. After telling Hannah the truth, I knew I had to tell Maggie as well. I figured now was as good a time as any.

"Maggie, I'm afraid I haven't been telling you the whole truth," I blurted. All at once, I felt a little foolish.

"Really?" Maggie asked. "What do you mean the whole truth?"

She stared at me, bewildered while I told them about Jan and Barb, and the whole nine yards. When I finished, I looked at Maggie. "Believe me, I did not know who you were until we were introduced. And even then I wasn't sure if I should stay or go."

"It's Kismet!" Hannah said with great enthusiasm until she looked at her niece. Her smile faded quickly.

"It's rot!" Maggie said, in an irritated voice. "So, you thought you'd get the scoop and leave, is that it? Have my aunt tell you personal family matters, then what? Give it to your magazine for a nice little cover story about the sad lives of the rich? Tell me why I should believe you?"

"Maggie, Jan and Barb told me you declined to meet with me, but I came up—"

"You came up to see if you could find me anyway, is that it? Even though I said I didn't want anyone here?"

I was getting tired of being cut off. "No, you self-absorbed little..." An appropriate word failed me. "First of all, I take wildlife photos. Unless a loon is in your lineage, which is a distinct possibility, I can't sell any photos or stories. I came up here because you have two friends who care a great deal about you who were worried sick. They honestly think something is wrong. Probably because of something you told them.

"I'm sure they could have easily told me, but because they respect your privacy, they did not say a word—only that you were a friend and in trouble. And since I am *their* friend and care about *them,* I thought maybe, just maybe, I might be able to help.

However, I can see now that you don't want any help." My heart was pounding. Christ she got me angry. "I think I'd better go." I stood. "I'm sorry I disrupted your lives today. Really, it was never my intention and I apologize for losing my temper."

"Nonsense, we have a great deal to discuss and you aren't going anywhere," Hannah said. "What we need is food. We need lunch! I'll be right back, and you," she said to me, "Stay put. I mean it!"

I stared in disbelief as she left the room.

Without looking at me, Maggie started. "I might have been a little out of line a moment ago. I don't know you and I thought the worst. I apologize. Jan and Barb are good friends and I know they care. When they told me about you, initially I thought of meeting with you, but I didn't want anyone involved in this. I'd like you to stay. I haven't talked to anyone about this. Maybe you can help. I don't know. There is so much going on and I don't quite know what to do." She stopped and looked at me.

"I don't think your aunt will let me leave, anyway."

"You may be right. Thank you," she said gratefully. "So, what else did Aunt Hannah tell you?"

I proceeded to tell her the whole conversation from beginning to end.

She sat quietly and listened. She interrupted only once when I related what Hannah had said about our lifestyles. She actually blushed. "You'll have to forgive Aunt Hannah, she means well. She's a very direct person."

"Yes, she is. She cares very much."

"So, do you still want to help, or do you want to eat and run? I wouldn't blame you if you did."

"Well, I can't leave without my dog, and since I have no idea where she is, I guess I'll have to stay for a while."

Hannah came back in the room, pushing another tray. This time it was filled with sandwiches and potato salad. All at once, I was famished.

"No more discussions until you've both eaten," Hannah ordered.

We sat in silence for a few minutes eating our lunch. I didn't say anything. I couldn't. I was stuffing my face with a wonderful roast beef sandwich. It appeared we all had ravenous appetites.

As I ate my lunch, I thought of my car. Don't ask me why. "When we're finished perhaps Bedford can take me back to the scene of the crime, and I can get my car."

Hannah looked down and said nothing.

"Hannah?" I asked, slowly.

"Your car's not there," she mumbled into her plate.

"Beg pardon? It sounded very much like you said my car's not there."

She looked up at both of us. "Well, it's been damaged and I thought Stan could fix it," she said. I heard the innocence in her voice and then realized there was nothing innocent about Hannah.

I gave her a confused look. "Who's Stan?"

"Our mechanic! He's very good and I'm sure—"

"You called a tow truck to come and take away my car? Hannah, I need my car! How else am I going to get home?"

"Aunt Hannah, Kate and I discussed it. She said she would stay."

"Oh," Hannah said. She looked down at her plate.

"No!" I said in disbelief as it dawned on me. "Tell me you didn't have that guy tow my car just to keep me here all day. Tell me you didn't do that, Hannah."

Maggie hid her face behind both hands; her shoulders were shaking as she laughed.

I looked at Hannah. "Hannah?"

"Well, you were going to leave and I didn't know what to do! So, I called Stan and had him tow your car." She looked at me with a sheepish grin. "So you might as well finish your lunch. I told Stan to call us later."

I stood dumbfounded. I had no idea what to say. I finally shook my head, sighed, sat down and did what I was told. I finished my lunch.

Kate Sweeney

CHAPTER FOUR

A t three o'clock in the afternoon, it started getting very dark and windy and the temperature dropped at least twenty degrees.

"It's getting a little chilly. Why don't we go in the other room and light a fire?" Maggie suggested.

"Need a hand?" I held out my hand and helped her up.

As we walked through the foyer, I looked out the window to see Chance snooping around the front yard. Maggie saw her too.

"Why don't you get her? I'm sure the poor thing is cold. Bring her in by the fire," she offered.

I opened the door and whistled. Chance looked up, saw me and started racing for the door. She was dirty around her snout so I knew she'd been digging at something. She came to the door and sat staring up at me.

I wagged my finger and tried my best role playing of mistress and canine. "Man, you better behave yourself or I'll put you right in the car."

Then I remembered I had no car in which to put her. So much for my threat. Chance followed me down the hall as I went in the direction Maggie had gone with her cane. I stood in a massive doorway and looked into an expansive room. The opposite wall had two big French doors, which led out onto a huge deck and the surrounding woods. A couch right in front of the fireplace and two overstuffed chairs to the left, separated by a table, gave the room a cozy, comfortable feeling.

Maggie stood by the fireplace struggling to get the wood. As she awkwardly gathered the wood, it was obvious her ankle was causing her pain. I thought I would offer my expertise. "Why don't you let me do that? I love playing with fire."

"Why does that not surprise me?" Maggie replied as she stood back.

In minutes, I had a roaring fire going. Fires were one of my specialties, and even I had to admire it. I turned to see my dog on Maggie's lap, sleeping.

Suddenly, there was a clap of thunder. Chance yapped and jumped off Maggie's lap and scooted under the coffee table.

"What a coward," I said shaking my head as I sat next to Maggie on the couch.

"Leave that poor dog alone," Maggie scolded and I turned to face her.

I was going to argue with her but was tired of quarreling. Besides, she looked exhausted.

"It's been a long day, hasn't it?" I asked quietly.

"Yes, and interesting," she answered. "While you were in the kitchen with Doc, Aunt Hannah told me your father was a detective. Are you following in his footsteps?"

"He wanted me to join the force. He came from a long line of policemen and firemen. Seems the thing to be if you're Irish and from Chicago. He could see I had a flair for it, but it wasn't for me. I think he was a little disappointed, although he never let on. I did, however, try my hand at being a private investigator for a few years." I stared at the fire, visions of that night flashing through my mind—*the dark cellar, Bob covered in blood, someone screaming in pain.* A cold shiver ran through me now when I remembered I was the one screaming. Lost in my thoughts, I didn't catch Maggie's question. "I'm sorry. What did you say?"

"I asked what became of your business." She watched me as if I were nuts.

"Oh, the fun went out of it." What a lame reason, I thought to myself. Looking at her, I could tell she knew I wasn't telling the truth. How in the world could I tell anyone? Dammit, why did she have to ask me? I'm fine when I don't think about it.

"Not talking or thinking about this will not make it go away. You have to face your demons, Kate," the hospital psychiatrist said, calmly.

"Don't patronize me! You don't think I know that?" I yelled and slammed my fist on her desk.

All at once, my heart started pounding in my chest and the claustrophobic feeling started. *Don't start this again,* I begged the gods above. But they didn't seem to hold me in very high regard these days. Beads of perspiration broke out on my brow and I hastily wiped them away and walked over to the fire. Maggie said nothing but I was sure she noticed the change. How could she not? I took a deep breath and turned back to her. She was sitting watching me and smiling slightly.

"I suppose I can't get away from my insatiable curiosity," I tried to explain. "I shouldn't be surprised when I find myself in this type of situation. I'm only following my instincts."

"And they led you here," she said quietly.

I smiled slightly and said, "I think so." We were silent for a moment.

"I'm glad they did. So, how long have you known Jan and Barb?"

"I've known Jan for almost eighteen years. We went to college together and became fast friends. She's a card. I met Barb after she started seeing Jan about two years ago. So, how long have you known them?"

"It's the opposite. I've known Barb for ten years. She was a nurse at Cook County. Thank God, she got out of that place."

"Ten years, did you meet her in grammar school?"

"Grammar school?" she asked frowning. "Say, what is it with you? First, it's 'my age' and now this. Do you have an age fetish? How old do you think I am?" she asked. I heard the anger rising. "Never mind, I don't think I want to know."

"Can we drop this? I'm sorry," I said quickly. This kind of conversation could cause nothing but trouble.

"So what else did Aunt Hannah and you discuss?"

"Nothing. Is there more?" I asked.

"N-no," she hesitated. "It's nothing."

"Why don't you tell me and then we can decide if it's nothing?" I asked.

She looked into the fire. I waited silently, hoping she'd open up.

"Margaret, if you don't tell her I will!" Hannah exclaimed as she leaned in between us.

I nearly jumped off the couch. As soon as my heart rate returned to normal, Hannah repeated herself.

"Margaret!"

"All right," Maggie started. "About two months ago—"

"Someone tried to kill her," Hannah blurted out.

My eyes widened as I stared in amazement.

Maggie tensed and said, through clenched teeth, "No one tried to kill me. It was an accident."

"Wait a minute…" I said.

"Good heavens, someone in the stable hit you from behind—knocked you out cold—and that's not attempted murder?" Hannah asked.

"Hold on, when—" I started.

"Christ, Aunt Hannah, this is precisely why I didn't want anyone to know. Christ!" Maggie said. I noticed her hands beginning to shake.

"Well pardon me for caring." Hannah turned to me. "We went to the police, and they were absolutely no help. They investigated but found nothing. Well, of course they found nothing. Whoever did it is a murderer, not an idiot!"

But before I could even open my mouth—

"And what about the woods?" Hannah asked. "Don't even tell me someone wasn't following you. Whoever it was scared you senseless on more than one occasion."

"Okay, ladies, if we could—" *I always wanted to be invisible.*

"Aunt Hannah, could we please stop this? I know what happened. I know you care and I know you're scared. Well, so am I dammit, and I don't know why it's happening or what to do!" She was on the verge of hysteria. "So please, can we stop this? I feel like I'm going insane." She laid her head against the back of the couch and closed her eyes.

Hannah sat on the arm of the couch and held her. "I am sorry, sweetie," she whispered, stroking Maggie's hair.

Maggie cried softy for a minute then looked up at her.

Her aunt reached down, dried her tears with the back of her hand and kissed her cheek.

I coughed softly.

"I'm sorry, Miss Ryan," Maggie said.

"Kate, please, and there's no need to apologize. We should take this step by step, don't you think?"

"So, where do we start?" Hannah sat next to Maggie, and held her hand.

"Well, obviously, we've got to figure out why someone would want to kill...uh, attack you. When did this start? Was there anything going on at the time that might offer an explanation?"

"I can't think of anything. I've been racking my brain for two months. Maybe money. All I have is money. But why now? It doesn't make sense. I've had money all my life."

I raised an eyebrow. "Really, how much money?"

She looked at me and grinned. "I'm a poor little rich girl. I thought you knew that."

The phone rang and Hannah got up to get it. "Don't talk without me," she said over her shoulder.

Of course, we did.

"Maybe it's my imagination. Maybe none of this is happening. Perhaps it's a coincidence. I swear, when I ran into you this morning and I fell, I thought, God please, not again. I expected to see your car race down the road away from me, but when I saw you and you looked so concerned I knew you weren't part of whatever this is."

"Was anyone with you during any of these attacks?"

"Why, do I need a witness?" she asked.

"No," I said. "But if there was someone with you, maybe they saw something you didn't."

She sighed and closed her eyes. "I'm sorry, I'm a bit jumpy."

Hannah came back into the room. "You're talking without me." She got no farther then five steps before the phone rang again. "Jiminy Christmas!" She turned on her heels. "No talking," she called over her shoulder.

I leaned over at put my hand on Maggie's, not surprised to find it freezing. "Don't worry, we'll figure this out."

"I'm not sure what it is. Sometimes, I think I'm going nuts. I mean I'm a reasonably intelligent woman and I can't figure out why this is happening much less who is behind it." She looked at me then. "You do believe me, don't you?"

I looked into the scared blue eyes. "Yes, I do."

Hannah came back in the room. She looked disapprovingly at both of us. "You talked without me. I could hear you in the other room. So, now you have to tell me everything. Go on." She sat down.

Maggie looked at her. "Who was on the phone?"

"Stan," she said, not looking at me.

I waited for her to tell me what he said. Then I waited some more. Finally, I took a deep breath. "Okay, what did he say?"

She sat there, dusting off her dress or picking lint or something. I have *no* idea.

"Hannah?" I asked.

"Well, do you want the good news or bad news first?"

"Bad news? There's bad news? How can there be bad news?" I asked.

She smiled and gave me an inquiring look but wouldn't say a word. I wasn't sure who was more infuriating, her or her niece.

I took another deep breath and caved. "Okay, give me the good news first."

"I knew you would be a good-news-first person!" she said triumphantly. "Shows you're an optimist. I always say, show me a person who is a good-news-first person and I'll—"

"Christ, Aunt Hannah, will you please give her the good news," Maggie said.

Here we go again, I thought. I said nothing. I was not in control with these two.

"Oh, all right. Well, the good news is that your car will cost next to nothing to fix." She smiled broadly.

I closed my eyes and rubbed my forehead. "And the bad news would be?" I was so frightened.

"He had to get a part for the bumper and it won't be ready for two days," she said as her voice trailed off to a whisper.

I leaned back on the couch and looked at the ceiling. The ceiling was beamed in beautiful, dark oak that reflected the warm light from the fire and made the room feel cozy and peaceful. It belied the bedlam in which I found myself.

The fire needed stoking. I dutifully put another log on, and it started to blaze again. I returned to the couch and was actually quite comfortable. I looked over to see both of them looking at me, with more than a little anxiety.

Hannah said in a voice as low, deliberate and calm as a doctor who was about to put a straightjacket on you, "We would love you to stay the night. We have plenty of room. Don't we Margaret?" She looked to Maggie for help.

"Of course we do, Kate." The straightjacket was coming as she continued, "It's pouring and Chance seems to be having fun."

I looked at my cur sprawled in front of the fire. "True, true. She does look comfy. That is important," I said.

"And it's getting late and you haven't eaten supper. And you two never told me what you were talking about when I was on the phone," Hannah added with a hopeful smile.

"And Aunt Hannah is terribly sorry she had your car towed. Aren't you, Aunt Hannah?" Maggie added, scowling at her aunt.

"Yes, very sorry, truly I am."

She did sound sorry. As I'm sure Murphy may have sounded right before his law went into effect.

Well, I thought, it could be worse. I could be on the side of the road, stranded in a storm. However, right at this moment...

"Please say something dear, you're making Margaret nervous," Hannah said with a wicked grin.

Oh, this woman.

I started chuckling. What else could I do? "Thank you, I'd love to spend the evening."

Hannah breathed a very heavy sigh of relief. "Good, now let's go into the kitchen, we'll make dinner, have a nice bottle of wine, and oh, I have a marvelous idea. We'll have a slumber party!" she howled with excitement.

I wasn't sure about Maggie, but I was dumbfounded.

Hannah laughed and conceded. "Well, let's start with a nice bottle of wine and then let the chips fall where they may!"

CHAPTER FIVE

I looked out at the pouring rain and was glad I wasn't out in it. I stood at the kitchen window, with my hands in my pockets, staring out at the darkness. Thinking of the day's events, I wondered if I was in over my head with this one. Helping Jan last year was one thing. This might be quite another. I'd now been away from the P.I. scene for four long years. My instincts were failing me and I wondered if I could be any help at all.

The wind was howling and the temperature dropped dramatically yet again. *I should go out to my car and get my sweater. I should remember I don't have my car.* I turned to see Maggie watching me as she sat at the table with her foot propped up on another kitchen chair.

"A penny for your thoughts," she said. "Or at your age, are you finding it difficult to gather them?"

I saw the mischievous grin and was about to say something, probably sarcastic, when Hannah started down the cellar stairs.

Maggie apparently didn't think it was a good idea. "Aunt Hannah, do not go down that steep staircase."

"Oh, don't be such a ninny. I'm fine. Besides, it's not as if you could go get us a bottle of wine."

I threw my hands up and started down the cellar steps, listening to the two of them bantering back and forth. I had such a headache.

It was dark in the cellar. I turned on the wall switch and a small light went on, which did not illuminate as much as I had hoped. As I walked down the stairs, the dampness hit me right in the face, and I shivered violently. Cellars gave me the creeps.

Through the dimly lit room, I saw a large wine selection in the far corner. There were boxes and old furniture in the other corner. There was a small cellar window at the top of that wall, which looked like it was in serious need of a cleaning. However, who could reach it? Next to it was a stairwell of six or so steps leading up to another door that I assumed led outside.

I turned my attention back to my task. I perused the selection before me. "Okay, if I were filthy rich, which wine would I choose?" Not knowing what I was looking for, I closed my eyes and randomly reached for a bottle. I looked at the label. "Rothschild Bordeaux 1958. It's got dust all over it. It's either very good or very bad. The Winfield ladies will tell me I'm sure," I said in a haughty tone and blew the dust off the bottle and headed upstairs.

They were both still babbling as I came back up the stairs. Hannah stopped her prattle long enough to give Maggie a scathing look.

"See what you've done," she scolded and Maggie glared at her and got the glasses.

I handed the bottle to Hannah who blinked several times. "You have excellent taste, Kate."

Maggie looked at the bottle and laughed as she opened it, then poured three glasses of the red wine.

"What? Isn't it a good year?" I asked, as if I have *any* idea what a good year was.

With a smug grin, Maggie handed me a glass. "Oh, it'll do. It comes out to roughly $88.00 a glass."

Now I blinked several times. I looked from the wineglass to both women. "Oh."

"Oh, indeed. A toast," Hannah said.

Oh God, I thought.

"Christ," Maggie grumbled.

"Shut up, dear," Hannah said to her without looking at her. We lifted our glasses. "A toast, to our new friend, Kate, a good sport and hopefully… a good cook."

"Here, here," added Maggie.

We touched our glasses together and not one of them broke. Maybe it was going to be a good night after all.

"Now," I said rubbing my hands together. "Apparently, I'm cooking. So, you don't mind if I invade your kitchen, do you?"

"God no," said Maggie. "I don't cook all that much, I leave that to Aunt Hannah."

"By all means dear, invade, invade!" Hannah said.

I went over to the refrigerator, opened it and found it completely stocked.

"Okay, what'll it be?" I asked.

"I bought some gorgeous steaks yesterday," Hannah said. "There's some asparagus in there and fixings for salad."

"Great, then steaks it is. Okay with you Miss Winfield?" I asked.

"Okay with me Miss Ryan," she said.

Hannah sat back. I noticed her smiling as she drank her wine.

After dinner, Stan the faithful mechanic came by and brought my suitcase and camera equipment.

"What a relief," Maggie said. "I thought you might have to wear one of Aunt Hannah's old nightgowns to bed."

"Oh, good grief, I don't wear those old things any more, I'm liberated. I sleep in the buff!" Hannah said.

"That's way more than I need to know," I said as I reached over and took Hannah's wine away from her. She laughed uproariously.

Maggie looked at her aunt. "I am going to have you committed."

"Yes, but not tonight." She was still laughing while reaching around me for her glass.

The phone rang when we started to clear the table. Maggie and Hannah both looked at the clock, then at each other. Neither made a move to pick it up.

I looked at them. "Want me to get it?"

"No," they said simultaneously.

I raised an eyebrow and continued clearing the dishes. The phone stopped ringing. One minute later, it started ringing again. And exactly the same thing happened.

"All right, what's going on?" I asked as the phone continued to ring. It was driving me nuts. Then it stopped.

"Nothing is going on, just because the phone rings doesn't mean I have to answer it. I mean it is my house, isn't it Miss Ryan?" Maggie asked.

She had a very snippy attitude. My patience was wearing very thin. "Look, I know you don't know me from Adam, or Eve for that matter, but if you'd like me to help, you need to let me know what's going on. So maybe we can set a few ground rules. First, do you want my help?"

"Yes," Hannah said quickly. She looked at Maggie and motioned with her head.

Maggie stood silent for a moment. "Yes," she finally said.

"Okay, then the foremost rule—please tell me the truth. I can't help if you don't." I looked at Maggie. "Otherwise, you'll wind up dead, and I won't have that on my conscience."

No answer. I rubbed my forehead.

"Look, I don't know if I can help you but you have to trust me. You simply have to. And I need to know I can trust you too. Dammit, this is serious. Now, why didn't you answer the phone?"

Maggie hesitated for a minute before answering. "I've been getting crank phone calls this past week. They seem to come at the same time of night. There's usually no one on the other end—only breathing. So, I told Aunt Hannah not to pick up the phone, and let the answering machine get it." She watched me for a minute and then softened. "I'm sorry, I need your help and I will level with you from now on."

I looked her straight in the eye.

"Pax?" she smiled and held out her hand.

"Pax," I said and took it.

"Well, now that that's settled," Hannah said confidently.

"I haven't even gotten to you yet, Hannah." I said.

"Me, what have I done?" she asked, horrified.

"Oh, nothing, Miss I Had Your Car Towed Because It Was Damaged. Do you understand me?"

"Yes, Kate."

"And by the way, who was the second phone call from earlier?"

Hannah put her hand up to her mouth and laughed. "Margaret, I'm so sorry. It was Allison. She wanted you to call her back." She stopped and looked at the clock. "An hour ago."

With that, the doorbell rang.

"Guess who?" I asked and picked up my glass.

I noticed Maggie got up, quite easily now and started for the door.

"Margaret, your ankle seems to be better, dear."

"It is much better, Aunt Hannah!" she called over her shoulder.

Hannah looked at me. "It does seem better."

"Boy, that Doc. He sure is a wonderful doctor," I said. I watched her as she blushed and laughed. "He is kind of handsome," I admitted truthfully.

"Handsome, nothin', he's, oh, what's the term the women use today? He's a …babe!" Obviously feeling the wine and sherry, she laughed out loud. Then she covered her mouth. I couldn't help myself; I laughed with her.

"She's what? Why?" Allison was obviously rather angry.

Hannah and me both stopped laughing and looked at each other. Then there were low voices—not a good sign.

"Call her a cab!" Was the angry, sarcastic response.

"Look, Al, I don't owe you any explanation at all. And as I recall, you never offered any to me. I had to deal with it. So, she's staying and that's that. Deal with it."

I was a little embarrassed and I said to Hannah, "Maybe I should go and straighten this out. I don't want to be the cause of anything here."

"Oh, no you don't!" She reached over and grabbed my arm. "I've been waiting for this moment. For six months, Allison has been making Margaret feel guilty. Telling her that if she would only forgive her, they could go back to the way it was. Never mind that Margaret caught her with someone in their hotel room while she and Allison were in England. Seriously, that's what I was going to tell you earlier in the kitchen. Well, I'll let Margaret tell you now. But that 'let me take care of everything' attitude—she only wanted one thing from Margaret—her money."

"Be careful what you say Hannah." I waved my finger at her.

"It's true. I know that Allison is having financial difficulties. No, she wouldn't have the nerve to try to hurt Margaret. She knows I'd have her—"

"Ah, ah, Hannah—"

With that, we heard Maggie's voice. "I've had enough. Look, I'm tired and this is pointless. Thank you for stopping by. I'll call you later."

Maggie came back to the table. "Not a word. Not one word," she said as she picked up her glass.

I looked at the clock. Only eight o'clock. It seemed like midnight and everyone had to be tired. I knew I was. I looked at my companions. "If you don't mind I need to make a phone call. I should call my sister. We were supposed to meet in Galena tomorrow for the weekend."

"Why don't you have her come here for the weekend? We have plenty of room. Your car won't be ready for two days. You said you and she always listened to your father's cases, maybe she can help as well."

"That would be fine, if you want to, Kate," Maggie said. "I feel terribly responsible for ruining your weekend. Maybe you can still salvage some of it."

"Well, I can call and check it out. Teri would be helpful. If you're sure?"

"Oh, good heaven's, of course! Will her husband be coming too?" Hannah asked, apparently excited at the prospect of more houseguests.

"Well, he was going to see if he could get away. Okay, let me call and scope it out."

"You can use the phone in the hallway if you like," Hannah said.

Mac, my adorable brother-in-law answered the phone. "Hi kiddo, how the hell are ya? Where in the hell are ya?"

I love Mac. His real name is Michael McAuliffe, and he is a wild Irishman who loves my sister madly. "In the rabbit hole, Mac." I laughed but heard nothing from him. "Hello?" I asked jokingly.

"Rabbit hole? I don't think I want to hear this. I'll get your sister," he said abruptly.

I briefly told my sister what was going on. I must admit it sounded incredible even to me.

"What have you gotten yourself into? Are you serious?" she asked.

I laughed at the tone in her voice. "Of course I'm serious, aren't I always?"

"No. God, that's horrible." Then she laughed. "She actually had your car towed?"

"Yeah. Look, the reason I called," I said and explained the situation. "What do you think?"

"I think it sounds like I'll be there about noon."

"Are you sure?" I asked again. "I have no idea what in the world is going on here, but I can feel it, Ter. This kid is in real trouble."

"You get yourself in the strangest predicaments," Teri said. "Oh, hell, I have to talk to Mac. Can I call you back in five minutes?"

I read her the number off the phone and went back into the kitchen. Hannah looked at me hopefully.

"Well, Teri will come for sure. She's talking to Mac now to see if he can come. She's going to call back in a minute to let me know," I said, and then looked at both of them. "Are you sure you want to do this? You didn't want anyone to know about this, now you're about to have half my family here."

"I'm sure, Kate. If they can help you then I'd like them to be here," Maggie said.

The phone rang and Hannah left the room to answer it.

Maggie was studying her wineglass and I could tell her thoughts were a million miles away. She looked up at me. "Sorry, my mind—"

"I understand. You know there's safety in numbers. This might be a good thing."

"I'm sure it will."

Hannah came into the kitchen talking on the phone. "That will be fine, Teri. You and Mac are welcome, please come whenever you like... Noon? That will be wonderful. I'll have your room ready... it's no problem at all. Well, see you tomorrow dear. Here's Kate."

She handed me the phone. I sat there with my mouth open staring at her.

She looked at me. "It's a portable phone, dear. You put it to your ear and talk."

As I took the phone from her, I heard Maggie chuckling in the background. "Hello," I said flatly.

Teri was laughing on the other end. "We have to come now. She promised pie."

I gave Teri the directions and was glad they were coming up for the weekend.

Hannah brought the coffee to the table along with what I had hoped was homemade pound cake. She also brought another decanter. This time it was cognac.

She looked at me and answered the questioning look on my face. "It complements the dessert," she said properly. She prepared the coffee, cognac and a piece of almond pound cake lavished with butter, for each of us.

"Everything all set?" Maggie asked tiredly.

"Yes, they'll be here around noon."

I went to the big bay window behind the kitchen table. The rain had stopped and now there was only a cool autumn wind rapidly blowing the clouds. As the clouds passed, I could see the near full moon shining brightly. I started thinking about the present situation, wondering what I could do to help. What did I know? I looked at the moon and through my reverie, I heard Hannah calling me.

Hannah looked at Maggie, who looked exhausted. "Look, I think we could all use a good night's sleep. Why don't you go to your room and take a nice hot bath, and go to bed? It's been a long day, sweetie," Hannah said.

"I have to take Chance out. I think I'll skulk around the back yard," I said.

Maggie whirled around to face me. "Don't, don't go out there."

"Hey," I said. "I have to get Chance out. I'll be right back."

"Promise you won't go into the woods?" she asked, putting her hand on my arm. "I'm not going upstairs until you come in."

"Okay, I'll be right back." I gave her hand a reassuring pat.

Chance had heard the word "out" and waited patiently at my side. "Come on, you mutt."

Once outside, I realized how cold it was. I waited for Chance to finish as I watched the woods. Maggie spooked me, thank you very much, and now I had an eerie feeling I was being watched, and not by Maggie.

It was cold and windy. The yard was unbelievably bright when the moon came out, then dark as pitch when it went behind the fast-moving clouds. As I looked out at the woods, my imagination got the better of me.

In the dark of the night, at the edge of the woods, I thought for sure I saw someone looking at me. Just standing, not moving—just looking. When I was about to pass it off as my imagination, Chance started to growl. Then she started to whine. I shivered uncontrollably and grabbed her collar more tightly, not wanting her to bolt into the woods. The hair on her neck was standing rigid. So was mine. I stood, perfectly still, and I swear I saw whatever— whoever—it was fade into the woods. The only sound was the rustling of the leaves.

Okay, that was enough for me. I turned, still holding Chance by the collar and, in a controlled panic, walked very quickly back to the door. I was too terrified to turn around, thinking that whatever it was changed its mind and was right at my heels. I fumbled at the door latch and almost cried out for help as it opened. I slammed the door behind me and locked it.

I turned around to see Maggie staring at me in horror. "What happened?" she asked.

"Nothing, everything is fine," I said. "It's freezing out there." I rubbed my hands over my arms.

Hannah appeared in the doorway. "Okay ladies, lights out, let's get to bed."

She turned out the lights as I checked all the doors and locks.

At the top of the stairs, Hannah stopped at a doorway. "Here you go, Kate. I put you in the room next to Margaret's. Everything is all ready, so have a good sleep." She came over and kissed my cheek. "Bless you," she said.

"Good night, Hannah," I said, warmly.

She then went over, kissed Maggie good night and went into her room at the end of the hall.

"Well, I appreciate all you're doing. I don't know why you're doing it but thank you," Maggie said.

"I'm not quite sure why I'm doing it either, but you're welcome."

I smiled and for a moment, she looked like she might say something, then she smiled as well.

"Well, good night," she whispered and opened her door.

"Good night, Maggie."

I went into my room and saw Chance sprawled out on the bed, sound asleep and snoring peacefully. What a life, I thought as I put my bag on the chair and went to the window. The wind had quieted and now the trees moved gently with the breeze. I peered out the window, wondering if my imagination had gotten the better of me. Did I see something? A shiver ran through me as I backed away from the window and drew the curtains shut. I went into the bathroom and looked at myself in the mirror.

"Getting a little grayer every time I look at you, Kate ole girl."

I also needed to shed a few pounds, but who didn't? What with middle age and all that. Overall though, I was content with my life and myself. I guess if I were more than six feet tall, my weight would be perfect. However, being five foot nine, several fewer pounds were in order.

I lie there with my hands behind my head, staring at the ceiling. Chance growled lowly as I gently nudged her out of the way.

What had I gotten into? Surely, something was going on, but what and why? I thought of Aunt Hannah's family history lesson. Who had control of the family business now that Maggie's father had died?

Then I remembered Hannah telling me, when we were in the kitchen, that Maggie's mother had *died* twenty years ago. I'd first thought she died from an illness. But then later, Hannah said she was *killed*. To me that took on a whole different connotation. I wondered if she were in some kind of an accident or something more. *More than what?*

Was there something going on or was this all Maggie's imagination? My instincts told me it was not, but then my instincts weren't what they used to be. I tossed restlessly and looked at the clock. Only 10:30.

But maybe, just maybe, Maggie and her aunt were just plain nuts like the aunts in the movie, *Arsenic and Old Lace*. They get rid of my car, then my dog, and then me. *First we get moose, then we get squirrel.* The immortal words of Boris Badanoff came to mind.

Wouldn't that beat all? I thought as I drifted off to sleep. Two crazy women...

CHAPTER SIX

I sat bolt upright in bed. Was I awake? My heart was pounding in my ears. I hate those dreams when you know you're dreaming but you can't wake yourself. Someone—something—in this dream had been shaking my bed, urging me to wake up.

I looked around until my eyes adjusted to the pitch-blackness of my room. I was awake and Chance was growling. She was no longer on the bed and, through the darkness, I saw her by the door.

Then I heard it—a shuffling sound in the hallway. I got up and put my ear to the door. I stood for several seconds before hearing it again. I haphazardly struggled into my jeans and sweater and slipped into my shoes, thankfully not falling flat on my face.

"C'mon, Chance," I whispered and the traitor jumped on the bed and laid there. "You coward! If I get killed, you'll be sorry." What was I saying? Nobody was getting killed.

It was dark but the moon cast a perfect light from the hallway window so I wasn't totally in the dark, as I opened my door.

Who the hell was I kidding? I was completely in the dark, and I knew it. I closed my door behind me and walked out into the hall. Putting my ear to Maggie's door, I heard nothing. I cautiously opened her door and peered into the darkness. I heard her breathing and snoring peacefully. I must have imagined the whole thing.

It was on my way back to my room that I heard a noise downstairs. My heart stopped. I turned toward the staircase and took a few steps. I thought I heard Maggie's door creak, so I turned around, but no, the door was still closed. I sneaked to the top of the stairs, leaned over the railing and looked around before I slowly descended. Occasionally, a stair would creak. Of course, they had to creak, since I was trying so hard to be quiet.

A shiver rippled through me. *Someone's walking over your grave.* My Irish Grandmother's words came back to me. Thanking

Granny for the gruesome mental picture, I reached the bottom of the stairs and turned into the hallway. It was freezing. I walked down the hall and into the living room.

Through the darkness, I examined the contours of each wall and then I saw it. The curtains were blowing wildly in the wind. The French doors were wide open. I had locked them myself. Someone was already in the house. I tried to swallow, but couldn't peel my tongue off the roof of my mouth.

I was terrified as I walked over to the doors. Then I felt something behind me, but I couldn't move. I opened my mouth to scream but nothing came out.

"You shouldn't be here," the voice came in a wicked whisper, touching my ear.

I do believe I may have screamed then, as I instinctively raised my arm and swung my elbow backward, catching the intruder at the head. As he grabbed me, we crashed through the French doors.

We tumbled out onto the deck and I felt something sharp pierce my shoulder. The intruder whined like some scared animal as he tried to gain the upper hand. My adrenaline was at an all-time high and power surged through me. I was almost on top of him, surprised to get the upper hand so quickly, when he broke free and pushed me off. It was enough for him to get to his knees.

As I struggled to get to my feet, the intruder picked up a piece of firewood and swung it in my direction. I tried to dodge the lumber, but it grazed my head enough so I saw stars and my knees buckled.

He slipped and fell on the wet grass as he took off running like hell into the woods.

I attempted to run after him, but fell to my knees instead. The back yard was spinning. I got to my feet and stood, bent over with my hands on my knees, trying not to faint. Of course, it started to rain—what else?—as I stood for a moment longer, trying to get my bearings. Actually, the light rain may have saved me from passing out.

Disgusted, scared, wet and a little shaky, I headed back to the house, trying to avoid the broken pieces of glass, and ran into Hannah.

"Good heavens," she said. "You're bleeding!"

"Call the police, Hannah. Now."

Hannah was at the phone before I even finished.

Maggie rushed into the living room. "What the hell happened?"

"Someone was in the house." I started shaking uncontrollably.

"Christ," Maggie looked around, as if ensuring no one else was there before looking back at me. "Kate, you're bleeding."

I impatiently waved her off. "We have to make sure there's no one else in the house."

With that, we heard sirens. Within a minute or two, there were police at both the front and back doors.

A policeman in full rain gear was standing in the middle of the room talking to Maggie. She gave me a very worried look. I looked back outside and saw two other policemen with flashlights combing the back yard. Thankfully, the rain had stopped.

One of them poked his head in. "Can you come out here, please?"

"No, Steve, she cannot," Hannah answered harshly.

"Hannah, I need—" Steve started.

I waved my hand. "Let's get this over with." I was freezing, wet and tired, and not necessarily in that order.

"You okay?" Steve asked me.

"I'll live," I said.

"What happened?" he asked.

As I told him everything, he wrote it down in his book. He then looked around the yard. "Any idea who it might be?" he asked as we made our way back inside.

"No, I don't, but earlier I thought I saw someone out in the woods when I was out with my dog. I thought it was my imagination, but I guess not." I looked over at Maggie, who threw a shocked look in my direction.

"I guess not," he agreed. "You're lucky. You could have been hurt. As it was, you handled yourself pretty well. So, whoever it was, was wearing black. That narrows it down."

I stared at the floor in contemplation. Something wasn't right.

He waited for a moment watching me. "Something else?"

I shook my head. "I'm not sure. It's just, well, he didn't seem that strong. I was surprised that's all." I scratched my head. "Maybe it was the adrenaline." However, I knew that wasn't it. It annoyed me. I was missing something.

Two other policemen had checked the house and, of course, found nothing. They checked the cellar and every room in the house. The only sign of the break-in was the shattered French doors. A third officer was dusting for fingerprints around the doors.

Steve looked at me. "Your forehead is bleeding, better get that looked at."

I felt the side of my head with my fingers. It was sticky with blood. As I turned away, I heard him continue.

"Hey, your shoulder is bleeding too. Hannah, you'd better call Doc Jenkins."

"I'm all right, I think," I said, looking at my right shoulder. I didn't want to move any farther, fearing someone would find I had sprung a leak somewhere else.

Both Hannah and Maggie were immediately at my side.

"Christ Kate," Maggie said as she touched the side of my face. She then looked through the rip in my shirt and examined my shoulder.

Steve slipped the small notebook into his vest pocket. "I'll have a deputy get some plywood on the window tonight, Maggie. Would you like me to take her over to the clinic?"

"No, thanks Steve, we'll take care of her."

"Well, Mike and I will cruise the area for the rest of the night and Ed will stay out in front." He turned to me. "I'm glad you weren't injured too badly. Goodnight, ladies, I'll keep in touch."

When he had gone, Maggie turned to me and, once again, I saw an irritated look. "You need stitches, let's go."

She made a phone call and grabbed her keys.

"I'm fine," I said stupidly but no one listened as they pushed me out the door.

"Miss Winfield?" We all turned to see Bedford limping out of the darkness. *Well at least he's off the list of suspects.* "I just talked with the police, Miss," he said to Maggie.

"Good, please be careful, Bedford. Someone nearly killed Miss Ryan. We're taking her to the clinic. Please, stay with the police. We shouldn't be long."

"I am sorry, Miss Ryan," he said.

"You and me both, Bedford," I replied.

He nodded and stepped back as I got into the car. I saw the concerned look on his face.

For some reason a shiver swept through me. Bedford gave me the creeps.

We drove a mile or so outside of town and pulled up to a two-story building that stood on the top of a hill, set back into the woods. It looked rather ominous perched up there by itself and set back into the woods.

We met Doc Jenkins who ushered me into a small emergency room. Hannah offered to wait outside in the small waiting room.

"Maggie, check her vitals," Doc said.

I was confused. *How can she do this?* She took my blood pressure and everything else that accompanies it.

"Are you a doctor or something?" I asked the obvious question.

"Or something," she said, continuing her work.

Doc smiled and used scissors to cut the sleeve of my shirt. "I'd say ten, maybe twelve, sutures. What do you think, Maggie?"

She looked and agreed. She was checking the cut on my eyebrow. She put some liquid on it that made me jump.

"Sit still, please," she said. She put her hand on my neck to hold me. I felt the warm fingers and felt my heart racing. *Don't take my blood pressure now.*

"So, you're a doctor?" I asked again, as I watched her, completely intrigued.

Doc answered for her. "Almost. If she'll get off her duff and finish her internship, she can take over for me and I can retire. That's the game plan anyway."

I noticed the affectionate exchange and I glanced around the room. "I saw a sign that read *The Winfield Clinic*. Hannah mentioned it earlier. The family business?"

Maggie nodded with a shrug.

"I understand your grandfather started it," I said and looked at Doc. I had a feeling I wasn't going to get any information out of Maggie right now for some reason.

"That's correct. Back in the fifties, Alexander Winfield, Maggie's grandpapa, spent big money to have a clinic started. Of course, it had to be in his name and nobody was going to argue with him since he had more money than anyone else in this town could ever hope to see," he said, preparing my torture.

"Which he got from his business?" I asked.

Doc glanced at me then nodded. "Hannah's been talking I see. Yes, Alexander was a very good businessman."

"So, he wasn't a doctor. Who ran it back then?"

"Well, Nathan and I were finishing med school. He told Nathan to run the clinic. I was here as well to begin with then started my own practice in town. It started out a small clinic but, by the sixties, it was as efficient as a small hospital. It took a while to get the state to approve it, but Nathan was proud of it, and he should be. He worked hard. I have to admit, as much as I hate to give credit to Sarah, she kept that clinic going and kept fighting for it. She was on the Board of Directors along with Nathan, Old Man Winfield, Jonathan and Hannah. How she wrangled that one I don't know."

"Wrangled? I don't understand? Isn't she a Winfield?" I asked, looking at both of them.

Doc shrugged and came at me with a huge needle. I leaned back. "Okay, forget I asked," I said seriously. I heard a small laugh from the 'almost' doctor. *Sure, now she laughs.*

Doc smiled. "This will hurt you more than it will hurt me."

After administering the anesthesia, Doc nodded. "Okay, look at Maggie if you're squeamish."

I'm not a squeamish person. However, I turned my head and looked at Maggie. She smiled slightly and put a warm hand on my shoulder. I felt a jolt that was not caused by Doc's suturing skill.

"So, you didn't tell me you were a doctor. You didn't tell me about the clinic. Is there anything else you haven't told me?" I looked at her with a good deal of uncertainty.

Her smile faded. "I wasn't aware that it was important."

"Someone is scaring the hell out of you, if not trying to kill you. It could be a disgruntled patient. It could be anything or anybody. It may not have anything to do with your wealth, Maggie."

Doc finished stitching me up and stripped off his latex gloves. "Maggie why don't you finish dressing this? You need the practice," he said with a wink. "And you, Miss Ryan, will be fine. Don't move around too much. Stitches can come out in a week. You can see your doctor at home."

Maggie bandaged both my shoulder and my forehead. As I struggled into my shirt, she gently pushed my hands away.

"Sit still," she said.

I sat staring off into space while my body reacted to the warm fingers on my neck as she smoothed my collar. *Okay, Ryan, deep breaths, deep breaths.* When I looked up, I saw her standing at my side, frowning.

"This is a nasty scar," she said.

Doc walked up behind me and gently pulled at my collar. "Hmm. Looks relatively new."

Okay, too much attention. I instinctively pulled my collar up. "It happened a few years ago," I said, very aware of their scrutiny.

I glanced up at Maggie who gave me a curious look but said nothing. All at once, I was exhausted. I lifted my arm and tried to get a feel for my range of motion. I immediately winced at the sharp pain that ran through me.

"He told you not to move it too much. My God, you're like a child," Maggie said, handing me a small bottle of pills. "Here, take two and—"

"Call you in the morning? I don't like taking pills. I'll be okay."

"Suit yourself, but you're gonna be sore." She shrugged and put the pills in her pocket as Hannah appeared in the doorway.

"How's the patient?"

"She'll live," Maggie said with a smug grin.

Doc laughed and went over to Hannah. "You okay?" he asked.

She nodded.

He gave her a hug and kissed her forehead. "Okay, everybody home and to bed," he ordered.

It was an eerie feeling to stand in the living room. True to his word, Steve had a piece of plywood over the pane of glass that had been broken.

Hannah had gone to the kitchen and come back with a broom and dustpan to begin sweeping up the shards of broken glass.

I went to the front door and looked out to see a police car right in the front. I felt a little better seeing a patrol car cruise by them. I looked at my watch—4:30.

"Well, are we going to bed or staying up?" I asked.

We all looked at each other. "Staying up," we said in unison.

"I'll make some coffee," Maggie said.

"I'll light a fire," I said, trying to maintain control. I quelled the urge to break into a dead run and go screaming into the night, never looking back.

"I'll get the cognac," Hannah said.

I stopped dead.

"I just wanted to see if you were listening," she said.

My body was turning against me as I bent over for the firewood. I groaned and grabbed at my shoulder.

Maggie came out of the kitchen and put the coffee on the table in front of the couch. "What's the matter, sore?" Her voice reeked with sarcasm.

I looked to at the ceiling and counted to ten. *What would I get for strangling a snotty rich kid?*

"Kate, you could have been badly hurt. What have we gotten you into?" Hannah asked.

"After tonight, nothing," Maggie answered as she pushed me out of the way. "Go sit down." She grabbed the wood from my hand and busied herself with the fire. "I will not have anyone else hurt over whatever this is. Call your sister, get your car and get back to your normal life." She slammed the wood into the fireplace and faced me. "Why didn't you tell me you saw someone in the woods? Didn't you think I could take it? Let me tell you, I've had a lifetime of this so don't treat me like a child. And another thing—why did you go downstairs? We could have called the police and stayed in the room. What if something happened to you? Did you think of that? No, you didn't. And now you're standing there, bleeding, bandaged up and…Christ!"

She got that all out in one breath. To say she was upset would be a drastic understatement.

"Look," I said indignantly. "I heard a noise from your room and went to see if you were all right. You were asleep. Then I heard a noise downstairs, so I went to check the locks again. I noticed the doors opened and whoever it was—was right behind me. I had no chance to do anything but try to get him off me. I didn't plan this. Good grief, you can be the most ungrateful—" I stopped and put my hand to my forehead.

Maggie turned, flew past Hannah and went upstairs. I heard her slam her door.

Hannah winced. "That went well. She hasn't gotten that angry since earlier this morning. You seem to be the common denominator. You must bring out the best in her." She patted me on the back as if I'd won first prize.

"So, now what?" I asked. "I wasn't trying to do it all by myself. It just happened. You must know she's not the easiest—"

We heard her coming down the stairs. Maggie appeared as white as a ghost, and her eyes were wide.

"Did you leave my bedroom door opened after you checked on me?" Maggie asked.

"No, why?" I said.

"Because when I heard the glass door break, I flew out of bed and had to unlock the door. Did you lock it?" she said, shaking.

"It was locked? From the inside?"

I moved her out of the way and ran upstairs and into her room. Her bathroom door and closet door were both closed. I began to get panicky all over again.

Both the Winfields were behind me. Maggie was holding onto the back of my shirt and making me nervous. Hannah was standing next to Maggie holding her hand.

We all moved as if we were glued together. We walked to the bathroom door. I reached for the knob, threw the door open and backed up, my arm extended as if to protect them. It was also to give whomever a fast and clear getaway.

Nothing. I poked my head around to check out the bathroom. The shower curtain was closed and of course, it wasn't transparent. Quietly, I walked into the bathroom with the Winfield family behind me.

I reached over and quickly pulled back the curtain, with a tad too much strength. There was no one in the bathtub, but in my adrenaline rush, I yanked the curtain off the rod.

I stood there with the plastic remains in my hands. "S-Sorry…"

Maggie merely nodded and took the curtain.

Back in Maggie's room, I flipped on the light and looked around. "Is everything in place?"

Maggie shrugged as she looked around. "I believe so."

Then she went over to her bed, sat down and grabbed a pillow to hug. A piece of paper fell off the bed and onto the floor. She bent to pick it up and examine it.

She looked up, stunned, and handed it to me.

"What is it, dear?" Hannah asked in a shaky voice.

I reached over and took the paper.

YOU SLEEP LIKE AN ANGEL

The realization made my stomach lurch. He had been in her room while she was sleeping. He *must* have been in there. I interrupted him when I opened Maggie's door. Christ, he was in the room the whole time.

Why would he lock her door? What was he planning to do? Leave the note or something worse? I looked at Maggie and Hannah. By the looks on their faces, I could tell they were thinking the same thing.

"Maggie," I started while she stared at the note.

She didn't answer, just continued to stare at the note.

I went over and gently shook her shoulders. "Maggie."

She blinked and looked up. She was beginning to scare me. Like I wasn't scared spitless all ready.

"Maggie, what is it?" I said.

"My mother used to say that to me when I was a young girl. That I slept like an angel." She had tears in her eyes. Hannah looked like she was about to faint.

I was still trying to figure out why he locked the door. I looked around the room. The only other way out was through the window. I went to the bedroom door and examined the lock, pushing the button on the doorknob. My mind raced with a scenario. "Okay, let's try this. He gets in through the French doors, comes upstairs to presumably leave the note, and hears me in the hallway…"

"But why lock me in?" Maggie asked as Hannah sat next to her on the bed.

"He can't merely slip out now. He could have heard me in the hallway and knew the only way out was the way he came in, through the French doors. So, he locks you in and comes downstairs, figuring he can get by me, but it would be difficult to get by both of us." I said. "Okay, no one goes anywhere alone anymore. We all go together. The police checked the house tonight so we're fine for now." I was trying to sound confident. I hoped it worked. "Give me the note, Maggie. We'll call Steve."

We went back downstairs and in our paranoia, we double-checked the doors and locks.

Hannah sat on the couch, looking scared, tired, and, for the first time, her age. I sat at the other end of the couch. Chance, the coward, jumped up on the couch and put her head on Hannah's lap.

Hannah smiled and ruffled her ears lovingly. Damn mutt was good for something.

Maggie had started the fire. She sat in the armchair next to Hannah. We talked for a while longer, and they both fell asleep.

I, too, nodded off, but couldn't sleep. I roused myself and looked at my watch. It was 6:45. They had been asleep for two hours. I got up, very stiffly, as my shoulder throbbed wildly. I took the afghan from the back of the couch and laid it over Hannah. I found another one, with a beautiful Native American pattern on it, behind a chair. I used it to cover Maggie, even as I wondered if there was some way it could mistakenly slip into my bag when I left.

It was a cool, crisp autumn morning with a light fog covering the ground. I decided to take a walk down the path and into the woods. Perhaps the intruder dropped something when he dashed through these woods last night. In the light of day, maybe I'd find something the police couldn't see last night. It was very creepy, walking in the light fog, but with Chance a good twenty yards ahead of me, I felt braver than wandering around alone. *Ryan, you big ninny.*

Chance was in doggie heaven with her nose to the ground and her tail wagging. She roamed back and forth in the same area. What was she doing?

I walked to where Chance was tenaciously nosing about. As I got closer, I noticed small pieces of what looked like material strewn about on the ground. I picked them up and realized it was burlap. I remembered when I first saw my crazy dog with the bundle in her mouth the day before.

As I picked it up, it almost immediately disintegrated in my hands. Whatever Chance dug up must have been buried for quite a while. I looked over at her. She still had her nose to the ground, sniffing.

"What is it girl? I'd give big bucks if you could talk right now!" I ruffled her ears and looked out into the woods. I fought the shiver that ran down my spine at the thought of venturing out there alone. "Let's say we take a walk, Chance?" She heard the word "walk" and ran around in circles. I saw a fine-looking path and decided to see where it led. Chance was in front of me, eager to go exploring yet again today. I wondered if she already knew where we were heading.

As I walked along, I noticed how quiet and peaceful the woods were. I'd only walked about three-hundred feet when I came up to the lake. I was amazed. I had no idea it was this close. It was beautiful. Straight across, I saw a flock of geese lazily swimming.

With Chance running ahead, sniffing, I had an eerie feeling and shivered slightly. *Okay, here we go again.* I had the feeling of being watched. I looked in all directions but saw nothing.

Then I stopped dead and noticed Chance. She was no longer nosing around, but sitting perfectly still with her head cocked to one side. She was staring across the lake. I looked but saw nothing out of the ordinary.

"Hey girl!" I called and the scary mutt sat there, staring at whatever. With that, I heard her whine as she lay down, still staring.

As I started for her, she took off running around the small lake and into the woods. "Chance!" I called after her. I must have been a little too loud. The small flock of geese honked up a storm and flew off the lake. Chance was braver than the geese *and* me as she ran around the lake. I saw a glimpse of her darting in between the trees. Fine, now I have to go get her. I hope she didn't find an animal or something. The squirrel incident last summer came to mind.

As I started in her direction, she came darting out of the woods with something in her mouth, shaking it.

I slowly walked up to her and she dropped the material without me asking, begging or pleading. There was something wrapped around the burlap. It appeared to be a necklace of some kind. As I picked it up, I noticed it was locket with a broken chain. Tarnished badly, it must have been out in the elements for sometime. I turned it over and noticed the inscribed initial M.

A few feet away something glinted. A watch, also badly tarnished. *What in the hell was this?* I carefully searched the surrounding area. When I saw more burlap pieces, I knelt down and picked them up. A ring fell out. I looked at it. It was a wedding band. On the inside was an inscription: *All my love, Jonathan. 6/3/65.*

I was shocked. I frantically looked around for anything else. I couldn't remember any places by the house that looked like she might have been digging. I searched for signs of her digging around here, but found nothing. Where did she find these?

Yesterday, she had something in her mouth, shaking it up. I looked at the letter on the locket. My curiosity was piqued, but I decided to give it to Maggie and let her take the first look at the inside. I carefully put all the findings in my breast pocket.

I started back to the house. I looked down and saw Chance staring at me, her nose in the air. I knelt down and she immediately snorted at the pocket of my shirt. I ruffled the fur on her head.

"Is this what you found, you bloodhound, you?"

As I watched my mutt sniff around, I thought of the intruder last night. My father's words were haunting me—everything is useful. Never discount a thing no matter how small it may seem. I was missing something.

What came to mind was how easily I'd fought last night's prowler off. Was I actually stronger than I thought? What were the odds of that? I'd heard of adrenaline rushes where people lifted cars and all that. Either I was Super-Adrenaline Woman or he was a wuss. I was desperately trying to remember some kind a distinguishing feature about the intruder.

What was it?

Kate Sweeney

CHAPTER SEVEN

I decided to walk to the stable. As I pulled the door opened and walked in, I noticed the saddles were hanging neatly on a ledge. Then over in the far corner, next to a small bale of hay, I saw what looked like a stirrup. I quickly walked over and saw the remainder of the saddle behind the bale. I turned the saddle over, picked it up and swung it over the ledge.

As I set it in place, I noticed the length of leather that held the stirrup to the saddle was cut almost in half. It was practically dangling off. Additionally, also cut almost completely, was the strap that goes under the horse to secure the saddle.

I looked around the stable and everything else looked normal. It all looked like what I'd expect a stable to look like. There were five stalls and five horses. A few pitchforks, a couple of shovels, some other tools and grooming supplies—the usual stable stuff, I'd guess.

Chance was nosing around, obviously enthralled with so many new smells.

I heard Thunder, the wild one, way in the last stall, huffing and snorting. A chestnut mare was in another stall, snorting and bobbing her head when she saw me. I walked over to her when I spotted a big burlap bag of oats that said Carson Grain and Feed on it. Carson? As in Allison Carson? Probably her father, I couldn't imagine Miss Carson owning a feed store. I took a handful and let the mare eat.

It was then the stable door opened. I turned around to see Bedford coming into the stable. He hadn't noticed me yet, but he had noticed the damaged saddle on the ledge. I watched him for a moment. He looked puzzled, which I found interesting. Last night he gave me the creeps. I wanted to know why.

It was then he spotted me. "G'morning Miss. I didn't see ya standing there."

"Sorry, didn't mean to startle you. Is that Maggie's saddle from yesterday? Looks like it's in bad shape," I said, looking right at him.

"Yes, it is. I was coming to fetch it and get it fixed."

I wondered how Maggie with all her expertise could miss the damage to the saddle. "Does Maggie saddle her own horse, Bedford?"

Bedford had gone over and was brushing one of the horses. "No, usually if I know she's going out, I do it."

"And did you yesterday?"

He glanced up. "No."

"Where were you?" I asked.

"I have Thursdays off, but Miss Hannah called me to come and get the horse." He continued brushing the mare.

"Don't you find it odd how an expert horsewoman like Miss Winfield can fall off a horse so easily?" I asked, leaning against the ledge.

"Strange things happen all the time Miss," he said. "I'm sorry I wasn't there to help."

"I am too. Bedford, where do you live?"

He motioned outside and said, "I live in an apartment above the garage. It's small but comfortable. It suits me."

"Well, last night was disturbing to say the least. I don't suppose you heard or saw anything?" I asked.

"No, Miss. When I heard the sirens, I came down but you were already inside with the police. Like I said, I spoke with them. Then I came around and found you and the ladies. I am sorry, I didn't come out sooner."

"Well, if you didn't hear anything how could you know? Funny you didn't hear the noise when we crashed through the French doors, though." I kept my eyes on him.

He frowned as he continued with his task. "You sure you're all right, Miss?"

"I'm not the issue here, Bedford. I would think you'd be worried about Maggie."

"I do worry, Miss," he said. He sounded sincere, but something didn't ring true.

"What do you think is happening?"

He looked at me over the ledge, and said plainly, "I don't know what's going on Miss. I just take care of the horses and the property."

"But surely, you've been here forever, you have to have some opinion. Let's take this for example. What is your opinion of this?" I held out only the watch I'd found. It was still in the burlap.

He came out of the stall and looked down at my hand. His eyes widened. He looked up and, with the brush in his hand, he looked right at me. He had a threatening look on his face. He took two steps toward me and pointed the brush in my direction.

"It's a watch, Miss. Now, if you're asking if I know whose watch it is, I don't know. I learned long ago not to ask questions or go nosin' around. You might do well to do the same."

I was a little frightened, but mostly angry. "That sounds a tad like a threat, Bedford," I said, trying to keep my voice steady. "A moment ago you said you cared about Maggie. Well, I care for her as well." I amazed myself at how easy that came out. "Something is happening around here, Bedford. Maggie and Hannah have asked for my help. I'm not sure what I can do, but I'm going to try."

He looked out of the open stall door and into the woods. "This is an old family, Miss…"

"With old secrets?" I prodded. He shot an angry look my way.

"Don't talk of things ya know nothing about."

"Who can talk of such things then, Bedford?" I felt as though I was getting somewhere with him.

He put the brushes away and turned to me. "Everyone has secrets, Miss. I'm sure even you."

We were having a good old-fashioned staring contest when I felt a presence behind me in the doorway.

I turned to see a woman, maybe in her late fifties. She was tall, slender and had salt-and-pepper hair she had pulled back into a tight bun, which looked a little too tight. What I noticed most of all, though, were her eyes. They were almost black. She was wearing riding clothes and had her gloves and riding crop in one hand. I had no idea how long she had been there or what she had overheard.

Chance barked at her, and then bravely hid behind me and growled.

"I don't believe I know you." She extended her hand. "My name is Sarah Winfield, I'm Maggie's aunt."

I took her hand. She had a good grip. If Hannah was the aunt everybody loved, this woman struck me as the aunt no one wanted to kiss.

"It's nice to meet you. Kate Ryan," I said.

She turned from me and glared at Bedford, who appeared as if he wanted no part of this conversation. "I was out riding and I think the poor creature has something stuck in his shoe. Bedford, please go and check."

Without a word, Bedford took a tool and left the stable.

She turned back to me and said rather coolly, "I understand there's been some excitement." She put her hand up to hair as if to straighten it. Why, I don't know, there wasn't a hair out of place. "I hope no one was seriously hurt."

"No, not seriously hurt, but it was a little scary. Do you have any idea what's going on?"

She looked at me for a moment. "No, Miss Ryan I can't say that I do. Are you investigating?"

"No, no, I just seem to be in the middle of whatever is going on and I'm curious." I was still standing by the sabotaged saddle. I held up the cut leather strap. "They sure don't make saddles like they used to."

Bedford came into the stable. "He's okay, just a stone in his shoe." He limped over and put the tool back.

I started for the door. "Well, Mrs. Winfield, it was nice to meet you. Perhaps I'll see you again."

"Yes, Miss Ryan that would be nice," she said.

It would be nice if I thought she meant it. I walked out of the stable and Chance barked at her again before following me out.

Chance ran ahead of me. I walked back to the stable door, which was open enough to hear their conversation.

"What was that all about, Bedford?" I heard Sarah ask.

"Nothing, she's just nosing around like her dog."

He thinks that's an insult. Chance has found out more than I have.

"Bedford, what did you tell her?" I heard the threatening tone in her voice.

"I said nothing, Miss Sarah. And where would I start? Mr. Alexander?"

"Don't piss me off, Bedford. I'm not in the mood."

With that, the stable door opened completely, pinning me between the door and the stable. *Shit!* I stood there frozen as I heard Sarah gallop away.

"Bitch," I heard Bedford grumble as he closed the stable door.

For a moment, I stood there plastered against the wall. *Well, that was interesting.* I quickly headed back to the house.

As I approached the deck, Maggie walked out with the afghan draped around her.

"Good morning," she said, with a sleepy yawn.

"Your ankle seems better," I said.

"It feels much better. It was a slight sprain. Besides, I'm a quick healer. How's the shoulder?" she asked looking out at the woods.

"Fine, good," I lied horribly.

"Nice try." She snuggled the afghan around her and smiled. "Thanks for the afghan."

"No problem, I was actually trying to think of a way to smuggle it out in my duffel bag. Guess who I just met? Aunt Sarah."

She looked surprised. "Really, where?"

I explained the stable incident. "She's a cool customer."

"She's always been that way—very distant and forbidding. I guess she's not a happy person. I don't know why, she's married to Uncle Nathan who is a nice, considerate man. He's a little weak where she's concerned but he treats her well. I have never been able to figure her out, though." She pointed to the woods to the right. "See that path? They live about a quarter mile behind the woods. It was my grandparent's house. This place is like a small compound."

I told her of my walk. Then I pulled out the jewelry and showed it to her. "Look what I found."

She reached out to take the ring and read the engraving. "This is my mother's wedding ring. I know that. I don't think I've ever seen the rest of it. Where in the world did you find these?" She was amazed and seemed at the same time to be very apprehensive.

"I went out with Chance. She found them across the lake, I believe." I pointed in the general vicinity. Maggie was studying the tarnished jewelry. "Maggie, I hate to ask you, but could you tell me how your mother died?"

She looked at me sadly and then gazed out at the woods. "She was murdered, Kate, twenty years ago. The police said it was a robbery. She was at the lake and the thief stabbed her and left her there." She stopped and put her hands to her face, as if to hide her tears.

Murdered? Crap. I reached over and put my hand on her shoulder. "Maggie, I'm so sorry to ask you this," I said. I put my arm around her and gave her a reassuring hug. I felt myself wanting to hold her. Instead, I quickly let her go.

She looked up at me, her eyes red with tears. "It's okay. I just haven't said that out loud in quite some time." She took a deep breath.

Murdered, I repeated again to myself. I looked at the jewelry. "Why would someone rob your mother then leave all the stolen jewelry in the woods?" I asked myself out loud. "Is this your mother's watch and locket?"

"Like I said, I don't know," she said. "Maybe Aunt Hannah will know."

Hannah was in the kitchen making coffee when we sat down and Maggie put the locket on the table.

"Good morning my darlings," she said cheerfully. She looked at the locket. "What's that?" she asked, putting the pot of coffee on the table.

"Aunt Hannah, look at it. We were hoping you'd know," Maggie said.

Hannah sat down and picked up the locket and studied it. Then Maggie showed her the other tarnished jewelry. Hannah's eyes got as big as saucers, and she looked up at both of us. "Where in heaven's name did these come from?"

She studied the locket while I retold the morning's adventure.

"Of course, it must be Miranda's. I seem to remember her wearing something like this. However, good heavens, that was more than twenty-five years ago, so I can't be absolutely certain..." her voice trailed off.

As of yet, no one had tried to open the locket. My curiosity was extremely piqued and I was getting very impatient. "Wouldn't you like to open the locket?" I asked.

Hannah looked at it sitting on the table. "Yes."

"Would you like me to open it?" I asked and she nodded.

I picked it up and tried to open it, but it had been out in the elements and wouldn't budge at first. After a couple of tries, it gave way and opened. I put it on the table. A lock of hair fell out and

Maggie moved to pick it up. I instinctively reached over and grabbed her wrist.

"Wait, let's not. Hannah, can you get me a plastic bag, please?"

I gingerly picked up the lock of hair, and put it in the bag. They both watched curiously.

"Though everything has been out in the elements all these years, you never know what this lock of hair might tell us. The less we disturb the better. I doubt there's anything, but let's make sure."

With the locket opened, Maggie picked it up. I figured it was out in the elements for so long, all fingerprints had likely long since eroded away.

"Why doesn't just one of us do this?"

They both nodded. "Go right ahead." I knew they'd spent way too much time around each other, since they kept doing and saying things simultaneously.

I very carefully opened the locket, keeping it on the table. I looked at the pictures; of course, I had no clue. It was a man and a little girl who I was sure was Maggie—the resemblance was too great. I gently spun it around for both of them to see.

They stared at it for a second then looked at each other, then back at the locket once again.

Maggie looked completely confused. Hannah was ashen. I was curious.

"Who are they?"

It seemed it took an eternity for them to answer me. Maggie shook her head in amazement and Hannah swallowed and took a deep breath.

"It's you and your father, right?" I asked.

Maggie looked at me. "No, it's me and Uncle Nathan." She seemed completely bewildered.

"Are you sure?" I asked. Maggie gave me an exasperated look and I felt the color rush to my face. "Of course you are. Sorry. I never thought a brother-in-law's picture would be in it."

Hannah still said nothing. I glanced at her and knew something was up. "Well, I assume the lock of hair is yours," I said, looking at Maggie.

She nodded. "I agree, though I don't remember this locket. Maybe I remember her wearing it occasionally, but I can't be sure. It was so long ago." Her eyes welled with tears and I felt bad for her. Then she blinked and they just rolled down her face, without her changing expression. I swallowed hard at the sad expression.

I looked at the clock, it was nine. I looked at both of them; this was taking its toll. "Well, why don't we discuss this further over breakfast? Breakfast is on me," I said.

"That's a good idea. I'll be ready in twenty minutes," Maggie said and got up. Hannah declined and I felt perhaps she didn't want to be part of the discussion.

"Would you mind watching Ole Yeller for me?" I asked, motioning to Chance, who was sleeping in the doorway.

"Not at all, Chance and I will be fast friends by the time you get back. She may not want to leave. Now go, go," Hannah said with a shooing gesture.

I took the tarnished jewelry and carefully placed it in a plastic bag. "Keep an eye on this, Hannah."

"Dear Lord, I have to fix up a room for your sister and brother-in-law. Good grief! You two have fun."

She got up, kissed my cheek and was out the door with Chance following her.

CHAPTER EIGHT

It was a nice cool, crisp autumn morning and I'm sure the scenery would have been beautiful, if I could have seen it. Maggie drove far too fast.

"You drive a car as fast as you ride a horse," I said, as I instinctively pressed my foot on the imaginary brake.

"And you complain too much," she answered and put her foot on the gas.

We parked in what I could only guess was the downtown of this small town and walked across the street to a little diner for breakfast.

As usual, I was starving by the time we sat in a booth by the window.

I started the conversation as the waitress set a coffeepot in front of us. "So you're a doctor." I eagerly poured both of us a much-needed cup.

"*Almost* a doctor," she corrected me.

"I appreciate you taking care of me Almost Dr. Winfield. Seriously, thank you."

"I should be thanking you after what you did last night. I'm sorry I yelled at you. I have a frightful temper, but you're the last person in the world I should be angry with."

As Maggie spoke, I noticed a man at the counter staring at both of us. He was the epitome of tall, dark and handsome. "Who's the guy at the end of the counter?"

She glanced over and grunted. "Christ, it's my cousin, Charlie. I thought he was out of town."

"He's very handsome."

"I think that's part of his problem. He even dated Allison once or twice," she said as she drank her coffee.

"Really?" That surprised me. "Maybe I got the wrong impression, but I thought you and she had a relationship at some point in time."

"Yes, we did. We were involved for four years. We were having problems for the last six months of the relationship and thought a vacation was in order. We were in England. She was buying antiques for her shop. We argued one day, and I stormed out. I walked around London for hours, knowing it was over, but not wanting to give up." She shrugged. I saw the dejected look.

"I know what you mean, Maggie. The realization hits you right between the eyes. You wonder what in the world you were thinking. How you could have been so foolish. It's a hollow feeling," I said and stared at my coffee cup.

Once again, the visions flashed through my mind. *How could I have been so foolish, so easily taken in?*

"Speaking from experience?" she asked. I looked into her eyes and for the first time in quite a while, I thought of spilling my guts.

Then the anxious feeling started once again coupled with the urge to get up and run. "Everybody falls in love, Maggie. I'm no different. So, you were in London..." I said, dismissing the topic. I felt the eyes of scrutiny upon me and drank my coffee. *Leave it be, Maggie, please.*

Graciously, she continued. "I went back to the hotel and found Allison with Charlie of all people. They were standing in an intimate embrace. They didn't even notice I was there. I took the first plane back. She tried to tell me I was imagining things, that we were all childhood friends and there was nothing intimate about Charlie, that I was being paranoid and ridiculous. I don't know, maybe I was. In any event, she wanted to try again. She's been persistent ever since."

"Why would she want someone else when she had you?" I immediately felt the blush rush to my face.

Maggie raised an eyebrow and grinned. "Well, that was an unexpected but nice thing to say."

"Well, you, I..." *No stammering, please.*

Luckily, my new best friend, the waitress, arrived.

Maggie looked at my plate in amazement. "Where are you going put all that?"

"Hey, I'm gonna need all the nourishment I can get. Getting thrown through a door takes its toll."

Her smile faded and she became very serious. "You shouldn't be involved in this. I don't even know you."

"Well, I am involved now, and you do know me now, so let's put our heads together and figure this thing out." I could feel her watching me as I ate a mouthful of pancakes. I was in the middle of a bite when I glanced up to see her looking at me. "Do I have egg on my face?" I self-consciously looked down at my shirt. I was afraid my feeding frenzy was out of control.

"It dawned on me that I know absolutely nothing about you. Except that you once had a private investigation business and now you're a photographer."

"What kind of photographer?" I asked, wagging my fork in her direction.

"A well-known photographer," she corrected herself with a slight grin.

"That's better."

She gave me a suspicious glance, which again, I ignored. She was about to go on when her cousin got out of his chair.

"Uh-oh, Charlie at three o'clock. Wait, that's nine o'clock to you," I whispered.

She gave me an exasperated look, and looked up to see her cousin standing next to our table.

He was indeed very handsome with deep brown eyes and a devilish smile, almost a smirk. In that respect, he looked like Maggie. Apparently, they came from a strong gene pool. He looked Irish, like a sea captain on the cover of one of those romantic novels.

"Hello cousin," he said.

"Hi, Charlie, I thought you were out of town. You've been gone for a few weeks, haven't you?" Maggie asked without even glancing up from her plate.

"Yes, I have, in London. I've got a few irons in the fire," he added with a grin before looking at me. "We haven't met. I'm Charlie Winfield."

"I'm sorry, this is Kate Ryan. Kate, this is my cousin."

"Nice to meet you," I said, trying to be polite. "I met your mother this morning."

"You met my mother first thing in the morning? You poor thing. I can't believe you still have an appetite." He turned his attention back to Maggie. "What brings you to town, Maggie? You haven't been in for quite a while."

Maggie said nothing, which I thought was either odd or rude or perhaps both.

"Would you like to join us?" I asked. Might as well get to know the rest of the family. You never knew who all was implicated in whatever this mess was.

"This is cozy," he said settling in next to Maggie. He poured himself a cup of coffee as he glanced at both of us. "I understand there was a slight problem last night," he said, looking at my bandaged brow. "Everyone all right?"

"I'm fine. Thank you," I said. Maggie wasn't saying much and I didn't want to start anything.

"Someone broke into the house and left a note on my pillow," Maggie finally said, never looking up. "It scared me to death, Charlie."

He was shocked. "In your room?"

As I told him about the intruder and finding the jewelry, I thought he looked a little uneasy.

He put his arm around Maggie and kissed the side of her head. "So, Miss Ryan, or may I call you Kate? Miss Ryan sounds like a schoolteacher, and you don't look like any schoolteacher I ever had."

Maggie and I looked at each other. I smiled warily.

He apparently caught the look. "Oh, am I barking up the wrong tree?"

I smiled and shrugged. "You can't win 'em all."

"But he'll try," Maggie said into her coffee cup.

It was not a joke. I looked down and stirred my coffee.

Charlie stiffened and gave her a side-glance. "Well, I should be off. Please let me know if I can do anything. We *are* related, remember." He held his hand out to me. "It was a pleasure meeting you, Kate. Perhaps we'll meet again soon. I'd like that."

Hell, he sounded sincere.

As I watched him walk across the street, I thought he was quite a gentleman. He did not look like someone who bullied little girls when he was a boy, as Hannah had said.

I was still watching when I saw Allison walking down the other side of the street.

"Uh-oh, Allison at nine o'clock—wait, three." I was all turned around.

Charlie crossed the street and walked right up to Allison. They stopped and exchanged a few words. She laughed and went on her way. He continued in the opposite direction.

Nothing special. No signs of anything between them, I thought. However, I didn't know them at all. Maybe that was to my advantage. I could be objective where it was obvious Maggie could not. This was something else to add to the growing list of things I didn't know.

We finished our breakfast and walked out into the bright sunshine of a beautiful autumn morning. I could tell Maggie was upset about seeing Charlie and Allison.

She must still care about her, I thought. Allison was an attractive woman, and they had spent years together, so why shouldn't she care?

I was so lost in my thoughts I nearly missed Maggie's next words.

"I don't suppose you can ride a horse?" she asked.

"Yes, I can. Why?"

"I thought maybe we could take the horses out," she said. "That is, if your shoulder isn't bothering you. I know at your age the healing process takes a while longer."

"You're asking for it, you know that don't you?" I asked. "Let's go, you little brat."

She laughed all the way back to the car. I tried to dismiss the feeling of contentment her contagious laughter made me feel.

CHAPTER NINE

As we saddled the horses, I remembered my conversation with Bedford earlier that morning. "Maggie, do you saddle your own horse? Or coming from obscene wealth, do you have Bedford do it for you?" I thought it was funny, but from the glare in the blue eyes, I could tell Maggie did not. However, she didn't answer. "You have Bedford saddle your horse, don't you?" I accused.

"He likes doing it for me," she said as she roughly cinched the poor mare. "He's very efficient, he had Thunder all ready for me yesterday morning. But yes, Miss Ryan I can saddle my own horse if need be. I can even feed myself on occasion."

"Okay, okay, it's just that Bedford told me you saddled Thunder yesterday."

"Aunt Sarah had him saddle both our horses yesterday. Why would Bedford lie, or do you think I'm the one who's lying?"

"Maggie, let's not get carried away. I don't think you're lying, but there is something odd here. Let's drop this for now. I see your left eye twitch, and that cannot be good."

We rode side by side but didn't take the trail that led to the woods. Maggie suggested we take the horses down by her uncle's house.

It didn't take a brain surgeon to realize she was avoiding the woods. I thought of telling her to confront her demons but thought better of it. I had no business telling her to do something, I had yet to accomplish myself. I glanced at Maggie, who looked deep in thought.

"A penny for your thoughts, Maggie."

She looked at me and smiled. "Touché. I was thinking about my mother. After she died, I had this dream of a faceless person chasing me through the woods. Suddenly, I'd be in the lake with water up to my waist, while someone grabbed my ankles. I couldn't move or scream. My mother stood on the other side of the lake, as if she were waiting for me. The harder I tried to get to her, the deeper I sank. As I was about to go under, I'd wake up." She looked at me. "Pretty nutty, huh?"

"No, not at all," I said.

My mind drifted back to that night four years ago and all the nightmares I'd had since. Through all the horrible nights, I'd wake in a pool of sweat, screaming. Suddenly, I felt my body shake as an anxiety attack started. I took a deep breath and it subsided. *I could show Maggie a thing or two about being nutty.*

I looked up to see her once again watching me with a curious look. "Last night, before I woke, I had a similar dream. It was almost like someone was trying to tell me to wake up, but I couldn't, you know?" I said.

She nodded while looking at the woods. "Well, whoever it was, I'm grateful. I don't know what would have happened if you hadn't come into the room when you did."

We were both quiet as I tried to dismiss the idea. I didn't want to think what would've happened if I hadn't woken when I did. I looked over at Maggie, noticing the forlorn look on her face. I felt something pull at my heart. I felt bad for this young woman and I only hoped I would be able to help in some way.

"Hey, can't we get some room to open up these horses?"

"If you think you're up to it."

"Just get me there."

I said my prayers, hoping I wouldn't fall off the horse. It seemed I was promising a great many things to the Man upstairs lately.

Maggie led us to a clearing and we stopped for a moment to enjoy the breathtaking view. Straight ahead was an open meadow and I could almost feel my horse chomping at the bit to break into a steady gallop.

I hadn't been riding for a while, but I'd spent many a time on horseback over the years, in many different states, getting perfect photos.

Maggie gave me a challenging look then did the ole giddy-up and took off. I watched for a few seconds. She was good. *Oh well, here goes nothing.* I struggled for a few minutes to get the feeling back. I wanted to make sure I was back in the saddle again, not out of it. My childhood hero, Roy Rogers, would be proud, but I knew my arse would be killing me later.

All at once, I felt a little more at ease on the galloping mare. However, my inner thighs were burning, my muscles clenching to stay in control. I was having the time of my life. I cannot remember how far we had gone before Maggie motioned to me to slow down.

"These horses aren't used to going so fast this long. Let's walk them," she said, a little breathless. We walked in silence for a time before Maggie spoke. "Okay, I'm impressed. I didn't think you could ride that well."

"I'm a little surprised myself. It's been a while and I must admit I was holding on for dear life there for a minute."

"Where did you learn to ride?" she asked.

"I've been on photo assignments all over the country, in such remote places you couldn't reach them by car." I shrugged. "Horseback was the only option. I love the untouched beauty of this country. There's so much out there the average person can't get to. I like to think through my photos, I'm giving them the opportunity to see God's creations before we muck it up with concrete and parking lots." I suddenly realized how much I had been talking and let out a nervous laugh. "Am I talking too much? I haven't talked like this in a long while. Sorry."

It was true. I hadn't talked about my job or anything else with anyone but my editor for quite a while. I realized how pathetic that was. I stole a glance at Maggie. She was easy to talk to. Maybe too easy.

"Why should you be sorry?" Maggie asked. "It's fascinating. I would love to see some of your work."

"Well, when all this is over, perhaps you can visit Chicago," I said.

"I'd like that," she said. It seemed as if she meant it, and I had to admit the idea appealed to me. Then again, it scared the hell out of me.

We walked the horses for a while longer. Enough time for me to think about the intruder again. Something wasn't right and it was nagging at me. What in the world was it and why the hell couldn't I think of it? I rubbed my forehead and ran my fingers through my hair in frustration.

"Okay, you're doing that thinking thing and you haven't heard a word I've said. What's bothering you?"

"I don't know. Something about the intruder last night that I can't put my finger on. I know I'm no Wonder Woman, trust me, but if he hadn't hit me in the head, I honestly think I could have subdued him. Something"—I ran my fingers through my hair again.

Then as we walked, a gentle breeze blew and Maggie's perfume wafted over my way. I looked at her and sniffed. I stopped as it dawned on me.

"Perfume! That's it!" I said.

She looked at me. "What, my perfume? I'm glad you like it."

"That's it!" I exclaimed triumphantly as I leaned over and stupidly sniffed her neck.

"What in the world?" Her face reddened as her hand instinctively went to her neck.

"What a colossal idiot!" I exclaimed while looking at Maggie, who glared at me. "Oh, no, no, not you. Me, I'm the idiot. That's what I couldn't remember. The minute I smelled your perfume, it occurred to me—the intruder was wearing perfume as well. Geez, I can't believe I didn't think of that before. My father is rolling over in his grave right now," I said and shook my head. "God, it was a woman."

"Are you sure?" she asked amazed.

"Positive. Let's get back."

We saddled up and headed back toward the house. Maggie suddenly pulled her horse to a stop.

"What's the hold up?" I asked.

She said nothing. I eased my horse up next to hers. Maggie was staring into the woods, so naturally, I followed her gaze. I didn't see anything.

"Maggie?" I asked, ignoring my quick shiver. "What's wrong?"

"I-I thought I saw someone in the woods, over there." She pointed in the direction we were looking.

"Are you sure, Maggie?" I asked.

"Maybe not. Let's get out of here, though."

The uneasiness in her voice had me looking once again. Then I saw something move.

Deep in the woods, a woman was standing alone. She was dressed in white that made her stand out against the dark woods. She stood so still, it was unnerving.

She was watching us.

I looked at Maggie, who had obviously seen her now, too. I grabbed her arm to steady her, or to steady me. Maggie leaned into me.

"Do you see?" she whispered.

Is she nuts? "Yes, I do. Why doesn't she move?" I asked. We were talking in whispers. "Is she looking at us? Who is she, can you make her out?"

"I can't tell. The trees are in the way. Kate, I'm frightened. We just can't sit here."

"Okay, let's go introduce ourselves," I said, not wanting to do any such thing.

I had a feeling Maggie felt the same as I saw the fear flash across her face. She then nodded.

As we started in her direction, the woman abruptly turned and faded into the woods. We stopped and looked at each other.

"Okay, did you see that?" I asked. Maggie nodded quickly and shivered.

"Let's see where she's going," I said.

We went off the path and rode in the direction the woman appeared to have gone. We were getting deeper and deeper into the woods.

All of a sudden, Maggie's horse reared and took off. As she galloped into the woods, I could see Maggie faltering, almost falling off the horse. She was pulling on the reins, trying to stop her horse.

I chased after, but soon lost sight of her. I stopped, listened and heard nothing. I suddenly realized I was completely turned around. I had the horse canter slowly while I looked for any indication of Maggie's direction.

I had to raise my arms defensively to fend off branches that seemed to come alive as they grabbed for me. I made my way through the heavy brush to a little clearing. I stopped and called out, to no avail. Just as I was about to call out again, an inner voice stopped me.

Leaves rustled to my side, and I turned to look. There was nothing.

Though it was still afternoon, the massive pine trees gave the woods an ominous darkness, allowing only a few rays of late sunlight through. I waited, straining to hear something, anything. As soon as the horse slowly started to lope, I heard the rustling to my right, once again. I stopped, and the rustling stopped. I continued, and the rustling continued. The woods and I were doing some kind of a macabre two-step.

Someone, something is walking right by me, I thought as I frantically strained my eyes to see. The sun had gone behind the clouds and the woods took on an even more menacing darkness. *Okay, don't panic. How far can she go?*

My shoulder started aching horribly. I was tired and scared and wanted to go home. *Nothing better happen to that brat.* I looked in every direction. I heard nothing, only my own labored breathing.

"Where did she go, boy?" I asked the horse.

Moving along slowly, I kept my senses alert for any indication of where she might have gone. Then I saw the brush moving and heard a muffled cry. Maggie's horse bolted through the woods, about fifty feet or so in front of me. I started in that direction, but quickly stopped when I saw Maggie lying on the ground.

Literally leaping off my horse, I knelt next to her, laid her head on my lap and held her. I looked around, hoping her horse would come back, but it was long gone—probably back at the stable already.

The woods were silent, too silent. I looked down at Maggie. Her long auburn hair was full of leaves and branches. She looked very much like Medusa. I picked the leaves out of her hair and whispered her name. Finally, she stirred and opened her eyes. She seemed confused and disoriented for a moment as she tried to get up.

"Easy," I said.

"What happened?" she asked, clutching my arm and pulling me close. I had no problem with that. I was petrified.

"I have no idea. Can you get up?"

"I think so," she said sitting up and rubbing the back of her neck. "I couldn't stop. She reared and I couldn't stop her. I think I hit a tree limb." She still looked a little groggy.

"Okay, let's see if you can stand," I said.

As she stood, her legs buckled. I put my arm around her waist to steady her and she stood still for a minute or two with her hands resting on my shoulders, her head against my chest. We stood there for a moment or two longer.

"Your heart is beating fast there, Miss Ryan," she whispered and looked up into my eyes.

"You scared the hell out of me, Miss Winfield," I said, hearing my voice tremble. I looked down into her blue eyes. For one ridiculous moment, I thought of kissing her. *Good grief, Ryan, she's nearly knocked for a loop, you're scared spitless, and your only thought is...* "Look, can you walk? I think we should get the hell out of here."

We walked to the horse. I had my hand under her elbow to steady her because she was definitely wobbling.

"Let's get you up on the horse," I said feeling as if the woods themselves were coming alive around us.

I steadied the horse and helped her up. I was trying not to panic and I felt very vulnerable in these woods.

Then I got my foot in the stirrup and got on behind her. I put my arms around her waist and held on tight. The last thing we needed was for both of us to fall off. I started in the direction of the house.

"This is like something out of a movie," she said as she leaned back against me.

"Yeah, an Abbott and Costello movie," I grunted and kicked the sides of the horse.

"My head, Kate. I'm sorry I think I'm going to pass out," she whispered.

"Maggie, stay with me. Are we going in the right direction?" I asked.

She lifted her head and nodded.

"Okay, hang in there—we'll be at the house in a few minutes."
God, please don't let me fall off the back of this stupid horse.

I rode, slowly, not wanting to jar her. Then, ahead of us, a man on horseback came into view. My horse got a little skittish and I steadied him.

"What in the world?" He looked at Maggie, clearly shocked. "Young woman, what are you doing?"

"Her horse reared and bolted. I lost sight of her and I guess he threw her. Who are you?" I asked.

"I am this woman's uncle, Dr. Nathan Winfield." He brought his horse closer. It was then I noticed the resemblance to Hannah.

Odd that he would show up at this time. Maggie was coming around but still had her head against my chest. He reached over, checked her eyes and felt her forehead.

"Okay, let's keep her where she is and get back to the house." He turned and trotted ahead of me, leading the way.

Hannah was standing on the deck in the back when we came through the clearing. Teri and Mac were standing behind her.

Nathan jumped off his horse, took Maggie from me, and helped her upstairs.

"What in the world happened, Kate?" Hannah asked, obviously worried as she looked at me, then in the direction Nathan had gone, clearly at odds as to where she should be.

"Dammit," I said disgusted with myself. "Her horse bolted through the woods and threw her."

Teri and Mac stood close by. "Are you all right?" Teri asked.

"I'm fine, Ter."

I explained what happened. Hannah put her hand on my arm. "You saw someone in the woods. I knew it. Someone *is* out there."

Teri and Mac were understandably confused and I promised to fill them in later. We talked as we went upstairs to Maggie's room.

I watched Maggie while her uncle examined her. When he finished, he motioned us all out into the hallway.

"She's fine," he said. "She's got a good bump on the noggin. Keep it iced for twenty minutes or so. She's awake and coherent. Let's keep her still. With head injuries, you have to be careful. Try to get her to talk and focus, but keep her still. If she wakes and starts vomiting, call me immediately." He spoke in a soft, caring tone and put his arm around his sister. "She'll be fine."

"I'll go sit with her," I said.

"We'll be downstairs," Teri said.

I went into the room and stood for a moment, watching her. I felt a hand on my shoulder and I turned to find Dr. Winfield with an icepack. He walked by and sat on the edge of the bed and gently placed the ice against the side of her head.

"She's got a hard head, it runs in the family. She'll be fine. Why don't you stay with her? Hannah is naturally upset. I'll go see to her."

We exchanged places as he left the room. I held the ice in place and gently ran the back of my fingers against her soft cheek. As she stirred and opened her eyes, I took my hand away.

She looked at me for a moment, as if trying to focus. She reached her hand up to her forehead and tried to sit even as I pushed her back onto the pillow.

"Hey, take it easy. You had a nasty fall," I said.

She blinked and looked at me. "I fell off my horse."

"Ya know, kid, you might want to find a better mode of transportation. This is twice since we've met that you've fallen off your horse. Of course, the fact I'm with you when it happens means absolutely nothing," I said with a grin.

She laughed and winced as I held the ice in place. "How do you feel? You scared the life out of me."

"Really?" She searched my face and smiled faintly. "Why?"

I looked down into her blue eyes for a moment. "Because I don't want to be the one to tell Hannah you broke your stubborn little neck, that's why."

"Oh. Well, I'm all right."

Did I hear disappointment in her voice?

"We did see a lady in the woods, didn't we, Kate?" she asked.

"Yes, we both saw her. I don't know who she was, but we saw her."

"I feel like an idiot, falling off my horse. Again."

I laughed slightly and avoided her glare. "Hey, the way your horse bolted, I'm surprised you stayed on as long as you did. However, if you like I can give you riding lessons some day."

She laughed, then winced, and put her hand to her head.

"Look, you need to keep quiet. I'll go downstairs and you can rest. Teri and Mac are here. You rest." I looked down into the blue eyes again. "Maggie I'm..." I had absolutely no idea what I was about to say.

"Yes?"

"I'm glad you weren't hurt too badly. Rest now."

Hannah, Nathan, Teri and Mac were sitting at the kitchen table drinking coffee.

"Did she come around?" Hannah asked.

"Yes, we talked and she seemed alert."

"Miss Ryan, Hannah has been filling me in on what's been happening. Thank you for helping out." Nathan said, drinking his coffee. I could tell his mind was elsewhere.

"I'm glad I could be here. Did Hannah tell you what I found?" I picked up the plastic bag that was still on the table.

"Yes, it's amazing. After all these years to have them turn up," he said.

"Dug up. Sorry, my insane canine went amok."

I searched his face—it revealed nothing. I glanced at Teri, who looked confused. I couldn't wait to fill her in. I handed the locket to Dr. Winfield. He took it and I saw a flash of sadness cross his face.

"This is Miranda's," he said. "I remember... when she wore this."

There was silence around the table for a moment. "Dr. Winfield, did you know your picture is in the locket?" I asked.

He took a deep breath and opened the locket. "This would be like Miranda. At one time we were close." He closed the locket and almost reverently placed it on the table. "To think they've been here all the time, all these years... Anyway, Miss Ryan, I understand you're an accomplished photographer *and* amateur sleuth."

I couldn't tell if he was being sarcastic or not.

"Perhaps you think you can figure out who would break into Maggie's house and leave that note," he said absently looking at his coffee.

I was about to ask him about that very thing, when he abruptly stood and kissed Hannah on the top of her head.

"Well, I should be going," he said. "Make sure Maggie stays quiet for the rest of the day. I think she'll be fine—she's a healthy girl. See you tomorrow, sis. It was a pleasure meeting all of you."

I watched him as he mounted his horse and easily rode down the trail in into the woods. I looked over at Hannah who was watching as well. She looked tired and worried.

"So, you're knocking this poor kid off her horse right and left, huh Kate?" Mac said proudly.

Hannah laughed heartily. "I like him."

"Want him?" Teri asked.

We seemed to relax for a moment, as we laughed at poor Mac's blushing face.

"Hannah, you just met Mac and already you have him blushing. Good girl!" I said.

"How is Maggie?" Teri asked.

I could tell by her look that she wanted to talk to me alone. She looked a lot like our mother, who had a way of looking at you so you knew exactly what she was thinking.

"She's resting. She'll be fine," I said. "She seems to have a hard head."

Hannah got up. "Well, I will leave you alone. I want to check up on Margaret."

Mac, Teri and I sat for a second staring at each other then Teri and I both started talking at the same time.

"God, you'll never believe what happened!" I said.

"Was I spooked when we drove up!" Teri said.

We both stopped and laughed. Mac rested his chin in his hand. "God, the Ryan sisters." He poured himself more coffee and sat back like a kid at the circus.

"When did you get here?" I looked at my watch: one o'clock.

"About forty minutes ago. Kate, as I said, I got the creeps when we pulled up here. Didn't I, Mac?"

"Yes, you did," he said.

"Why?" I asked.

"I looked out into the woods and you know me, I got that feeling of a presence, something was there. I just felt it," she said and Mac and I fell silent. "Well, that's what usually happens when I bring up the supernatural with *you* two. So, what's been going on around here? Hannah—and we have to call her Hannah—started to tell us but then you came back. What the hell happened?"

I explained everything that had happened since I talked to them last night—as well as everything I'd figured out about before.

"Good grief, are you all right? How many stitches, Katie?" she asked, sounding very much like our mother. It was truly scary.

"I'm fine." I said. "Now, more importantly, on our ride today, before Maggie got bounced around, my brain caught up with me and I finally figured out the intruder was a woman. She was wearing perfume."

Teri was amazed. "A woman? Do you think it was the same woman in the woods? Tell me about her."

"It was kind of eerie. She was there, and then she wasn't. I got the same feeling last night, when I thought I saw someone at the edge of the woods. Whatever it was, was there, then gone. Whaddya think?" I asked.

"Well, I don't know. If and when she turns up again, it'll be interesting," Teri said.

"To say the least. Man, I'm glad you two are here." It struck me then, how lucky I was to have them. Teri was 48. She was sophisticated but also down to earth. She was about five foot six, an adorably full-figured redhead with beautiful blue eyes and a great sense of humor. Being married to an ex-Marine like Mac, she needed it quite often.

"Maggie and you both saw the same person?" Teri asked.

"Yes, but I saw her clearly. Maggie said she couldn't get a good look. You know what I'm thinking? All the time I had Maggie on the horse, I felt like someone was watching us. Then, boom, the uncle shows up. What are the odds?"

"Well, it's his property, he might easily have just been out for a ride," Teri said.

"True. I guess I'm getting paranoid, here. That woman spooked me."

The vision of the woman in the woods stuck with me. What was she doing there?

Mac was playing with the plastic bag. "So, this is what Chance found?"

"Yep. Chance dug it all up. I don't exactly know where, but I know it was on the other side of the lake. It was very spooky how it happened." I explained Chance's odd behavior from last night and then this morning.

"And she came back with everything?" Teri asked.

"Yep. She had the burlap and the jewelry. It was freaky."

"Why did she bolt around the lake?" Mac asked and looked at Teri.

"I think Chance knew where to go. You say Chance sat there and stared across the lake?" she asked and I nodded.

"It was as if—" I stopped dead and without finishing my sentence, Teri understood.

"As if what?" Mac asked, looking at both of us.

"As if she saw someone or something. Mac you know perfectly well, dogs have that sense."

"No, *you* have that sense, Teri," I chimed in. It was true.

Teri has that sixth sense that scares the hell out of me. She downplays it, but never denies it. Some call it intuition, but those who know Teri, know it's much more.

"Okay, don't tell me: You're traveling through another dimension..." Mac started.

"Next stop: The Twilight Zone," I said in my best Rod Serling imitation.

Teri glared at both of us. "Very funny, children."

Kate Sweeney

CHAPTER TEN

Being the gracious hostess, Hannah made sure we'd have dinner then she joined us on the deck.

"Kate, Teri was telling me about the woman in the woods. Who could she have been?" Hannah asked.

"I don't know. It was a little unnerving." I ran my fingers through my hair.

"So now what, Sherlock?" Mac asked.

"I need to know more about Miranda's murder. Last night the sheriff—Steve, I think his name was—seemed like an affable guy. I think I'll take a skip into town, maybe he can shed some light on this."

"It was twenty years ago, do you think he knows anything?" Teri asked.

"I don't know," I said.

"Want us to come with?" Mac asked.

"Would you mind if I went alone? I'll only be an hour."

"Okay, Mac and I will stay with Hannah," Teri said.

"Can I borrow the Jeep?"

Mac and Teri laughed. "It's not funny. I have no idea where my car is," I said as Mac tossed me the keys.

I walked into the small police station and noticed Steve in his office. He waved me in.

"Hi. How're ya feeling?" he asked. His thick, sandy hair flopped forward, making him look like he just woke up. His short-and-stocky build also made me think of a high-school football player.

"I'm fine, thanks. Can I bother you for a few minutes? I have two issues. One, I remembered something about last night's break in." I told him all about my realization of the intruder being a woman, and how Chance found all that jewelry.

"I remember you saying last night there was something that didn't sit well with you. You're sure it was a woman?" He wasn't challenging, just asking.

"Well, in this day of unisex cologne, I can't be completely sure. However, Steve, this was definitely a woman's fragrance. So, if it quacks like a duck…well, you know what I mean. That coupled with the strength, I'm saying it's a woman. Now, onto my next issue. Can you tell me anything about Miranda Winfield's murder?"

He looked at his watch. "How 'bout a cup of coffee? I can tell you what I know."

We sat at the same diner where Maggie and I'd had breakfast.

"You look done in, Kate. What's your deal here? How is it that you're in the middle of this?"

I told him, vaguely, about Jan and Barb and their concern for Maggie. "I never expected to fall into the middle of something like this."

"You're not trying to play Nancy Drew are you? I care a great deal about that family."

"That's not the case, I assure you. Besides, I'm too old for Nancy Drew." I gave him a reassuring smile.

He slid the old folder he had been carrying across the table. "It's the police file on Miranda Winfield's death. You can take a look at it today, but I'll need it back tomorrow."

"Are you sure you should be giving this to me, Steve? I mean, you don't know me," I said, though I was itching to take the folder and run.

"My father was the sheriff back then, Kate. If he were still sheriff, I think he'd do what I'm doing now and give you the file. He'll be here tomorrow for the Fall Festival, maybe we can talk to him then."

As we walked out of the diner, we bumped into Allison. It was obvious she noticed the folder. Giving us a curious look, we exchanged hellos and good-byes and she scurried off.

"I'll make sure I get this back to you as soon as I've read it, Steve. Thanks."

I wanted to see the lake again, from the other side. I drove the three miles then saw the sign for Cedar Lake and turned right. Surrounded by woods, the road was worn but drivable. I came to a fork in the road and took the road to Cedar Lake. There was a small parking area for no more than three or four cars, and didn't look like anyone had used the lot in quite a while.

Grabbing the file, I walked down a path that led to the lake. It was beautiful. The autumn colors that lined the shore were breathtaking. The path probably led all the way around the lake, so I followed it for about fifty yards.

I saw a makeshift bench close to the shore. Someone had taken a long birch log, about six feet, and planed it flat on one side so you could sit on it.

I leafed through the pages, and then I came to some gruesome photos. When I saw these, I was a little prepared, but shocked nonetheless. I hoped Maggie or Hannah had never seen these.

Miranda's bloated body was completely clothed. She was laying on the lakeshore. The upper torso and neck had several stab wounds. I quickly went to another photo. I scratched my head. I looked up and scanned the lake.

The report was short. A young couple that was walking around the lake found the body. It was determined that the body had been in the lake for two days. She was last seen on October 31, 1986. I stared at the date. She died on Halloween. I shivered violently, for the hundredth time this weekend.

Christ, I thought, not that there is a good time to be murdered, but Halloween? I read on.

The coroner, Dr. Walt Jenkins, determined that the cause of death was loss of blood due to the severed carotid arteries. The victim died within minutes. It was also determined that the victim had been killed at the lake.

She had been stabbed with an extremely sharp instrument; however, no murder weapon had been found. Unfortunately, it was impossible to get the exact time of death, due to the weather conditions at the time. An unexpected warm spell and heavy rains marred any exact determination.

Doc Jenkins was the coroner. I guess that wasn't too unheard of. Hannah said he was more or less a brain, and in a small town, you have to wear many hats other than town doctor.

I turned the page and there was the report from Steve's father, Sheriff Tom Caldwell.

The victim was Miranda Margaret Winfield, found on November 2, 1986. She was the victim of an apparent robbery. Her body found in Cedar Lake, by a young couple walking in the area, had multiple stab wounds. Mrs. Winfield had no jewelry, purse or any other belongings on her person, but victim's house and car keys were in her left pants pocket. The crime scene and surrounding area was sealed. The robber was clever enough to leave absolutely no signs, or any evidence.

Sheriff Caldwell's signature was at the bottom on the page. I turned the page over and someone had scribbled—*Murderer too careful. If a drifter then why didn't they take keys?*

I sat there for a moment or two. Why would a murderer take the time to steal all the jewelry, take her purse and money, but not check her other pocket and notice the keys? Why in the world would you rob and kill someone then leave the evidence all over the woods?

Then I realized they didn't leave it all over the woods. Chance dug it up. The question now was why would someone bury it and not take it with them and then dispose of it, or better yet, sell it if that was their intention, for drug money, or whatever.

Someone was scaring Maggie and causing these accidents. Someone definitely sabotaged that saddle. Who would want her harmed? Who is the woman in the woods and what connection does she have to a twenty-year-old murder?

And why am I sitting at the crime scene by myself?

CHAPTER ELEVEN

I went back to my car, trying to shake off the feeling of being watched, and fumbled to the put the car in gear. *Good grief, Ryan, calm down.*

I glanced in the rear view mirror and saw her. She was standing right behind me in the same white dress she'd had on earlier. I jumped out of the car, but she had already vanished without a trace.

The woods were totally still. *Okay, that's enough.* I jumped into the Jeep and sped away, occasionally glancing in the rear view mirror.

When I returned I found Maggie and Hannah in the living room where a repairman was replacing the French doors. They both looked up when I came in.

"Good, you're back," Hannah said. "Teri and Mac went for a walk with Chance."

Maggie ignored me completely for some reason. I looked at Hannah but couldn't tell what in the hell was going on by the look on her face.

"Good. Well, I stopped into town and—" I started.

Maggie interrupted me. *Good grief, these people!* "Where did you go this afternoon? Allison called. She told me she saw you coming out of the diner with Steve. She mentioned that perhaps I shouldn't trust you. With you sneaking off to Steve and thinking I was lying about the saddle, I'm not so sure she's wrong." She had that defensive look again.

"Margaret that's enough," Hannah said.

Maggie stared at me, completely ignoring Hannah.

I was getting a little tired of that look. I closed my eyes and rubbed my forehead. I was beyond tired and had had enough. "First of all I don't sneak. I'm trying to find out what's going on and what it has to do with your mother's murder. So trust either your girlfriend or me. Which is it going to be?" I turned away and looked out the door. Christ she was infuriating. I looked at my watch; it was nearly four-thirty. I'd been gone longer than I thought. I turned back to Maggie, who was standing by the fireplace.

She looked tired, lonely and worn and I felt bad for the way I'd reacted. "Look, this is a very unusual situation, Maggie. Things are beginning to unravel here and I don't want it to get away from me. My fuse is a little short, I apologize," I said.

She turned to me with tears in her sparkling blue eyes. Now I felt worse. I hated that look. "No, I apologize," she said. "You're right, too much has happened in the last twenty-four hours. My nerves are a little shot, too."

"Okay, let's forget it. Did you meet Teri and Mac?" I asked.

"Yes, are you sure you want your family in on this?" She gave me a worried look.

"Well, you've met Mac. I may ask you the same question."

"They're very nice. You have a great family, Kate."

"They're so disgustingly in love," I said.

Maggie laughed openly and once again, I chuckled along with her contagious laughter.

"Boy all this is yours? I'd hate to have to mow that lawn," Mac said as he and Teri walked up to the porch.

"Bedford's been doing that for almost thirty years, he does takes care of this place," Maggie said.

Hannah walked out onto the deck and smiled happily. "Well, did you enjoy your walk?"

"It's beautiful. Someone is burning leaves," Teri said.

"I remember when we were kids. I loved that smell," I said.

"When I was a little girl, Bedford would rake the leaves and let me play in them and ride my bike through them," Maggie said. I noticed a sad tone in her voice.

All at once, I felt bad for her. Growing up in an Irish neighborhood you took for granted that you had family and friends to play and fight with. I wondered if she was lonely as a child.

"I remember when I was young, we would have piles and piles of leaves, smoldering for weeks at time," Hannah said.

"So you're the one who screwed up the ozone," I accused.

We all had a good laugh as Hannah shook her head. "You nut. I'm going back to the kitchen. Oh, Margaret, don't forget to remind me to call the caterers tonight. We have the party tomorrow after the

Fall Festival," she said over her shoulder, and disappeared into the house.

"Fall Festival?" Mac asked and looked at Maggie.

"Yes, it's in town during the day. Aunt Hannah prides herself on her one big bash of the year afterward," she said. "Now, what did Steve tell you, Kate?"

"Let's go in and I'll fill you all in."

Mac and Teri walked ahead of us, I gently held Maggie back.

"What's wrong?" she asked.

"Maggie, Steve gave me the police report to read and there are certain aspects of your mother's murder... Well, I don't want them to upset you. Or Hannah."

I realized I was holding her hands in my own. We were silent for a long moment and all I could think of was how soft her small hands felt. I let go of them and got back to the matter at hand. The poor kid had been through a great deal and I didn't want to add to it if it were at all possible.

Maggie then reached down and grasped my hand, once again. "Kate, I've been living with this my whole life. I'd like it cleared up so I can move on. I know my mother was murdered and I know there are gruesome details. I can handle it, if that's what you're worried about."

"I'm sure you can. I just want you—" I stopped, not knowing what I was going to say.

Maggie gave me a curious crooked smile. "You want me...?" she prompted.

When I didn't say anything, she smiled and caressed by hand before she let it go.

"Well, you'll have to finish that sentence, but, thanks, I'll be fine."

I looked down into her eyes and frowned. I realized I had no idea how to finish that sentence. This little woman was beginning to ...

"Kate, the fireplace looks awfully lonely," Hannah called from the doorway.

I had the fire blazing within minutes and we sat in comfortable silence staring at the mesmerizing flames. Chance, of course, was sound asleep, once again sprawled out in front of it.

"Okay, Kate, what do you know so far?" my sister asked.

I began pacing in front of the fire. I'm a pacer. When I think, I have to move.

Hannah came into the living room and set down a tray of all sorts of goodies. "Mac, will you tend bar please?"

Mac got up and rubbed his hands together. "My pleasure," he said and went over to the bar. "Okay gals, name your poison."

I was pacing, not paying attention. "Don't mind that two-headed nature lover. She's in another world," Mac said, handing Maggie a drink.

Staring at the fire, I thought of how to piece together what I knew. I forgot where I was and thought I heard Teri say to Maggie, "She's in her thinking mode."

"I've noticed that," Maggie replied.

Hannah said, "Sshh! Let her think."

"Kate's mind: a finely honed machine," my smart-ass brother-in-law said.

I gave him a sarcastic grin. "Thanks. Okay, here's what we know: First, someone murdered Miranda twenty years ago, on Halloween."

Mac stopped pouring and looked at me. Teri's eyes got as big as saucers. I glanced at Hannah and Maggie. Maggie gave me an encouraging nod, so I continued.

"For some reason, the murderer buried the jewelry soon after the murder. Yesterday, Chance dug it up, from where I don't know, and brought it back here, where I found it today.

"In the police report, Tom Caldwell stated that the murderer took everything but didn't bother to look in her pocket to find her car and house keys. He found that a little odd. I agree with Tom Caldwell, but we'll get back to that. Now, two months or so ago, weird things start happening to Maggie. She got knocked on the head in the stable and stalked through the woods. Then yesterday morning, I come along and she got thrown from her horse." I cleared my throat and avoided eye contact with the smug doctor as I continued. "The saddle, I discovered, had been tampered with—the stirrup had been cut almost clean through. I found it hidden in the stable earlier this morning. Bedford said he was coming to 'fetch it and get it fixed' I believe." I looked at Hannah and Maggie. "I know Bedford has been with you for a long time, but I think he knows something and I need to find out what. Maybe I'll have a chat with him later. So, to continue, last night, well we all know what happened last night: An intruder broke in and whispered in my ear that I shouldn't be here. She also left a note on Maggie's pillow. Today, we see a woman in the woods and Maggie's horse bolted and then"—I stopped and took a deep breath—"I saw the woman in the woods again this afternoon. It was quick, I could be mistaken, but when I looked in my rearview mirror, I saw her. When I got out of the car, she, of course was gone."

Maggie's face lost all color. "What in the world is happening?"

"It's a good thing you saw her," Teri said.

We all looked at her as if she was crazy.

"How do you figure, sweetie?" Mac asked.

It dawned on me. "Because if this woman, whoever or whatever she is, wanted only to scare the life out of Maggie, or hurt her, why show herself to me? Or, if Maggie was the only one who saw her, we'd all have a very good reasonable doubt as to Maggie's state of mind." I looked at Maggie. "We *both* saw her. You weren't imagining anything. She's real."

Maggie said, "So this means…"

"You're not nuts!" Mac declared through a mouthful of cheese.

Teri shot Mac a horrified look. I hung my head and Maggie laughed out loud.

"I like him," Hannah reaffirmed with a wink.

"Who do you suppose this woman is?" Teri asked, still scowling at Mac.

"I don't know, but I'd bet big bucks she's not trying to harm Maggie. I just get that feeling," I said, looking at Maggie.

Maggie nodded. "I have to admit when I saw her I was shocked, but I wasn't afraid. I wanted to know who she was."

Teri had that look on her face as if she knew something but didn't want to say.

Maggie apparently saw it, too. "If you think of something, please go ahead and share. As Kate said, this is an unusual situation. So please, don't hold back."

"What did this woman look like and what exactly was she wearing?" Teri asked.

Maggie started, "Well, from what I could see, she had long brown hair and wore a white dress, but with the trees in my way, I didn't see much."

I had to agree. "She was standing there looking at us, but not in a malicious way, just looking. Like she was waiting for us to do something. I don't know. The minute we started in her direction, she turned and faded into the woods—somewhat like last night when I saw whoever or whatever at the edge of the woods. Maybe that's who I saw last night." I turned to Maggie. "Did you ever see her before? Think—at any time, did you or Hannah ever see her?"

"No, dear. I have to say I've never seen anyone like that," Hannah said and looked to Maggie.

"Not before today, though I don't venture to woods too often," Maggie said.

"Okay, let's move along. Chance, who seems to be doing all the leg work here, finds the jewelry—Miranda's wedding ring, watch and a locket that has Maggie's picture in it, but also has her uncle's picture as well." I looked at Maggie and Hannah and asked, "Why would Miranda have Nathan's picture in her locket?"

Maggie shook her head and stared at the fire. "I have no idea." She looked at Hannah.

I figured this was as good a time as any. "Hannah, what do you know about the locket? Please tell me, if you know anything or even if you think of anything," I pleaded.

Hannah looked at her glass. "Kate, it is all speculation. I knew Miranda and Nathan were close. As I said, back in those days we were all close to Miranda, because Jonathan was always gone. She was in this big house alone for most of the time. I discussed it with Nathan and Walt. None of us liked to see her all alone. I was with Miranda constantly after Maggie was born. I haven't thought about it in years."

I looked at Maggie. "There's a connection between your mother's murder, your father's death and what's been happening to you. It doesn't take much too see that." I looked around at the tired and confused faces. "Let's take a break, shall we? This is a lot to absorb right now. Hannah, how's dinner?"

"Should be ready in half an hour," Hannah announced.

Teri got up and grabbed Mac's hand. "Well, I think Mac and I will unpack." They went upstairs.

I stood looking at the fire. Chance was lying at my feet and I sat down on the hearth and ruffled her ears.

"Well, I'm stumped pooch. I can feel I'm close but..." I grunted and rubbed the back of my neck. I was exhausted. I went out to the back porch. It had turned very cool, and as I turned to get my sweater, Maggie came out and handed it to me.

"Thanks," I said. I looked up into night sky. There were a few stars; the moon would be up in a while. I smiled wistfully, thinking how much I loved being in the outdoors. The scenery here was beautiful.

Maggie interrupted my thoughts. "It's getting chilly. How are your shoulder and your head? I feel responsible for this," she said with regret as she looked out at the woods.

"Don't be silly. I'm a little accident-prone. You should see me when I'm working. I can't tell you how many times I've tripped, fallen—you name it. I think I have a scar for every state of the union. Teri and Mac wince every time I pick up my camera."

"I'd probably worry, too, if you came back all banged up after an assignment. Maybe you should get a nice, safe desk job," she said and I laughed at the idea.

"Wouldn't matter. I'd staple myself to something," I said.

"So, I take it you and a letter opener would not be great friends?" Maggie asked through her laughter.

Once again, her contagious laughter pulled me right in as I let out a good laugh and nodded in complete agreement.

During all this, I looked down to see my hand covering hers. Maggie noticed it as well.

"This is a good feeling," Maggie said as she moved her fingers through mine.

"Y-Yes, laughter is a good relief mechanism. I-It releases stress and, and helps, um..."

Maggie chuckled and shook her head.

"C'mon, it's getting chilly. Let's get back inside."

I tried to get ready for dinner in peace. That was not going to happen. There was a soft knock at my door and Teri poked her head in.

"I wanted to see your room. Ours is huge. It's like being at a hotel. Do you have your own bathroom?"

"Yep," I said and motioned to the door.

Teri was looking out the window. "So, what do you think is happening?" She looked back to me.

"Ter, I don't know. For some reason, someone is trying to scare the hell out of Maggie or maybe even kill her. Whoever it is, they're sure doing a good job of scaring me. You should have seen that saddle. If Maggie had been riding any faster, she'd have broken her neck." I rubbed my neck and yawned wildly. "I need to sleep."

"You're right," Teri said. She went back to the window and looked out. "Who is the woman in the woods, Kate?"

"I wish I knew. It spooks me. I was petrified when I saw her in my rear view mirror this afternoon. It was definitely the same woman. She looked content, you know, not scary or dangerous. I don't know."

"Well, I was going to ask this earlier, but I don't want them to think I'm a psychic nut or something, but I'd love to see what Maggie's mother looked like. I have a feeling, Kate." She shivered and walked over to me.

I could feel my eyebrows getting lost in my hairline. "You think the woman is Maggie's mother?" I wished I would quit shivering.

She nodded. "I do."

"Maggie's mother," I repeated, making sure I understood her. "Maggie's dead, murdered, mother," I said again.

"Yes, I do."

I found a chair and eased myself into it. "Crap."

CHAPTER TWELVE

Dinner was wonderful; we ate like kings and queens. Hannah beamed when she saw all the empty plates. Mac sat back. "Hannah that was delicious."

Teri nodded in agreement. "I can't remember when I've had such a good meal."

Maggie got up and cleared the dishes. "I'll get the coffee."

Teri offered her help and followed her into the kitchen.

The rest of us went back to the living room and Mac got the fire going again. I sat in the huge chair by the fireplace and put my head back.

"Kate you need to sleep tonight, you haven't slept at all," Hannah said, giving me a worried look.

"I will tonight, thanks Hannah."

Teri and Maggie came in with the coffee. Maggie handed me a cup and sat down by the fire. She looked tired and drawn. I looked at my watch. It was eight-thirty. Once again, it felt like midnight.

"So, Kate, are you sure the intruder was a woman?" Mac asked.

"She wasn't strong enough to be a man and she was wearing perfume. Do you know any men who wear women's perfume?" I looked at Mac.

"Nope, do you?"

"No," I said.

He looked at Maggie, who shook her head. "I don't know many men at all," she said and I had to laugh out loud.

"Well, I knew a young boy who liked to wear his mother's hats," Hannah said absently.

We all stopped laughing and Maggie hung her head. "Aunt Hannah, please don't tell that story."

Teri and I were intrigued. "Go ahead, tell us," Teri begged. We leaned toward Hannah.

"Well, Eddy Walsh lived on our block. Walt, Tom, Nathan and I would go over to his house and there he'd be walking around in his mother's hats." She started to laugh, so did Teri and I, although we had no clue why.

Teri said, "And?"

She gave us a confused looked. "And what, dear?"

"And what did he do then?" I asked.

"Nothing, he just wore his mother's hats," Hannah said.

Teri and I sat there with our mouths open. Then we looked at each other and sat back. I looked at Maggie and she gave me an "I told you so," look.

Hannah stood and stretched. "I'll get the apple pie ready. Mac, my darling, can I bribe you for some assistance?"

Mac followed her into the kitchen. "Hannah, for pie I'd follow you anywhere."

"Don't speak too soon, Mac. You haven't tasted my pie. I could be a murder suspect."

Teri and I stared at the kitchen door and I blinked a couple of times.

"Well, that's Aunt Hannah," Maggie said.

"She is adorable. You're very lucky," Teri said.

"Yes, she has been a Godsend. That's for sure," Maggie agreed as she played with the ring on her finger.

"Do you have any idea who's doing this?" Teri asked.

"Teri, I wish I did. I've been racking my brain," Maggie said.

I got up and started pacing. I saw Teri lean over to Maggie, "She's in her thinking mode. Pretty soon she'll—"

"Run her fingers through her hair and rub her forehead," Maggie interrupted her.

Teri nodded. "She's already done that, I take it."

Maggie nodded with a wink and I could feel her watching me.

Mac and Hannah came out of the kitchen with dessert and Hannah fixed everyone a plate while we talked.

In the middle of our conversation, Hannah walked to the French doors.

"What's wrong?" I asked and followed her look.

"I don't know, I thought I saw a light down at the stable. My imagination, I guess."

Now my curiosity was piqued. I got up and went to the door. Then I saw it too. It was a faint light coming from the stable.

Mac was standing behind me. "What is that?" he asked.

"Shit! The stable's on fire!" I turned to Hannah. "Call the fire department."

When we got to the stable, the huge door was ajar. As I opened the door, smoke billowed out. The hay had caught fire. I quickly searched for something to put it out.

Mac and Teri grabbed a couple of horse blankets from the ledge and tried to smother the flames. There was smoke everywhere. I heard the horses and realized I needed to get them out.

Maggie and I ran to the stalls and opened them, then went in and opened the back door so they could run free. The last stall was Thunder. He stomped and reared as I approached. I looked through the smoke and saw something heaped in the corner of his stall. I tried desperately to get past Thunder. I couldn't see a thing. I got closer and Thunder reared again and, as his hoofs came down, I jumped out of the way.

It was then I realized the heap in the corner was Bedford. I needed to get Thunder out of that stall and out of my way so I could get to Bedford.

Maggie apparently realized this as well, and ran around to open the outer stall door. She grabbed Thunder's bridle and pulled him out of the stable so he could run free.

Maggie and I struggled to pull Bedford out of the stall. I looked up to see Mac and Teri, who were completely disoriented. The fire was out of control. If we didn't move fast, we'd all go up in flames. "Mac, forget it! Take Teri and get out!"

Maggie and I pulled Bedford safely away from the burning stable, but I couldn't see Mac or Teri. "Stay with him," I yelled to Maggie and headed back into the stable.

Just as I got into the stall, a heavy beam collapsed in front of me, blocking my way. I jumped back, knowing I couldn't get in. The smoke engulfed the stable and the flames seemed to be everywhere at once.

I ran around the front of the stable and was shocked to see the doors closed and a shovel jammed through the handles. I yanked the shovel free and pulled the doors open.

The smoke billowed out and Mac and Teri stumbled into the fresh night air.

In the distance, we heard the sirens.

"Ah, the cavalry, just in time," I said.

Mac and Teri were coughing as they collapsed on the ground, gasping for air.

Firefighters rushed onto the scene, trying to control the burning stable. The paramedics had Bedford on a gurney, wheeling him toward the ambulance with Maggie at his side.

"Bedford, you'll be fine," I heard Maggie say as I approached and stood next to her. He reached up and grabbed Maggie's wrist and pulled her to him. "Please Bedford, lie still," she said.

"I never told," he whispered. I leaned in, as did Maggie.

"Never told who?" Maggie asked. Bedford coughed violently and kept his vice grip on her wrist.

"Secrets, so many secrets." His voice came out in a desperate whisper.

Then he said something else that both Maggie and I could barely hear. It sounded to me like he said "love." I leaned back as he closed his eyes.

I stood there numbly staring at Bedford's still body. Finally, he let go of Maggie and the paramedics lifted him into the ambulance.

Behind us, the fire department soaked the smoldering rubble while Steve and his deputy directed the traffic. Mac was standing now, with his arm around Hannah, who was sobbing. Teri was close by.

We watched as the ambulance drove out of sight.

"You three look like hell," Steve said. "What happened?"

"Not now, Steve," Maggie said quickly. "I need to get Kate and her family to the clinic. You can drive. We should have gotten another ambulance. Aunt Hannah, please stay here."

"I'll leave my deputy with her," Steve said.

We drove in relative silence to the clinic. The ambulance was already there. The paramedics met us at the door as they were coming out. Maggie talked to them for a moment or two. When I saw her shoulders slump, I knew. I felt the tears catch in my throat.

"Let's go. You all need to get checked out. Doc's with Bedford," Maggie said in a tired voice. She looked at our questioning faces and shook her head.

She examined Mac and Teri first. "You're next," she said, and beckoned me into the small examining room.

I sat on the table and Maggie snapped on another pair of gloves. She reached up and pulled the dirty bandage off my forehead and I caught my breath and flinched.

She winced. "Sorry," she whispered, surprisingly gentle.

When she was finished, she stripped off the gloves, tossing them in a nearby wastebasket. She then turned to me. I took a deep quivering breath and, as I reached up to rub my forehead, she held my arm.

"Don't do that, you're filthy," she said.

Then, unexpectedly, she reached up and brushed the hair off my forehead. Her fingers lingered for a moment.

She gave me a worried look. "Are you all right?" she asked.

I nodded. "And you?" She said nothing, and when I saw her bottom lip quiver, my heart broke. "Bedford's dead, isn't he?" I asked. The tears welled up in her blue eyes and I whispered, "I'm so sorry, Maggie."

Maggie put her hand on my shoulder. "I know. I can't believe it. What a horrible accident, Kate," she said.

I thought of the shovel wedged through the handles of the stable door, and, of course, thought of everything else that has been happening since I drove into this town. "I don't think it was an accident, Maggie."

I looked into her eyes and saw the realization there. She blinked several times but said nothing. She just flopped down on the table next to me. Instinctively, I put my arm around her small shoulders and pulled her close. She clung to me and quietly cried for a moment or two. She looked up then with sad eyes and I reached down and ran my thumb over her cheek, wiping away the tears.

"C'mon. We need to tell Steve," I said.

Doc was talking with Mac, Teri and Steve when Maggie and I came out.

"Your family told me what happened, Kate. Could you see how the fire started?" Steve asked.

"No, but I don't think it was an accident, Steve," I said, and now all eyes were on me.

After everyone cleaned up, we sat at the kitchen table.

"Okay, Kate. Let's hear it," Steve said.

"After Maggie and I got Bedford out of the stall, I tried to go back in to get Mac and Teri. The stall entrance was blocked, so I ran around to the front of the stable. There was a shovel wedged through the handles of the stable doors. I had to yank it out in order to open them. It doesn't take a great detective, which I am not, to know someone put it there. And I'm thinking whoever it was started the fire."

There was silence around the table. Steve took a deep breath. "Any ideas?" he asked.

"Well, I think the only one who knew was Bedford," I said. I then thought of my conversation with him earlier in the day. "I had a talk with Bedford this morning after Chance found Miranda's jewelry. He said he talked to you and the deputies outside after the intruder incident. He was cryptic—"

"Who? Bedford? I didn't talk to him. I didn't see him until he was walking up to Maggie's car," Steve said.

"Okay, then he was not being cryptic, he was lying," I said.

"Why lie about that?" Maggie asked and I shrugged.

"Maybe he didn't want anyone to know what he was doing," Teri offered.

"What could he be doing at that time of night?" Mac asked.

"Well, because of his limp, he couldn't be the intruder, that's for sure," Steve said, and I nodded in agreement.

"But if he was outside, wouldn't he have seen something?" Maggie asked.

As I listened to everyone, my mind raced recounting the conversation with Bedford once again. "Yes, I think he probably would have," I said. "I think Bedford knew much more than we'll ever know. For instance, he told me that Maggie saddled her horse that morning. Maggie told me it was already saddled and ready for her. Did he lie? Perhaps. He lied about talking to Steve. What else was he lying about?

"After I met your Aunt Sarah, I overheard them. Sarah asked Bedford what he had said to me. He told her he said nothing, but then for some reason he brought up Alexander Winfield," I said and looked right at Hannah.

It was then I realized the Hannah had been conspicuously silent. I looked at her as she sat at the head of the table. Our eyes met and for an instant, I got that old feeling. Though it had been many years since my investigating days, I could still recognize that look.

Hannah knew something.

Kate Sweeney

CHAPTER THIRTEEN

W hat do you think, Hannah? What did Bedford mean about your father?" I asked.

Hannah's face showed no emotion. "I'm not quite sure, Kate. He could have meant anything."

"Well, Sarah sounded concerned he'd say something. And I have to tell you, Maggie and I heard his last words," I said.

Hannah looked at me then. "What did he say?"

"He said, 'I never told.' When Maggie questioned him, he said, 'secrets, so many secrets.'" I looked to Maggie for confirmation.

"That's exactly what he said," Maggie said and looked at her aunt. "What does that mean, Aunt Hannah? What secrets about Grandfather?"

I watched Hannah. She looked old and tired. I reached over and took her hand. "Hannah, I think whatever Bedford knew is connected to this whole mess. Please, whatever you know, however innocuous, now's the time."

"Aunt Hannah," Maggie said. "I understand our family's dynamics. No one knows this better than I do. I remember Grandfather being an unapproachable, bitter old man. I remember Father being the same way. But Aunt Hannah, what does Aunt Sarah have to do with Grandfather?"

"Your Grandfather favored Sarah with a seat on the Board of Directors at the Winfield Clinic. I don't know why, and I never asked," Hannah said and I heard the dismissive tone in her voice.

"Hannah, I don't like to press you about family issues, but someone is trying their damnedest to scare the hell out of Maggie, if not downright kill her. Bedford is dead and the fire was no accident," I said, in a stern voice. Maggie shot me a disapproving look, which I ignored.

"Which is where I come in, Hannah," Steve said. "I agree with Kate. Someone started that fire, and when the fire marshal comes out to investigate, I'm sure he'll determine it was arson."

"Perhaps nothing was said at the time, but what do you think was going on between Sarah and your father?" I asked. I was getting very impatient with this whole mess. I was tired, sore, and I just wanted to go home.

Hannah looked right at me with determination. "Knowing my father's lack of integrity and Sarah's greed and ambition, I always thought there was something between them."

"An affair?" Steve asked and Hannah closed her eyes.

"I don't know, but I assumed," she said.

Nothing was said for a moment or two. Steve then stood. "Well, it's very late and I think this is enough for one night. I'll be in touch with you." He said his good-byes and was gone.

"Aunt Hannah, why don't you go to bed? You look exhausted," Maggie said, urging Hannah out of her seat.

Mac and Teri followed, which left Maggie and I sitting at the kitchen table.

"Well, this is an interesting turn of events," Maggie said in a tired voice.

"I agree and it won't be the last, I'm afraid."

"Well, I think a good night's sleep is in order, Miss Ryan. Doctor's orders," she said and stood.

I groaned as I hoisted myself out of the chair. "I'll obey that one. But only that one."

"Why does that not surprise me?"

"Perhaps you're getting to know me," I blurted out but quickly recovered, "and I should keep my mouth shut and go to bed. Good night."

As I sat on the bed, I heard a soft knock on the door. Letting out a small groan, I took the long hike, all of three feet, to the door.

"Didn't we just say good night?" I asked with a wide yawn.

Maggie stood there and motioned me into the bathroom. I obediently followed her; she had forgotten to check my shoulder. Her hands were shaking and I could tell she'd been crying, which wasn't surprising since so much had happened in the past two days.

I could only imagine what her life had been like for the past twenty years, growing up alone and scared.

She fumbled with the gauze and tape and then dropped it on the floor.

We both bent to pick it up and clunked heads. God, what a weekend we'd been having.

"Boy, I'm running out of body parts here," I said chuckling as I rubbed my head.

She laughed almost too hard. It'd been my experience that when someone laughed that hard at seemingly nothing, especially one of my jokes, crying is not far behind.

All at once, the crying started. It sounded as though it came from her soul as she covered her face with her hands.

I instinctively put my arms around her and whispered, "Maggie, let it go."

She sobbed openly and I said nothing. What could I say? Her tears subsided after a moment or two then she stepped back and I let her go. I picked up what she dropped and placed it on the sink, then handed her a Kleenex and she dried her eyes.

"Okay now?" I asked.

She nodded, taking a deep, quivering breath. She finished re-taping my shoulder.

"Thanks, Doc."

"You sure you're all right?" she asked, fidgeting with the first-aid kit.

What a little woman she was, I thought as I watched her. A little woman with a fiery temper. Something pulled at my heart then. It was something I hadn't felt in a long while, and I didn't even dare put a name to it. I realized I was staring at the diminutive doctor.

"Just a flesh wound, ma'am," I joked again.

She rolled her eyes and pushed me into my room. She came out of the bathroom with a glass of water and a capsule.

"No arguing. Take this, you'll sleep better," she said with authority.

I grumbled childishly and took it—and slept like a baby.

I don't think I moved once all night. It was only six-thirty when I hauled my aching body out of bed. A hot shower revived me and I felt ready to tackle this mess.

Being the only one up, I went into the kitchen and made a pot of coffee. Okay, I thought, let's get started. I got a pencil and paper, and wrote down Miranda's name on one side and Jonathan's on the other, and then I got to work. I poured a cup of coffee and began.

Miranda is murdered on Halloween, 1986. Made to look like a robbery. She was stabbed several times. No sign of a struggle, all wounds in her chest. *That doesn't sound like a thief to me. This was a brutal act for Christ's sake.* The criminal was smart enough not to leave fingerprints or any evidence of any kind. *Why in the world be so methodical, and then take the time to bury the jewelry and run the risk of getting caught. This doesn't make sense.*

My daffy mutt sniffs around, finds jewelry. That night we have an intruder and it's a woman. I am sure of that. *It's the only thing I'm sure of, right? Shit!*

I shook my head in disbelief as I continued with my list. Miranda's wedding ring her watch and her locket, which contains a photo of Maggie at about five years of age and her Uncle Nathan. The way the pictures are situated, it's as if they're looking at each other. *Why does would Miranda have a picture of her brother-in-law in locket with her own daughter?*

Then I started with Jonathan's list. He died in a hit-and-run six months ago. Three months later, all this starts happening to Maggie. This list is shorter, than Miranda's, but I know his death has something to do with all this.

I wrote down: Who gets his business? Who gets the clinic? It's a family thing. Does Maggie get it? What could that mean?

I sat back and looked at my list. These two people die twenty years apart but they are never closer than they are right now. It's all connected. I could smell it, as my father used to say. I sat there drinking my coffee feeling every bit of my forty-three years and then some. I looked outside. The sun was coming up and would soon burn off the light fog that hung over the yard. It was beautiful and the fall colors were radiant. It was so peaceful.

"Good morning."

I jumped and spilled my coffee on the table. Christ, my nerves, I thought as I looked up to see Maggie. She looked tired but her blue eyes still sparkled. *Why am I constantly noticing those eyes?*

"Good morning," I said.

She handed me a napkin and poured herself a cup of coffee. "Mind if I join you?"

"No, not at all," I said moving my notes. She watched with raised eyebrows. "I was making a list of what we know." I handed it to her and she read it, thoroughly.

"Did you sleep well?" I asked.

"Honestly, no. How about you?" she asked and gave me a worried look.

"I was drugged, so yes, I slept fine. You witch, what was that?"

"It was a very mild sleeping potion. I perfected it at the Witch's Convention. You needed it," she said. "You know, you have a very good sense of humor." She laughed and drank her coffee.

"When all else fails, get 'em laughing," I said, reading the notes. "Maggie, I am sorry about Bedford. I don't know what he was doing in the stable. I wish we could have saved him."

"I do, too, Kate. I remember the day Bedford started working for us." She stared out the kitchen window absently and continued. "He's the one who taught me to ride. He was an excellent horseman back then," Maggie said sadly. "Who would want to kill Bedford?"

"It's speculation, but like I said last night, Bedford knew something and somebody killed him to shut him up. The fire in the stable was supposed to look like an accident."

With that, Hannah came into the kitchen. "Good morning, my darlings. I thought I smelled coffee." She poured herself a cup. She looked terrible. I could tell she'd had a rough night as well. She sat down with a groan. "These old bones."

Mac and Teri came down soon after. Mac looked rested but Teri looked tired.

Hannah said, "I feel horrible about Bedford. He was like part of the family."

We were all silent for a moment before Teri spoke. "Bedford must have known something. What do you think, Kate?"

"I think that's a given. He told me it doesn't pay to ask questions. I think he knew too much. This is no coincidence. There is a connection between the fire and what's happening to Maggie. I *will* find out what it is."

Out of the blue, Hannah let out a small cry. "Goodness, I almost forgot the Festival! Perhaps I should cancel in light of all this."

"No, don't cancel," I said quickly. "It might be a good idea to go to this festival. Besides, Steve said his father would be there. I'd like to talk to him."

"Let's get ready and go into town. The festival starts in two hours." Hannah sounded excited and a little life came back to her face.

We went up to our rooms. Thank God, I'd been planning to be away for the entire weekend so had enough clothes. It was a beautiful Indian summer day, so I threw on my favorite flannel shirt with a white turtleneck and jeans. I grabbed my tweed blazer, just in case, and looked at myself in the mirror.

"Hmm, not too bad, I've looked worse. I think," I said. I instinctively grabbed my camera case as I headed downstairs to rejoin the others.

Of course, I was the only one ready. I went out on the deck and watched Chance dart around. I looked around, reminded again of the beauty of the area. I could see the lake not too far off. I opened my bag and took out my camera.

I put on a stronger lens and scanned the lake for a good shot.

As I was scanning the lake, I thought I saw something on the other side. I took the camera away from my face, and looked again. In a panic, I reached in my bag for the strongest lens I had with me. It took me a second, but I attached the long, heavy lens. I scanned the lake again and I saw it much clearer. It was the woman—the same woman.

My heart was beating like a drum as I tried to swallow, but my mouth had gone dry. I took several deep calming breaths to steady my hand. I stood, frozen as I took the picture. I let the shutter go several times. She stood there dressed in white. Her long, dark hair blew with the gentle breeze. Hand her arms were folded in front of her as she gazed out at the lake. When I took the camera away and then looked again, and she was gone. I stood for a second and then I felt something behind me.

"Boo!" Maggie and Teri said.

I must have jumped ten feet as I screamed like a woman.

"I'm sorry."

At least that's what I thought Maggie said. Who could understand her, with her laughing so hard?

Teri looked at my camera. "Wow. Now that's a lens. What in the world are you looking for?"

"Maggie, Teri I..." I stopped and swallowed hard.

"What?" Maggie asked. *Now she stops laughing.*

"Are you all right?" Teri asked. Mac came out on the deck.

"What a beautiful morning." He stopped and looked at us. "What the hell is the matter with the three of you?"

"I saw the woman on the other side of the lake. I must have taken ten pictures of her," I said.

"You're kidding!" Maggie looked out into the woods. "Who *is* she?"

"You didn't get a good look at her yesterday did you?" I asked.

She shook her head. "There were too many trees."

"Well, do you have a photographer in town? Maybe I can drop off the film so they can get it to me as soon as possible."

She told me of an editor of the town paper, he was an amateur photographer and had a dark room. We could see him this morning.

I gathered my camera equipment and we went inside. Maggie took a step back and gave me an appraising look. I felt the heat rise to my face, under her smiling gaze. She looked as if she might say something when Miss Bubbly came downstairs.

"Well, I'm ready. Kate, you look good. Green is definitely your color, that shirt almost matches your eyes perfectly," Hannah said approvingly.

"I was about to say the exact same thing," Maggie concurred in a low voice.

That tone made my heart skip, dammit.

Teri beamed. "Ha! Great minds..."

"...Are obviously not in this room!" I finished, slightly embarrassed by their compliments.

Mac laughed and gave me a good slap on the back as Hannah laughed wildly and slipped her arm in mine.

"Come, Kate, let us away!" she called out happily.

I laughed as I held onto her hand.

"Yes, madam, as you wish," I replied obediently.

For a little while, we were all relaxed and carefree. However, the gods would not let that feeling linger for long.

Kate Sweeney

CHAPTER FOURTEEN

It turned out to be a gorgeous day. The sun was shining and there was a hint of fall in the air.

Mac and Teri took their own car so they could do some shopping before meeting up with us at the beer garden. Maggie parked in front of the little photo shop, to see Maggie's editor friend. He was a tall lanky redhead, with his sleeves rolled up and a pencil behind his ear and freckles everywhere.

Maggie introduced us as we shook hands. He gave me an odd look. "Do I know you? Your name sounds familiar. What'd ya do, fall out of bed?" He looked at the bandage on my forehead.

"I don't think we've ever met," I said politely.

He hadn't let go of my hand yet.

"Oh, sorry. What can I do for you?"

I explained my predicament and in the middle of what I was saying, he snapped his fingers. "I knew it. Wait a minute."

He disappeared behind a huge desk that had papers and a magazine covering it in what I assumed was his organized mess. It looked like my desk at home. I admired the lad.

He came back with a magazine and leafed through it, found a page, and slapped it with the back of his hand.

"This is you, right?" he asked hopefully, as he showed the magazine.

I went cold. I looked at the page and gave him a sick smile. "My, my, I thought that no one would ever see this. Wherever did you find it?" I asked.

Hannah squeaked. "Let me see!" She took the magazine from me. "Yes, this is the article I read too, Jack. Kate, you're very photogenic. Isn't she wonderful?"

I was completely embarrassed.

"Okay, can we get on with—?" I started.

Maggie interrupted by taking the magazine from Hannah. She looked up at me amazed. "You took these pictures?" She looked impressed.

Now, suddenly, for some reason I didn't mind the attention.

"And you wrote the article too, right?" the redhead asked.

"Yes, I did. Now, if you could—"

Interrupted once again; it is now my goal to be interrupted by everyone in this town.

"I want a copy of this magazine. Jack, where can I get one?" Hannah beamed happily.

I gave a glance at Maggie, who was reading and not saying anything. *Why did it matter what she was thinking?*

"Oh, keep it. I have a couple others. They did a whole layout of you in this issue. Boy, if I could take pictures like these," he sighed and motioned to the magazine.

"Thanks, but could we get back the matter at hand?" I asked and actually managed to finish without one interruption.

Jack eagerly agreed. He would try to have the film developed by late afternoon. If not, then in the morning.

He shook my hand and, for one horrifying moment, I thought he would want either my autograph or a kiss. I was extremely grateful he wanted neither.

We walked down the main street. There were people and vendors everywhere and Hannah was buying everything in sight. I had brought my smaller camera that was easy to carry and was ready for a good shot.

"Where's my magazine?" Hannah asked.

"I've got. I've got it," Maggie assured her, patting the pocket of her blazer.

It was almost noon when we met Steve. "Mom and Dad are over at the beer garden. I told them to save a few seats." He took me aside. "I told Dad about what was going on, he'd like to talk to you, too. We'll meet you over there later."

I agreed enthusiastically and he walked away.

"It's about time I sat down. You girls have fun. I'll save you a seat," Hannah said with a wink.

Then it dawned on me. "Hey, Hannah. What about my car?" I asked.

"What car, dear?" she asked seriously and walked away.

I stopped laughing. "Hey Hannah, that's not funny." I looked at Maggie. "Tell her that wasn't funny. They have my car, right?"

She laughed and pulled me along.

"It's good for you to laugh," I said.

"Thanks, you make it easy. Although you can be the most frustrating person I know."

"I must bring out the worst in you. It's a gift," I assured her. "I don't know why, but we start out fine, and then we wind up arguing. It isn't my intention to argue with you all the time."

"What *are* your intentions?" she asked with a cocky grin.

I blinked several times and felt the blood rush to the face and other various parts of my anatomy. I must have looked like an idiot.

"Uh…" Yes, and I sounded like an idiot.

"Why, hello you two," a voice called out.

For the first time all weekend, I was grateful for an interruption.

It was Allison, however. I looked away and gave a disgusted grunt.

"Hello, Allison. Enjoying the festival?" Maggie asked politely.

"It's wonderful. Mags, I heard from your aunt about last night about poor Bedford— how awful." She reached over and touched Maggie's arm. "Are you all right?"

"Allison, I'm fine and yes, it was horrible about Bedford," Maggie said sadly.

Allison had enough grace to stop talking for a moment.

"How are you Miss Ryan?" she asked sweetly when she ran out of grace. "You don't look too much the worse for wear."

"I'm very well, thank you," I replied and bowed slightly.

"I understand you brought your whole family here," she said sarcastically.

"Nah, just my sister and her husband. The rest come up in a few days. I'm bussing them in."

She ignored my sarcasm and continued. "Boy, things started happening once you arrived on the scene the other day."

So that was her opinion: I was the cause of the last two day's events. I guess I couldn't blame her. She was in love with Maggie and protecting her.

"Well," Maggie started, trying to diffuse the situation, I was sure. "We were just going over to the beer garden, everybody—"

Allison interrupted her. "How do you explain that, Miss Ryan?" she asked.

"I have no explanation for it. However, I'm sure you have an opinion and you're dying to impart your theory."

"Okay ladies, let's not get into—" Maggie started, but Allison interrupted her again. It must be in the water they drink.

"Well, of course I'm not a great detective," Allison said, "but it doesn't take Charlie Chan to figure out you might be the catalyst for all of this."

She was *really* beginning to annoy me.

I'd had enough and said as calmly and quietly as I could, given the fact that I wanted to belt her, "I assure you, Miss Carson that I am only here to help. If you think differently, I'm sorry. Frankly, I could care less what you think. I would hope you care enough about Miss Winfield to help rather than hinder. Either way, I do not want to have this kind of discussion with you again."

Mac and Teri were standing right there. My heart was racing and my blood boiling as I continued, "Now if you'll excuse me, I'm going to join Hannah. Maybe I'll see you there." I looked at Maggie. "I'll see you over there." I didn't wait for a reply as I walked away.

Mac and Teri followed me. "Hey, wait up."

"Who was that?" Mac asked. "Wow, she's—"

"Yes, she is. And I'm wondering if she could be a part of this mess," I said.

"Do you think she could do that?" Teri asked.

I shrugged. "I'm not sure, but she annoys me."

We found Hannah at a picnic table with Doc, another older couple, and Steve. Hannah saw us and waved. "Where's Margaret?" she asked.

"With Allison," I replied.

"Ugh," she groaned and I laughed. "Kate, I want to you to meet Tom and Lily Caldwell."

I reached over and shook hands. Tom looked like Steve with white hair. "Mr. Caldwell, the resemblance to your son is striking."

"That's what everybody says. I don't see it though. Please, it's Tom and Lily."

I sat down next to Hannah.

"So, Hannah tells us you're an accomplished photographer. That sounds fascinating," Lily said.

After a few minutes of idle chatter about my job, the conversation went to Hannah and Lily. Tom tapped me on the shoulder.

"So, I understand it's been pretty dicey around here," Tom said. He looked at the bandage on my forehead.

I instinctively reached up to it. "Well, it's been interesting." I told him I read the report and filled him in on all that had happened as Maggie joined the group and sat next to me. Allison sat by Mac and Teri.

"So, what have you done with the jewelry?" Tom asked.

"It's back at the house in a plastic bag," I said and looked at Maggie. "I want to talk to Tom about your mother. I don't want you to get upset," I whispered to her. I was dying to talk to Tom.

"I'd like to hear," Maggie said. "I never heard exactly what happened. I think I need to hear this." She swallowed with difficulty.

Tom busied himself with his mug of beer. "So, you read the report?"

"Yes, I did. No evidence was ever found, no clues no weapon, no murderer. Sounds like a typical murder in Chicago," I said.

"It may be typical for a big city but not in Cedar Lake and not while I was sheriff." He looked at Maggie and me. "I'm an organized person, Kate. I put the top back on the toothpaste. I straighten pictures. I like to have things in their place. So when a citizen in my town gets brutally murdered, especially someone I know and admire, then nothing is in its place. We never found anything to go on. However, we never closed the case. And now in light of what you found, I'm given renewed hope of finding the murderer." He continued sipping his beer. "Steve tells me your father was a Chicago cop."

"Yes, he was for thirty years. He was a good, honest man."

"Steve seems to think you have his genes. He told me what had happened. What's your slant on this, Kate?" he asked.

"Okay, if I'm a robber, I'm a sneak by nature. I would come up from behind my victim and, I'm sorry about this, Maggie, but if I'm going to stab somebody, I want it to be a surprise so there's no struggling. So, I come from behind." I shook my head, ran my fingers through my hair and thought for a moment. "Tom, according to the police report, Miranda was stabbed from the front—she had to see her attacker. If I saw someone coming at me, I'd be running. If I turned and started to run, wouldn't the entry wounds be different? I mean the angle." I looked at Doc.

He looked a little uneasy for some reason. "You're right. The angle of the wound would be different. Miranda's attacker came from the front."

"So what do you think?" Tom asked.

"Okay, let's take it step by step," I said. "Now, I might sound like I'm beating a dead horse, so bear with me here, folks. If you can't, then feel free to take a nap. So, Miranda was at the lake. We know this. This was where the attacker stabbed and robbed her. We know the attacker was in front of her, and there were no defensive wounds."

I looked at Doc for confirmation and he agreed.

Hannah frowned as she spoke, "So, twenty years later, your dog digs up Miranda's jewelry. The attacker wrapped it in burlap. Why would he steal the jewelry, kill Miranda and then bury the jewelry? It was expensive."

The hair on the back of my neck bristled. "It was expensive. So, why wouldn't he take it? Because logic says, he didn't need it. It wasn't robbery for money. It was a murder of passion. Okay, now, once again bear with me," I said, trying to keep my train from derailing. I stood and started pacing. "If you're walking in the woods, by yourself, and you see someone coming toward you that you don't know what's the first thing you do?" I went around the table.

"I'd probably get nervous and try to avoid them." Teri shrugged.

"I'd be apprehensive but I'd continue," Mac said.

"I agree with Teri," Maggie said firmly. "I'd be very nervous. I'd head back to my car. But, hell, I'm not sure I'd be in the woods alone by myself to begin with."

"I guess I would agree with Mac," Doc said.

"I agree with Maggie, I would never be in the woods by myself. I don't care how well I knew the woods," Lily said.

I looked at Tom. "I agree with the boys," he said.

Hannah was next. She looked at me and exclaimed, "Good heavens! Who in their right mind would go out in the woods, at night, alone?"

"Exactly!" I said, emphatically.

They all gave me a curious look as I looked at Maggie.

"Was your mother a brave woman?" I asked.

Maggie frowned. "I don't remember, but I don't think brave would fit." She looked at Doc.

"I would not say Miranda was a brave woman. She was stubborn and that part of the gene pool, Maggie bathes in. But brave, I would say not."

I let out a hearty laugh. "Bathes in it," I repeated as Maggie glared at me. I cleared my throat and looked at Tom. Both he and Lily agreed.

"Miranda was not brave in that sense, but she was stubborn," Hannah said.

"If this is all true, then why in the world would she be in the woods, alone at night, and not be afraid if she saw someone coming up to her?" I asked as I looked around at the confused faces.

In my heart, I knew with my next words events would quickly start unraveling. I needed to choose those words very carefully.

Kate Sweeney

CHAPTER FIFTEEN

M iranda was unafraid because she knew her killer."
Everyone at the table looked at me and I continued.
"This wasn't a random robbery. It was a violent
murder. He then made it look like a robbery and took everything.
He missed the keys, though. He didn't take them because he didn't
need them; robbery was not his motive. That was his only mistake,
but it wasn't enough to continue the investigation. Was it, Tom?" I
looked at him directly, knowing I was not wrong.

"No, believe me I tried, but then I didn't have the evidence you
have now."

"Kate found my mother's watch and wedding ring," Maggie
said. "And the most curious thing." She looked around the table.
"She found a locket, with Uncle Nathan's picture and mine in it,
with a lock of my hair."

Tom looked at Lily; they both looked at Doc and Hannah. "Does
anyone have a clue as to why Mom would have Uncle Nathan's
picture in her locket?" Maggie asked boldly.

This kid had guts. "I was wondering the same thing myself," I
added. "What was happening back then, twenty years ago?"

Tom was the first to speak. "When Jon brought Miranda home
everybody instantly fell in love with her. She was that type of
person—always helping people. She was a volunteer at the clinic for
a long time. That's back when Doc and Nathan were both working
there, it was way before you were born Maggie." He smiled and, as
he continued, I stole a glance at Lily. A faint sad, smile flashed
across her face.

"You know we all grew up together—Doc, Nathan, Jon, Hannah
and me. When we were kids I always said I wanted to marry
Hannah." He looked at Hannah and smiled. "But, Hannah always
said she wanted to marry Doc. Then a cute little blond girl moved

into town, and she hooked me. Took her to a dance one year and that was that."

Husband and wife exchanged light laughter, then Lily continued, "Jonathan was gone a great deal of the time. Miranda was alone, in that big house. We all went out together quite often. She was a sweet woman. Such a tragedy—so young. Well, back then, Nathan and Miranda were very close. There was no secret about that."

I noticed a wistful smile flash across Hannah's face. "When Maggie was an infant," Hannah said, "I remember Nathan and Miranda taking her to the lake. We all had picnics by the lake back then."

"Um, so where does that leave Miranda and Nathan?" I asked and looked around the table. "And what does it have to do with the locket found in the woods?"

"So, maybe Miranda kept his picture for sentimental reasons," Lily offered with a shrug. "Miranda was like that."

But no picture of her husband?

"But no picture of my father?" Maggie asked. *Fine, now she's in my head.*

Maggie looked around the table for the answer I feared she would get. In my heart, I knew that answer.

"Margaret, your father was like my father, not very sentimental," Hannah admitted then looked at her watch. "Look at the time. The caterers are at the house by now. I should be going."

She walked away with Doc. Tom and Lily rose to leave. "Keep all the evidence in the bag and in a safe place. Steve will pick it up tonight at the party," Tom said.

With everyone else gone, I looked over and noticed Allison talking to Teri and Mac. I had forgotten she was even there.

The catering company was indeed there. They were all over the house. Bedlam ensued.

Decorated for Halloween, the house was festive from the inside out. The dining room was setup for a buffet. I went into the kitchen and found an attractive woman at the stove hovering over a pot that had a heavenly aroma coming from it.

"Wow, what's cooking? That smells wonderful." I sighed and sniffed the air.

"Hollandaise and I don't want it to curdle." She looked at me and grinned. "Would you like a taste?"

"Sure," I said and rubbed my hands together in anticipation.

She placed the sauce on a silver spoon and gently blew at it to cool it off. She looked up and winked.

"I wouldn't want you to burn your tongue and ruin your day," she said and held the spoon to my lips. She finished in a seductive whisper, "Or your night."

I started choking and the sauce spilled down my chin and onto my shirt. The sexy cook grabbed a towel.

"Hold still, you have sauce on your chin," she said, watching my lips as she wiped the tasty sauce away.

"You have a bit more right here," she said and took her thumb to run it across my bottom lip. *I love Hollandaise sauce.*

I laughed and looked up to see Maggie standing in the doorway, arms folded across her chest, sporting a smug grin.

"Oh, hey. Um, we, she…" I stopped and licked my lips. "It's Hollandaise sauce."

Maggie glanced at the blushing cook. "My aunt needs you at the buffet table, Sharon. I'll finish cleaning up this mess," she advised evenly.

The young cook smiled sheepishly and quickly skirted out the swinging kitchen door.

Maggie picked up the towel and stood in front of me, looking up, but avoiding my eyes. I stood there, obediently. *What else could I do?* She lightly wiped away the remains of the dastardly sauce.

"I'm not sure I like you flirting with the hired help, Ms. Ryan," she scolded and only then did she look directly into my eyes.

"I'm a sucker for Hollandaise," I said with a helpless shrug.

"I'll remember that, now go get cleaned up. Mac is tending bar and he has a maniacal look on his face."

Mac was mixing some strange concoction at the bar. Teri was watching him suspiciously.

"What is he doing?" I asked warily as I joined them.

Teri shook her head. "I have no idea, but when he gets that demented look in his eyes… He's been shaking that one drink for three minutes." We watched as Mac checked his watch then nodded to himself. He picked up three small-stemmed glasses and poured.

Maggie came into the room and joined us.

"What did he make?" she asked.

Teri and I shook our heads as Mac pushed the drinks in front of us.

I stepped back and shook my head. "No way." He looked hurt.

"Katie, you're my best guinea pig." Then he looked at Teri.

"I love you sweetie, but I'm thinking, no," she said staring at the drink.

Finally, he looked at Maggie. She gave him a very doubtful look.

"Don't you dare make her drink that," Teri scolded.

The three of us stared at the cocktail then each other and then looked at Mac's pitiful face. I shrugged and picked up a glass, as did Teri and Maggie.

"A toast…" I started.

With that, Hannah came out of the kitchen and screeched, "You're toasting without me?" She hurried over to the bar. She honestly looked hurt.

"Hannah, I apologize. Just a minute," Mac said seriously. He turned his back to us and mixed another batch. Then shook it and shook it, and shook it again.

"Oh, will you pour the drink already," I said quickly.

Mac sneered at me and poured Hannah a drink.

"A toast…" I started again and the doorbell rang. "Oh, for Christ sake's, skip it. Cheers."

We all touched glasses and very cautiously took a sip. Hannah drained hers in one gulp.

"Ooh, that was good. I have to see what they're doing in the kitchen," she said and hurried away. The rest of us stood watching her.

I looked at my glass, took a deep breath and sipped it. I think it was a daiquiri. I nodded to Teri and Maggie. "It's good, not poisonous. Go ahead."

They did and we all applauded as Mac took the obligatory bow.

The caterers, after doing their job, quickly exited, leaving the cooks and servers. I went into the kitchen; it was humming with a couple of chefs. I was completely in the way so I made a hasty retreat.

Maggie was on the deck with Teri and Mac. It had gotten cool and no one had started a fire. *Geez, these people.* I got a fire blazing, sat down in the huge, overstuffed chair and put my feet up. I laid my head back and closed my eyes.

I felt a hand on my shoulder. Maggie came up to me with a glass of wine and I started to get up.

"Stay put. You look too comfortable."

She wore a pair of navy tweed slacks with a navy sweater and white turtleneck. She had her thick long hair pulled back with a white silk scarf; she looked good, very good.

Mac and Teri came in and sat by the fire.

Teri looked at me. "Uh-oh, Kate's by her beloved fire, she'll be asleep in ten minutes."

We all laughed, knowing she was right and now that she mentioned it, I blinked a couple of times and yawned. We talked about nothing of any importance for a while and I was indeed getting tired.

I looked down at Chance. "Wanna go for a walk?" I asked and the lazy cur laid there looking up at me.

I went out on the deck then walked down to what was left of the stable. It was pretty much a mess. The charred shell was still standing, well, leaning. Mac, Teri and Maggie came down to join me.

"We took a vote, no one goes anywhere alone anymore," Maggie said sternly.

I frowned and looked at Mac and Teri. They nodded in agreement.

"Well, I vote no," I said.

"Well, maybe you don't get to vote," Maggie said frowning.

"Well, maybe you can't tell me what to do," I said childishly.

Am I forty-three? She's irritating me again. One minute, I'm looking into her blue eyes, the next, I want to strangle her. This young doctor was becoming a thorn in my side and I think a judge might be lenient in my case.

I stood near the area where Maggie and I pulled Bedford out. *He must have seen quite a bit. He had to see something and either threatened to expose whoever it was, or maybe he tried blackmail.*

No, Bedford didn't look like the blackmailing type.

As I turned to walk away, I stepped on something. Looking down, I noticed it was a black leather glove.

"Why, Sherlock Holmes, what the devil are you doing over there?" Charlie asked in a ridiculous British accent.

I jumped. Teri and Maggie screeched.

"Dammit!" Mac groaned and grabbed his chest.

"Charlie, come here, look what I found." I showed him the glove. We all knelt down and stared at it.

"What is it?" he asked. "Why, it's—it's a glove!" he said in mocked astonishment.

We stared at the glove for a minute.

"Is it going to do something?" he whispered, hopefully, and Teri laughed again.

She liked him and I knew why. Charlie definitely had our father's sarcastic sense of humor.

"You idiot, can you go up and get a plastic bag? I'll put it in there," I asked.

"Yes, inspector, I shall return," he said eagerly and walked away.

I stared at the glove. The murderer could have been wearing it. Perhaps during a struggle, the glove came off.

Charlie came back and I carefully placed the glove in the bag.

Back at the house, we examined the bag under the lamp on the desk.

Maggie looked at it. "It looks like a woman's glove."

"How can you tell?" Charlie asked.

"It's too small to be a man's glove. I can't be sure, but it looks leather, maybe expensive," she said and Teri and I agreed.

"Be right back," Maggie exclaimed and dashed upstairs.

I went to the desk, opened the bottom drawer and reached way into the back. I took out the plastic bag of jewelry from where I had placed it earlier for safekeeping.

Hannah came into the room and Mac explained what had happened. Hannah's eyes were as big as saucers.

Maggie came down breathless and smiling. She handed me a pair of gloves that looked exactly like the one we found.

"I got these three years ago. They're actually riding gloves."

Teri and I looked at them. "These are expensive," Teri the shopper said.

"Where did you get them?" I asked.

Maggie hesitated. "From Allison. They were a birthday present."

"Are you thinking what I'm thinking, Kate?" Charlie asked.

"What are the odds of that happening, Charlie?" Maggie snapped at him rudely.

There was a moment of extreme tension between the two.

Hannah was watching them. "That's enough, children," she said sternly.

"You know, cousin, you and I need to clear the air and we need to do it now," Charlie said, almost fatherly in his tone.

"Why, what's the point? I saw you both so let's drop it."

I knew that look, she was getting angry. Mac, Teri and I busied ourselves with the bags of evidence.

"Well, I think I'll go into the kitchen and—" Hannah started to say, but she was interrupted by Charlie and Maggie. We all stepped back to a safe distance.

"You saw us doing what? There was nothing going on, Maggie."

"Oh, please Charlie, don't play the innocent, it doesn't suit you. Allison told me exactly what happened." She stared right at him.

He looked confused. "What did she tell you? Never mind, I can only guess. Let me tell you what happened in London," he started but Maggie interrupted him. *Why should he be special?*

"I don't want to hear about it, Charlie," she said, angrily.

"I've had enough of this, Maggie. You've been riding me for a year. Look, I know you and I have never gotten along, but like it or not, we're family. Now, I'm going to tell you and you're going to listen."

I waited for the blow up. Boy was he in for it. She said nothing. I was shocked, I must admit.

"Make it fast," was all she said.

"I was in London on business when she called me. She said she was there buying antiques. She did not tell you were there as well. I went over to her hotel and she was crying. I will be honest with you. I was attracted to her. She's a gorgeous woman." He looked to Mac and me for help.

We nodded stupidly, agreeing with him.

"She's very attractive," Mac offered.

"Really gorgeous," I said, trying to help him.

Charlie continued. "Whatever you're thinking didn't happen. I walked into her room and she hugged me. That was all. Believe it or not, when you walked into the room, I was shocked. You didn't even wait long enough for me to say anything. You've been pigheaded ever since, cousin." He looked at her affectionately. "It's the truth Maggie. I don't know what she told you, but if it was anything different than what I just said, then, I'm sorry, she's lying."

Maggie was standing with her arms folded in front of her, staring at the fire. I could tell by her face she knew that Charlie was telling was the truth. I felt bad for her, so much was happening, all at once.

She said nothing. I looked at Charlie. He gave a disappointed shrug and shook his head. He turned and went over to Hannah.

"Well, I'm going to go get ready for the festivities," he said to her. "I'll see you later, auntie." He bent down, kissed her cheek and started for the door.

"Charlie, wait," Maggie called, and went to him. "I'm sorry. I should have asked you long ago. I do believe you. I just didn't want to believe it." She looked down at the floor.

"I know and I don't blame you. Realizations can be hard to take." He gave her an affectionate hug. "I'll see you later," he said and was gone.

She turned, wiping away her tears, and went out on the deck. We stood watching her as Hannah came up behind us.

"She's lost. So much has happened to her." She sighed and went into the kitchen.

Mac and Teri were sitting at the bar talking. Guests would be coming soon and this place would be buzzing.

"Maybe I should go out and talk to her," I said.

"I think that would be a good idea," Teri agreed.

I grabbed Maggie's sweater and went out on the deck.

Maggie stood looking out at the woods, shivering.

"You forgot your sweater, Maggie."

She threw the sweater over her shoulders. "Thank you," she said.

"I think Charlie's telling the truth, don't you?"

I didn't know what else to say and I felt awkward. I'd been out of the loop, as it were, for four years, emotional detachment and all. I wasn't always so detached. But regardless, I made an inept attempt to rejoin the world.

"I mean, I can see where he'd be attracted to Allison," I said.

That was definitely the wrong thing to say. I should have stayed in my own detached loop.

"Hell, is that all that matters? That she's attractive? Christ!" she said and put a hand to her forehead.

"No, no. Hell, you're much more attractive than Allison and you're much more appealing." I stopped abruptly as I realized what I said.

Maggie shot a surprised look at me, which I avoided completely.

I tried to make conversation but stumbled over every word. She watched me as I continued in agony.

"Sorry, I'm not very good at this Maggie," I said. "Been out of the loop too long. I'm better with my camera and nature." I fought the pang of emptiness.

"Ah, I see," she said softly and looked up at the moon. "It's safe behind the camera lens and nature is always a constant."

I didn't know how to reply to the truth Maggie had spoken. I felt the scar on the back of my neck and remembered the last woman I was involved with. I shook my head.

"What's wrong?" Maggie said, not looking at me.

"Oh, nothing. I was just remembering a past incident. I lost myself in someone, who as it turned out, was not quite all there—if you get my meaning."

"What happened?"

I didn't know why I'd brought it up. "Crap," I mumbled and Maggie smiled slightly. It seemed my awkwardness amused her. "Some other time. Suffice it to say, I allowed myself to be taken in and I paid for it dearly."

Maggie gave me a curious look, but thankfully let it go.

"So I know how you feel," I said. "I know what it's like to be in love and then betrayed."

"Well, this is a first for me," she said shakily, tears welled up in her eyes.

We heard the doorbell and Maggie quickly dried her eyes.

"I am sorry, Maggie. Truly I am," I said, surprising myself at the tenderness in my voice. I pulled out a hanky and handed it to her.

She gave it a surprised look, and then took it from me.

"Well, you don't see these much anymore. Thank you," she said, wiping her eyes.

"My mother taught us well. Never leave the house without a hanky." I put my arm around her small shoulders, fighting a wave of contentment. "C'mon, company's coming."

In moments, people were everywhere. Maggie was telling me who was who as everybody from town came. She and I were passing out candy as if we were some kind of assembly line. I never saw so many children in my whole life. Maggie recruited a youngster to take over.

I leaned against the stair railing and watched in amazement. "Is it like this every year?" I asked.

"Just about. Although, I don't remember this many people," Maggie said.

Hannah appeared from the dining room. "Goodness, I hope I have enough food. Where did all these people come from?"

I looked out the door and saw Doc coming up the walk. He stopped at the door.

"Trick or treat." He smiled wickedly at Hannah and she blushed.

"Walt, get in here before you scare the poor children," Hannah said, smiling. Doc looked down at her and kissed her cheek.

"How's my gal?"

"She's doing fine, now that you're here. Now, let's get this evening started."

This was going to be some evening, in more ways than I cared to think about.

CHAPTER SIXTEEN

B y six o'clock, the party was in full swing.

Charlie came in with some beautiful woman on his arm.

"Kate, Teri, Mac, I'd like you to meet Shirley," he said with a sly grin.

I gave him a curious look. "Hi, Shirley, nice to meet you," I said and offered my hand.

"A pleasure." She was chewing gum.

When she shook my hand, she reminded me of a blond bombshell from the 1940's. Charming and…unassuming I think is the politically correct way to describe her. I glanced at Teri and Mac, who were just staring at her. I nudged Teri; she blinked.

"Oh, I'm sorry. Shirley, it's nice to meet you." Teri smiled and introduced Mac, who was still staring.

Charlie took Shirley's coat and she had on a strapless black velvet dress that was very revealing, but she wore it like a glove. I didn't know which way to look. So, like any red-blooded American lesbian, I stared.

"Holy crap," I said slowly and Mac nodded in agreement.

Maggie joined us, and her eyes widened for a split second, but she recovered quickly, much better than I did, when Charlie introduced her to Shirley.

Hannah saw us from across the room and waved.

"Aunt Hannah, this is Shirley," Charlie said with an impish grin.

"How very nice to meet you dear," Hannah said, wide-eyed.

"Your nephew told me so much about you. Can I call you Aunt Hannah?" Shirley asked sincerely.

"If you must, but only if you must."

Shirley let out a shrieking laugh that turned every head in the room. "Your aunt is a hoot, I tell you, Chuck, just a hoot." She slapped his back.

He appeared genuinely amused and said to Hannah, "You're a hoot. I mean a hit."

I looked around the room, mostly trying to avoid drooling over Shirley. I saw Nathan and Sarah having a conversation in the corner. He looked ragged and tired, like most doctors did at the end of the day, I suspected.

Sarah looked like she was nagging him about something. I thought of Allison and immediately thought of the intruder the other night. Could it possibly be Allison? I hoped it wasn't. Why would she do such a thing to Maggie? My mind went back to the glove. Whose glove was it?

Then I saw Allison come into the room. I had to admit, she was good looking. She looked elegant in a simple black dress and pearls. She immediately flew to Sarah's side. What was up with those two? Allison talked, and Sarah listened without looking at her. When Allison was done, Sarah patted her on the arm and handed her empty glass to her. The little toady went and got it refilled. I glanced over to her and she was staring right at me. I smiled, nodded, and she smiled back. At least I think it was a smile.

I looked around the room and saw Tom, Lily and Doc talking. They, too, looked a little worn as they talked seriously. The magnitude of the events of the past few days suddenly dawned on me. I was looking at it like a puzzle, trying to quench my insatiable curiosity. I had forgotten this was a family and a community that loved Miranda, a person who had been brutally murdered. It occurred to me how I'd pushed my emotional side to the background in the last few years and I considered the reason for it. The anxious feeling crept through me once again as it did every time I remembered.

"But I did, Doctor. Don't you see? I made the decision and now one person is dead and my partner nearly lost his life. I did that..." I said, pleading with her to understand.

"And you blame yourself?" she asked in a quiet, calm voice that made me want to leap across the desk and strangle her.

"Yes! I blame myself because I did it!"

She shook her head. "Kate, Kate..."

"Kate?" Mac gave me a wary look. "What's up?" He smiled and put his arm around me.

"N-nothing." I wiped my forehead with a trembling hand.

"C'mon, give. What's wrong?"

"I don't know, Mac, I think I'm in way over my head. Look at all these people, look how tired and worn they look. Christ, Bedford is dead. Someone's trying to kill Maggie by sabotaging her saddle and/or trying to drive her nuts. Sarah and Old Man Winfield probably did the dirty deed, and for all we know Miranda and Nathan had an affair as well. Oh, and let's not forget the woman in the woods. Who the hell is she? If my darling psychic sister is correct, it's Miranda! Who, by the way was murdered twenty years ago. So... does that about cover it?"

"Uh, pretty much, yeah," Mac agreed.

"What in the hell am I doing? Who do I think I am?" I asked. No one heard me but Mac. Teri and Maggie were talking alone by the bar.

Mac turned me to him. "Look, kiddo, you have your dad's gift, and you know it. Don't be afraid to use it. I know your mom didn't care for you and Teri trading horror stories with your dad, but it rubbed off on you, Kate. You have a knack for this. Hell, you spent almost ten years proving it." He looked me right in the eyes and continued. "Maggie needs you, Kate. I don't know whom else she can count on. I don't know her very well, but I can tell this is taking its toll. You don't know her that well her either, but can't you feel it? We—you have to solve this, quick. So, quit feeling sorry for yourself and get to work."

Before I could reply, Teri and Maggie walked up to us. As I looked at Teri, I remembered what I had just said about Miranda. "I've been thinking about the woman in the woods. Do you have a photo album? I think we need to look at one."

Maggie gave me a curious look. "Well, I know Aunt Hannah has a few she's kept over the years. Why?"

"Well, I'd like to see a picture of your mother, that's all," I said, and couldn't hide the hesitation in my voice.

"All right, I'm beginning to know you. Right now, you're lying to me. Why do you want to see a photo of my mother?" She looked at me, and by the look on her face, I knew it dawned on her. "You think the woman in the woods is my, my mother?" she asked in astonishment.

I winced and looked at Teri, who said calmly, "I think it's your mother, Maggie, not Kate. I just want to make sure. Kate saw her twice and you, once. Wouldn't you like to know for sure?" she finished, looking right into Maggie's eyes.

"Y-yes, I do. I just never thought of this." She gave Teri a curious look. "How can that be?"

"Maggie, there are things that happen all around us that we can't explain—"

"Like the Chicago Cubs," I chimed in then cleared my throat. "Sorry."

"Who knows why they happen? I believe that occasionally, not very often, but occasionally, God allows those who have passed on to hang around to make sure their loved ones are safe. Maybe Miranda won't rest until Kate solves this. Maybe I'm wrong, I don't know, but I'd like to find out." She patted Maggie on the arm.

Tears filled Maggie's eyes as she pulled out the hanky I'd given her.

"I would like to know, too," Maggie replied.

I looked over at Charlie and Shirley. "Boy, where does Charlie find 'em? That dress fits like a glove," I said.

"And Charlie seems to love the glove," Maggie agreed as we all laughed.

Then it came to me. I stared at the desk, where the bags of evidence were. I turned to Maggie. "When we were trying to listen to Bedford, what did you think he said?" I asked urgently.

"I thought he said 'love.' I know it doesn't make any sense."

"Maggie, he said 'glove.' He was trying to tell us about the glove. I will bet during whatever struggle there was, he got the glove and held onto it for dear life. Now, with the jewelry, DNA and fingerprints might prove useless. The jewelry is too old, and left out in the elements far too long. However, this glove may be different. DNA testing may reveal something. Who knows? I've got to tell Doc. Steve should take the bags. I don't like the idea of them in the house."

With that, Allison walked by and said hello on her way to talk to someone. She gave all of us a scathing glance. *Yep, she's annoying.*

"She gives me the creeps," Teri whispered to Mac.

"Why does she hang around your aunt so much?" I asked curiously.

"She always has," Maggie said. "Her mother died when she was little, even younger than I was. It seemed like she was always around Sarah. I guess I never thought of it before."

Just then, Tom and Doc walked up, each balancing a plate full of food. "This is wonderful grub. Your aunt outdid herself," Tom said. He looked at me. "Well, what have you been up too?"

I explained to them about the glove and my theory. They both looked at the desk.

"I agree Steve should take it, but I'd like to see it first," Tom suggested.

Because it was a beautiful night, most people were outside, which gave me time to retrieve the bags from the desk. We went into the library for privacy.

I saw Allison walk toward us. Maggie, bless her, called her and asked her for help getting wine from the cellar. As they walked away, Maggie gave me quick wink.

Steve had joined his father, Doc and me. Teri and Mac made sure we weren't disturbed. Steve and Tom examined the glove, careful not to handle it too much. I watched all the reactions. When Doc looked at the glove, he frowned. He knew something, I could feel it.

With Mac and Teri, settling in, I started as Maggie rejoined us and took a seat. "Given what we already know, I think we can safely presume that Maggie is the catalyst for all that is happening. Now, hear me out, please. I think the common thread in this whole mess is the secrets that surround this family. I'm tired of having unanswered questions. Like: What brought Miranda to the lake that night? We should assume it was at night because one of you would have seen her and missed her, if it were during the day. What was her relationship with Nathan? Why was his picture in her locket and not her husband's? After all these years, why is it that my dog finds the evidence that re-opens an unsolved, brutal murder? And while we're on that train, let's look at all the violence. I don't know how Alexander Winfield died, but Jonathon was the victim of a hit-and-run with no driver ever found. His wife, Miranda, was brutally stabbed in the woods, right across the lake. Bedford, the victim of arson. Somebody wedged a shovel through the handles of the stable door. Their intent was clear: To keep Bedford inside the burning stable. Why? Because he knew something. Another family secret.

Something about Alexander and Sarah. I know this because I overheard it."

I looked at Doc, who had gone a little pale. Tom was frowning, seemingly confused. However, no one said a word as I continued.

"And we all know what has been happening to Maggie in the last few months."

Tom spoke. "It seems that all this started once your dog dug up all the evidence. Smart dog."

I noticed Teri. I don't think she was buying Chance's superior intellect.

"No Tom, I'm afraid I don't have Chance the Wonder Dog. Are you all telling me that there are no other dogs in this community? No animals in the woods that would dig?" I remembered Chance yesterday morning, doing the scary dog thing. I looked at Teri and she looked me right in the eye. My blood ran cold as she nodded slowly. I knew she was thinking the same thing. "Who is protecting the woods?"

Well, if that didn't scare the hell out of everybody…

We all sat in silence for a moment, to digest what I had put forth. Suddenly, a cold shiver ran through me. I looked at Teri again. "Please tell me somebody else can smell that."

Everyone looked at each other. "What is that?" Doc asked. Tom sniffed the air.

"I don't know," he said.

"I smell it, Kate," Teri said.

"What is that? It smells so familiar," Maggie said as she sniffed the air.

With that, the library door opened and Sarah walked in.

Is it my imagination, or had the fragrance dissipated? I got the creeps.

"I'm sorry to interrupt. Doc, Nathan wanted me to tell you he was just paged. Apparently an emergency surgery in Dubuque. He'll call you in the morning."

Glancing at Tom and Doc, they seemed almost relieved. "Thanks, Sarah. I know the patient. Nathan asked my opinion the other day," Doc said.

Sarah smiled thinly. "Well, I'm sorry I interrupted. Please continue with your meeting." She gently closed the door as she left.

There was an awkward silence. "Well, I have one question," Maggie said. I noticed the stubborn look and held my breath. "Does anyone else but me think Uncle Nathan and my mother had an affair?"

Even though the question was long overdue, it took courage for Maggie to ask. I looked around the room at the dumbfounded expressions and nearly laughed. Teri and Mac said nothing. What could they say?

"I, for one, think it took great courage to ask that question. I think it deserves an answer," I said. Still no one said a word.

With that, Maggie stood. "It does deserve an answer, Kate. I suppose I'll find out for myself."

With a steady gait, she walked out of the library, passing Hannah on her way.

"Heavens, what's going on in here? Tom, Lily is looking all over for you and Steve. You all better continue this later."

We all left the conversation hanging, rejoined the party and mingled around the buffet table. As I was talking to Teri and Maggie, I caught the scent of the familiar perfume. I quickly looked around as the scent faded.

"Kate, what is it?" Maggie asked.

"Dammit. I smelled it again."

"You mean from the library?" Teri asked.

"No, the perfume the woman who tossed me through the French doors was wearing," I said and frantically continued looking.

The room was crowded with both men and women. Allison, Sarah, and Hannah were all standing in the same small circle of women, chattering away. It was impossible to figure out who it was.

"Shit," I cursed and turned back to the buffet table.

I noticed Allison standing by Maggie. "Well, where have you been? It's a beautiful night, c'mon, let's take a walk."

I didn't like her leaving with Allison, but I could say nothing. They went out on the deck and into the yard. As I watched them, that damned fragrance hit me again. I turned to see Sarah standing and looking at me with a half smile on her face.

"Mrs. Winfield, good evening. Are you enjoying yourself?" I asked politely, hoping she didn't see the look of sheer panic on my face. Swallowing right then was impossible.

"Yes, Miss Ryan, Hannah knows how to throw a party. How are you feeling? I understand quite a bit has happened in the last few days." She looked at me with her dark, almost-black, eyes.

"Oh, I'm fine. It's awful about Bedford, though. Who would want to kill him?" I asked looking at her while regaining my composure.

"Who? I thought he was unfortunately caught in the stable fire. It was a horrible accident," she said thoughtfully as she gazed at the fire. She was silent for an instant, but then said, "So this is good news. Tom can open the case again, and find Miranda's murderer. Maggie must be very happy." She stared at the flames as if in a trance. "Well, I think I'll go see if Hannah needs any help. Have a good time, Miss Ryan." With that, she walked away.

"Whatever," I said and turned to see Mac and Teri approaching. They watched Sarah's retreating figure.

"Man, she gave me the willies," Teri said.

I agreed. "Doesn't she look like Mrs. Danvers from the movie *Rebecca*? Oh, and she knew about Tom re-opening Miranda's case."

"You told her?"

"Nope."

Teri frowned. "Then how did she…" she stopped.

"Yep. The toady, Allison," I said. "Sarah wasn't there this afternoon. Allison must have told her. That's why she ran over to Sarah earlier this evening. I bet my log cabin on it. Sarah knows something too. They all do. Somebody's covering up for somebody, and her conversation with Bedford yesterday at the stable is nagging at me. Alexander Winfield…"

I looked around for Maggie. She was nowhere in sight and I got a little worried.

Charlie came out with his date and they sat down to eat. He seemed to sense my concern when he said, "Where's Maggie?" He looked out into the woods.

"She went for a walk with Allison," I said as I looked up to see him frowning.

"And you let her?" he asked.

I gave him a curious look. "Let her? Since when does anyone *let* your cousin do anything? Why shouldn't she go for a walk?"

He said nothing.

"Charlie, what in the hell are you doing? You're being way too evasive, what's going on?" I was getting angry. Too many people knew too many things and no one was talking. I felt myself close to the edge.

"I saw Allison this morning; I went riding with her and a couple of friends. She broke a nail and blamed it on her riding gloves—which she had lost." He looked at us.

Panic set in as we all looked around. Maggie was nowhere in sight.

CHAPTER SEVENTEEN

I'm going to look by the lake," I said quickly.

"We'll check the front," Mac said and then was gone.

Charlie and I split up and I went down the path that led to the lake. The moonlight easily led my way and, when I got to the lake, I heard Maggie and Allison talking. I stood still and could hear my heart pounding in my ears.

"Why don't you listen to your aunt, Mags? She knows what she's talking about, and you know it, too. All this happened right after she came here. She knocked you off your horse for Christ's sake. How do you know she hasn't been doing these things all along? Did you see an intruder? No. Did Hannah? No. Now, miraculously she finds your mother's jewelry. C'mon Mags, use your head. You don't even know her or where she comes from, or who she knows."

As I listened, I had to admit it was a compelling scenario. Looking at it objectively, I could see where someone would believe her.

"Allison, I care a great deal for you, but unfortunately you're a liar. You've lied to me continuously for the past two years and I don't trust you. You lied to me about Charlie, Allison."

"You're making a big mistake, Mags," she said angrily. "Okay, I admit about Charlie, but this is different. I believe your aunt."

"I'm sorry you do. This discussion is over, Al," Maggie said, ending the conversation.

"No, it's not. I can't let you be taken in like this!" Allison said. It sounded threatening to me.

"Don't Allison, don't make it worse."

As I walked down the path, they came into view. Allison was close to Maggie and I wondered how I'd get in between them.

"There you are. Hannah's looking for you, Maggie," I said as I walked toward them.

155

Allison held her ground, not letting Maggie by.

This could get nasty. It's been a while since I've been in a good cat fight.

"I might as well let you know, I don't trust you, Miss Ryan. I think you are a big part of the problem. You may have turned Maggie's head, but I know what you're doing," Allison said with an air of confidence.

"Well, thank you for letting me know," I said evenly then looked at Maggie. "Ready?"

Unfortunately, Allison was not.

"You think you're smart, don't you? You don't know the situation as well as you think you do," Allison said, angrily.

"That's possible," I agreed simply, looking right at her.

"And you certainly don't know Mags as well as you think."

"Oh, now that's *quite* possible," I agreed emphatically on that point and sported a wide grin. That did it.

Allison was fuming as she stormed passed Maggie. We watched her make an angry retreat.

"What does Aunt Hannah want?" Maggie asked as she started to walk away.

I grabbed her arm to stop her. "Hannah doesn't need you," I said, heatedly. I was angry because she'd scared the daylights out of me. "What's the big idea of coming out here alone in the woods with that woman?"

"What in the world…?"

"After telling me that none of us were to go anywhere alone anymore, you go off with her and don't tell anyone." I was steaming and my heart was pounding.

Mac, Teri and Charlie had come down the path. I barely knew they were there.

I continued angrily, "Are you crazy? Do you *want* to get killed?"

"Look, don't yell at me. It would have seemed pretty unusual if I didn't go with her."

"Did you have to go into the woods, for Christ's sake? Don't ever do that again," I said vehemently. "I can't figure this out and watch out for you, too."

"Well, who the hell asked you to watch out for me? I can take care of myself," she said.

"Oh, really, is this how you show it? Going into the woods, with her? Crap!"

"Stop yelling, the whole town will hear you, for God's sake!" She put her hand to her forehead and sat on the bench.

I turned to see the three others standing there gaping at us.

"I found her," I declared sarcastically and started back to the house. Teri stopped me.

"Kate, go back there. You can't leave her sitting on a bench."

"Watch me," I said childishly.

"Katie..."

I looked at Mac; he gave me that disapproving look I just loved to ignore. I took a deep breath and Charlie put his hands on my shoulders.

"We'll meet you back at the house," he said, turning me around and giving me a gentle push.

Dammit, she was crying. I put my hands in my pockets and stood next to her, my detached loop screaming for me. I coughed nervously and she sat up and dried her eyes.

"Boy, that hanky is getting a workout," I said stupidly. What an idiot. I cleared my throat and cautiously sat next to her. "Look, I was scared when we couldn't find you. I thought all sorts of horrible things. I-I'm sorry I yelled at you. You just scared the bejesus out of me," I said truthfully and continued, "and, after this weekend, I'm not sure how much bejesus I have left."

She sniffed and dried her eyes. "I'm sorry too. You were right. I made a point of telling you not to go anywhere alone and then I did it." She put her head back and stared at the sky.

We said nothing while watching the moon. It was gorgeous — full and yellow—a beautiful harvest moon.

"Handsome moon," I offered.

"Yes it is," she said with a quiet sigh. "When will this be over?"

"Soon, Maggie, I promise."

"I believe you. You have a way about you, Miss Ryan, that's very reassuring," she said and sniffed again.

She then cautiously reached out her hand. Instinctively, I took the small, cold hand in mine.

"You have warm hands," she whispered.

I swallowed hard as I stared at our laced fingers but said nothing.

"Thank you, Kate. I'm not sure I could do this alone."

I gave her hand a reassuring pat. "I'm glad to do it, Miss Winfield. Now, let's get you back."

For a moment, I could hear my heart pounding as we sat there in the moonlight, in a somewhat tender moment. I tried to remember what that was like.

I stood and promptly tripped on a boulder and smacked my knee on the corner of the bench. I grunted in embarrassment more than pain. *Geez, I just wanna go home.*

"Are you all right?"

"Yes, I'm fine," I said, through clenched teeth. "Go ahead, laugh. I can almost hear the peal of laughter."

"Good grief, you *are* accident prone," she said, as I limped back.

"Kate, Steve is getting ready to go. Where are the bags of evidence?" Tom asked.

I heard the worried tone in Tom's voice as I looked over at the desk. "We were in the library, and we left the room. Don't tell me they're not there?" I ran to the library.

We searched the room. They were missing.

"Dammit!" I bellowed.

"Okay, hang on. Maybe Doc or Hannah took them," Tom said, firmly.

No such luck; they were missing.

I ran my fingers through my hair. I was upset with myself to say the least. I had been so careful up until now. Dammit.

Steve put his hand on my shoulder. "Don't beat yourself up over this, we'll find them. Let's split up and search the house room by room."

We split up into twos. Maggie and I took the library and den. Mac and Teri helped Hannah with the rooms upstairs. Tom and Steve checked the yard and Sarah and Doc took the cellar. Charlie and his date took the kitchen and living room. This was one time I was grateful for so many people.

It took the better part of an hour and we found nothing. The evidence was gone. We all sat in the kitchen. Hannah put on a huge pot of coffee while we sat in disgusted silence.

"It's my fault," Steve said. "I had them in my hand and put them back on the desk. I went to see Mom. We talked for a while then, when I went back, they were gone."

"It's no one's fault," I said, then a thought occurred to me. "But it does add a new wrinkle."

I could tell by the look on Tom's face, he knew what I meant.

"What? What new wrinkle?" Hannah asked.

"Whoever took the evidence obviously didn't want any testing done on it," Tom said looking around the room. There was an unbelievably heavy silence.

What I was about to say was unnerving, to say the least. "Hannah, one of your guests this evening was a murderer."

An eerie silence blanketed the room as we all looked at one another. Then, Shirley, her eyes wide with terror, leaned into Charlie.

"Why would a sweet lady like your aunt invite a murderer to her party?" She was completely serious.

Once again, we all looked at one another.

Charlie stared at her, with his mouth wide open. He then shook his head. "I don't know, darling. We're an eccentric family," he offered affectionately and kissed her forehead.

"Oh."

The only sound that could be heard was the snapping of her gum.

Kate Sweeney

CHAPTER EIGHTEEN

It was nearly midnight when Tom and Lily offered to give Sarah a ride home. She kissed Maggie and Hannah then looked at me.

"It is unfortunate the way this turned out, but I'm sure the jewelry will turn up."

"Don't worry, this will all work out," Lily said.

"We're not through. This is just a setback. You're on the right track, don't you feel it?" Tom asked. I shrugged in defeat. "Hey, don't give up now. You have your father's cop blood in you."

Hannah was standing at the door saying good-bye to Doc. He bent down and kissed her. Hannah kissed him right back. Maggie and I stared at the ceiling.

"Now, that was a kiss," he said looking down at Hannah.

"Oh, get out of here," she said, blushing. She gently pushed him out the door.

She turned around smiling and looked at us. "What? Do you think two old people can't kiss? You think youngsters have cornered the market on romance. You two should take a lesson from us instead of playing the cat and mouse game with each other." She sported a smug grin and walked away.

I stared after her. "What's she talking about?"

Maggie rolled her eyes. I heard her mumbling under her breath as she walked away.

With everyone gone, the five of us sat at the kitchen table. I was exhausted and completely deflated.

Teri gave me a confident look. "Kate, this doesn't mean anything. You can still figure this out without that jewelry and glove. You just need a good night's sleep to clear your mind. You know you do," she said in motherly way.

"Yes, Mom," I said.

She put her head on Mac's shoulder. Watching them, and seeing how much they loved each other, made me realize how I missed having someone in my life. However, it had been four years since… God, I still couldn't say her name. I vowed— *never again, I'm too old. When this mess is finished, I'm going to my log cabin in the north woods and hide myself for a while.*

Maggie came back with a photo album, and sat next to Hannah, who apparently recognized it and sighed happily.

"I put that together ten years ago. I can't remember when I looked at it last," she said with tears in her eyes.

Poor Mac was fading fast. Teri kissed his head. "Honey, why don't you go to bed? We're gonna look at pictures for a while."

He agreed, said his goodnights, and was gone.

That left the four of us. Before Maggie opened the book, Teri explained to Hannah what she thought. Hannah sat there, wide-eyed, listening.

"You think the woman in the woods is Miranda?" Hannah asked.

I laughed inwardly at her incredulous tone. *My sentiments exactly.*

Teri thought for a moment before she spoke. "I don't think that is too far fetched at all. However, since I arrived, and heard about what has happened, I admit I've had a feeling of some presence around me. When our mother died, Kate and I felt the same thing. It is a strange feeling. You don't know if it's happening, or your mind and heart are wishing so hard, and missing them so terribly that you think they're there. I will tell you, whether it happens or not, it is a comforting feeling. I truly believe the deceased are allowed to hang around for whatever reason," Teri finished.

Maggie and Hannah looked at me. I shrugged. "I believe anything is possible. The whole idea spooks me, though."

"Now, Kate and Maggie, what exactly did this woman look like, please tell me again," Teri said.

"Well, I didn't see much of her, but she was in a white summer dress and she had long dark hair. I never saw her face—she was hidden by the trees and vanished when we started after her," Maggie said and looked at me.

"I saw pretty much the same, though I remember her hair. The dress was white and sleeveless, like a summer dress, and her hair was long and …"

I looked at Maggie for a moment.

"Like yours: beautiful, long and wavy," I said and continued to look at Maggie, who smiled and gave me a raised eyebrow. I blinked a couple times. "B-But darker," I said.

Hannah's face was ashen. She took the album from Maggie.

"What's wrong?" I asked, panicking just a little.

Hannah leafed through a couple of pages, and stopped at one page. She looked at Maggie and put the album in front of me.

There was a picture of the woman. She was wearing a white summer dress. Her auburn hair looked like it was blowing in the wind. Her arms were folded in front of her as she stared off at nothing. With the woods behind her, she stood by a huge oak tree. She appeared to be in her mid thirties and a looked great deal like Maggie. I stared at the picture and looked up at Maggie. Both she and Hannah had tears in their eyes. I showed the picture to Teri, who didn't seem at all surprised.

"This is the woman in the woods. Is this your mother?" I asked.

Maggie nodded, but Hannah spoke. "It was taken a few days before her death. We all walked around to the other side of the lake that day and had an end-of-the-summer picnic, Miranda's idea. We took that picture when we were down at the lake. I've always loved it. She looks so far away, but happy." Hannah smiled as she looked at the picture.

Suddenly, a light fragrance wafted my way. I sniffed and turned to Teri.

"Do you smell it?"

Teri nodded. "It's the same scent as in the library."

Hannah shivered. "What happened in the library? What is that?" She hesitantly sniffed the air.

I briefly explained what had happened. "It is the same." I looked at Maggie who agreed.

The fragrance was getting a little stronger. We all sat there, stupidly smelling the air.

"I think it's lilacs or something," Teri said.

I nodded. "Like honeysuckle, sort of sweet."

Maggie shook her head, "No, it's not that sweet. God, what is it and where in the world is it coming from?" She looked around the kitchen.

Hannah looked at me. "Kate, please tell me that this is not the scent on the intruder." She looked ashen. Maggie put her hand on Hannah's arm.

"Aunt Hannah, what is it?"

I closed my eyes and sniffed again, trying to remember. I shook my head confidently. "No. No, this is not the smell. That perfume was heavy, the kind that makes you sneeze. I believe Sarah was wearing it tonight, but I don't think she was the only one." I remembered the small group of women at the party. I sniffed and smiled. "This is almost a clean…"

Teri interrupted me. "A spring-time smell. I'm telling you it *is* lilacs," she insisted.

Hannah looked at Maggie. "Hyacinth," was all she said.

Maggie now lost all color in her face.

I looked at Teri who was studying both faces. She appeared to understand. I'm glad someone did.

"Okay, what is it?" I asked impatiently, the fragrance filling the room now. I was getting the creeps. Where was this coming from?

"When Maggie was a little girl, about six or so, Miranda and she planted purple and white hyacinths around the house. They spent the weekend laughing and planting."

"I barely remember, but I was happy and I remember my mother laughing as we planted. When we were finished, she said, 'They'll come up every spring and we'll watch them together.' I remember now." She stared at the picture. "We watched them come up, every spring. We would sit at this table with the window opened and the smell of hyacinth filling the kitchen. I remember sitting here, as a little girl, watching Mom make breakfast, humming and laughing."

Hannah smiled and took Maggie's hand, saying nothing.

"Well, we're not imagining this. We all smell the hyacinth." Teri smiled affectionately at Maggie and Hannah. Teri was so calm. I was so… not.

Maggie took out my overworked hanky, dried her eyes, and looked at the picture again. "I have felt several times in my life that my mother was near. I feel that now. I know it sounds stupid, but I do."

"Maggie, it's not stupid. I have several friends who have experienced the same thing that we are right now. I don't know why it happens, but I believe Miranda is here," Teri said softly.

"This is almost too much for me." Hannah sighed.

"Me too, Hannah," I said as I shivered.

"I do remember when dad took this picture, though," Maggie said.

"Margaret, your father wasn't there that day, honey. Don't you remember, he was in Chicago and didn't make it home?" Hannah asked.

Maggie frowned at her. "Of course it was Father." She looked around the room, confused. "It was a long time ago. But, who took the picture?" She looked at Hannah.

"It was your uncle, sweetie. He and I were standing by the shore remember? And he said Miranda looked beautiful and took the picture."

I sat there for a moment and looked at Teri. I could tell by her look she was thinking of something.

"Do you have a picture of your dad?" I asked casually.

Maggie seemed confused as she leafed through the pages and I looked at a man who was handsome, tall with lighter colored hair than Maggie. He looked... I don't know. I couldn't put my finger on it. There was a family resemblance between him and Nathan and Hannah.

I leafed through the pages. There were pictures of all family members: Charlie and Maggie when they were kids, the aunts and uncles, mothers and fathers as grown-ups and when they were younger.

Then I recognized the picture of Nathan. He sat with Maggie on his knee; they were smiling at each other.

"This was the picture of the two of them in the locket," I said and looked at Maggie. "When was this picture taken?"

Maggie looked at the picture. "I was six I think. It was a party like this. I used to love to sit on Uncle Nathan's lap. Doc too, I felt safe. Like a grandfather, you know?" She looked at me and Teri with tears in her eyes, and Teri smiled at her affectionately and nodded.

"The same year you planted the hyacinth?" I asked.

Maggie thought for a moment. "Yes, I think it was."

Something was here—this was a piece of the puzzle, I could feel it.

They sat in silence. I looked at all the photos in the album; I leafed through them, back and forth.

As a photographer, I don't think of the people in the picture but, instead, of who was taking the picture. All of the pictures of Maggie had Nathan or Hannah in them. I never saw her sitting on her father's lap. I never saw Miranda with Jonathan. Never saw the three of them together, happy and smiling, as Maggie was when she was sitting on her uncle's or Doc's lap. Who was taking these pictures? I could only think of Miranda taking pictures of the people she loved.

I knew what a photograph was worth; it stopped time. For an instant, it made the impossible, possible. Take a moment and freeze it in time. Take a picture of the man you love, with your daughter on his knee and put it forever in a locket, wear it around your neck and close to your heart.

Suddenly, the hair on the back of my neck stood up. Too many loose ends, I thought. I needed a common thread to pull it together. Then I remembered my common thread was all the secrets in the Winfield family.

Poor Hannah was still looking a little frazzled over the picture of Miranda.

"So, you think Miranda was in the woods?" she asked staring out the window.

"I wasn't completely sure until I saw that picture. Now, yes Hannah, I do," I said gently. I reached over and held her hand tight for a moment.

"I think I feel good that she is here, looking out for Maggie," Hannah said.

All at once, she started crying. Maggie put her arm around her and they both quietly cried for a minute or two. *These Winfield women can turn on the water works.* I handed each of them a napkin.

I looked at Teri and she, too, had tears in her eyes. Soon we were all sitting there either crying or tearing.

I took a deep breath and wiped my eyes. "Okay, if we don't quit, we'll flood the kitchen."

We all laughed and took a few deep breaths. We all noticed the fragrance of hyacinth fading. I got a little sad, it was comforting, in a way. In another way, it scared the crap out of me.

"Well, let's go to bed, for heaven's sake." Hannah got up slowly. She looked exhausted.

It was almost two in the morning and I was more tired than I thought. My shoulder ached wildly and, when I yawned, I thought my jaw would crack.

"Kate you looked absolutely done in. Go to bed. Goodnight," Hannah ordered.

"I'm going to check the doors and windows," I said and Teri and Maggie followed me. "I'm just going to check the cellar door. I'll be right back."

"Oh no, you don't. I'm coming too," Maggie said and I grunted.

Teri declined graciously and went off the bed. As she was leaving, she gave me that look again and I nodded my understanding. I'd see her before I went to bed.

Maggie followed me down the cellar stairs.

It was a bit creepy. I didn't like cellars. As we descended into the darkness, the musty, damp smell transported me back to that other dark cellar years ago. I begged the gods above as I desperately fought the vision and the wave of nausea that always accompanied it.

Lying face down in a pool of blood, I couldn't move. Through my haze, I heard gunshots. I opened my eyes to see her lying beside me, a mirror image; her lifeless eyes staring at me as if looking into my soul.

I stopped and ran my hand across my eyes. The vision, having it done its damage, vanished. I stood at the bottom of the stairs and realized Maggie was holding the back of my shirt.

"Okay, all clear, let's go," she said in a hurry.

"Will you let go of my shirt? You're panicking me, woman." I slapped at her hand. "Let me check the door, then we're done."

I walked up the four or five steps to the cellar door and gave it a confident tug. To my surprise and horror, the latch was open, the door was unlocked, and it flew open and out of my hand.

Maggie suppressed a scream. I did not.

I pulled the door closed, slammed the latch and shivered violently. "Dammit, who the hell opened that door? Did the caterers have to use this door at all?"

"No, no reason for them to use it," Maggie said, shaking her head quickly.

"What happened when you and Allison came down here?"

"Just what do you mean?" She frowned indignantly.

"Did you leave her alone down here at all?"

"Oh. No, we picked up four or five bottles of wine and we left, together," she said.

"Well, it's locked now. Let's go to bed. This place gives me the creeps."

Still unnerved about the cellar door, I rechecked all the doors and windows downstairs. I left a small light on in the kitchen and another in the living room. Maggie followed me around like a shadow.

"Good grief child, go to bed."

"Don't call me a child and I'm not leaving you down here alone. You'll probably trip over something and break a leg." She smiled sweetly.

"Very amusing, I see you've been talking to Teri. I knew it was a mistake to bring them here."

"Well, we did have a very pleasant talk this evening."

"Really? About what?" I asked absently. I stole a glance her way then checked the French doors.

"Nothing. Just that she and Mac love you and they think you spend too much time alone at this log cabin you keep talking about," she said casually. "You must like your solitude."

Mental note: Strangle sister. "There's a lot to be said for being a recluse."

"She also said you were reticent."

"There's a lot to be said for that, too. Now, you missed your calling. You should have been a psychiatrist. I could have used you a few years ago."

"I wish I knew you then," Maggie said quietly and walked upstairs, leaving me with nothing to do but follow her.

I stood in the doorway of my room and saw my faithful cur, sound asleep on my bed. Chance lifted her head and let out a yawn.

"Oh, go back to sleep, you lazy mutt."

We stopped at Maggie's door. "I'd like to check you room, if you don't mind."

"No, help yourself." She opened her door and I went in and checked the closet and windows, then the bathroom.

"All clear?" She smiled.

"Go to bed. Goodnight," I said lazily and yawned.

"You need a good night's sleep, Kate."

"No, I am not taking any more witches' brew."

For an instant, we stood there looking at each other. I found myself mesmerized as I looked down into her blue eyes; they sparkled wildly. Then I stepped back into the hall.

"Well, um, have a good sleep," I said.

"Good night," she said and closed her door.

I walked over and knocked on Teri's door. She immediately opened it and I jumped. Teri laughed as she pulled me inside.

"Okay, I saw the look. What the heck do you want, ya blabbermouth?"

"Blabbermouth? Oh, you mean Maggie?" She waved impatiently. "Forget that. Now, are you thinking what I'm thinking?"

"I don't know. What are you thinking? I'm so afraid to ask."

"Well, weren't you thinking about the picture of Nathan and Maggie? I think Miranda was in love with Nathan, that's why his picture was in her locket."

"Of course that's why it was in her locket. Everybody is afraid to say it. Jonathan sounds like a heel and from what I can gather, Nathan and Miranda got on pretty well," I said, yawning. "What was that with the hyacinth? I gotta tell you that spooked me bad."

"I know, but it happened. I never thought I would experience it. Did you feel like she was in the room?" she asked eagerly.

"Honestly, no. However, don't go by me. You're more in tune with that sort of thing than I am. God Teri, I'm glad you two are here." I shivered. "What if this isn't a good thing? What if it's *not* Miranda? Remember the movie *The Uninvited*? There were two spirits and one was not friendly."

"Go to bed before you scare yourself," my dear sister said. "Hey, do you think maybe Nathan was in love with her and then stabbed her to death because she wouldn't leave Jonathan? Then he tossed her body in the lake? Or maybe Jonathan found out and killed her, leaving her there, dead. Don't you think someone would have said this before? I mean isn't it kind of obvious?"

"I think it's glaringly obvious, but, as I said, this family is chock-full of secrets. And who in the hell would want to admit their uncle, father or brother, was an adulterer or murderer? Now, on that peaceful note, I bid you pleasant slumber, ya blabbermouth."

Sleep was impossible. My mind was all over the place with this mess. On top of that, Maggie's face kept flashing in front of me. I took the pillow and held it across my face and let out a muffled scream.

Suddenly, Chance jumped off the bed and barked at the window. "Shhh, you'll wake up everybody. What's the matter, girl?" I asked and ran to the window.

Out in the late moonlight, I saw nothing, but then I heard it. A banging noise outside, that sounded like something hitting the side of the house. *Shit, now what?*

I slipped into my clothes and walked out into the hall.

Maggie greeted me. She pulled her robe around her. "Did you hear that?"

"Yes, stay here."

"No way," she said firmly.

The coward, Chance, retreated to the bedroom as we headed down stairs. I heard it again. It sounded like someone wanted to get in and it was coming from that damned cellar.

"Look, I don't know why you won't stay put. I'm going to…" A loud banging noise interrupted me. Maggie looked at me and grabbed my arm.

"It's the cellar door," she said in a terrified whisper.

"Stay here," I said as I started through the kitchen.

All the lights were out except a small light over the stove. I stopped and Maggie bumped right into me. I jumped and turned around.

"Shit. Stay here," I whispered again.

We both jumped when Mac came into the kitchen.

"What's…" he started to say, while rubbing his head.

I put my fingers up to my lips to quiet him.

"What are you two doing up this late?" he whispered with a smile. "Shame, shame. I'm telling Aunt Hannah."

I gave him an exasperated look. "Mac, I think someone is trying to get into the cellar."

His smile faded quickly. "Are you sure?" We heard to door bang again. His eyes widened.

"Is the door locked?" he asked and I nodded.

I started for the door to the cellar.

"You're not going down there again," Maggie whispered vehemently and grabbed my arm.

"Maggie, let me go. I'll be right back," I said, confidently. I took her hand off me and Mac grabbed her shoulder gently.

Whoever it was, was in the back by the cellar door. I swallowed hard, and opened the door in the kitchen that led down to the cellar. I didn't turn on the light, but slowly descended the stairs. Mac and I started down, it was completely dark and we heard nothing.

Once at the bottom of the stairs, I stopped and stood completely still and listened. Mac went by me and stood close to the door. I thought I heard something outside. Then I felt something behind me on the stairs. I braced myself for another attack. No one was going to throw me through a door this time.

As before, I turned around, but this time I grabbed the intruder by the front of his shirt. I reared back and was about the throw whoever it was out of my way... It was Maggie.

I could see she was about to let out a blood-curdling scream so I put my hand over her mouth.

"Sshh," I whispered. "I think there's someone outside. Go back upstairs."

Her eyes widened and she shook her vehemently.

"Maggie, don't argue with me," I whispered.

She wrenched my hand away. "I'm not leaving you two alone," she whispered and stood firm. I wanted to strangle her, but I could see she was unwavering. I angrily pulled her down to the bottom step.

It was completely dark, but the full moon shone through the two small cellar windows. I saw a shadow pass by one window, then the other. We both stared at the steps that led up to the door. The silence was deafening. Someone or something pulled at the door then stopped, then tugged harder—almost angrily—and stopped again. Then there was one last frenzied yank and a bang. I thought for sure the bolt and latch would give way and the door would fly open. I was petrified and so was Maggie. Mac stood by the door perfectly still. There was nothing but absolute silence.

It was an eerie sight when the shadow passed by the window and vanished as if it had never been there.

Kate Sweeney

CHAPTER NINETEEN

I wish you would have called me, sooner," Steve said as we sat around the kitchen table, which was getting a workout. "I'm glad neither of you went outside. I don't need another unsolved murder in Cedar Lake."

I could hear the defeated tone in his voice.

"So the door was unlatched from the inside when you two checked it and you locked it?" Steve asked.

I nodded. "Someone had unlocked it, or maybe it's always been opened."

"Nope. I checked that door myself the other night, after your lady intruder showed up. It was bolted and locked tight," he said firmly.

"Then someone had to unlock it. Who's been in the cellar since Friday morning?" I asked and looked at Maggie.

"Well, I was down there with Allison, but we got some bottles of wine and came right back up. She wasn't down there alone," Maggie said.

"I didn't see anyone go down there, but with all the people here, honestly, who would be watching the cellar?" I asked. "Anyone could have gone down there at anytime and opened it."

"Well, Doc and Sarah checked the cellar this evening when we were looking for the jewelry and glove," Steve said. "Tomorrow morning, I'll ask them if they noticed the door was unlocked," he said as he stood. "It's late, why don't you all get some sleep? I'll have my deputy patrol the house...again."

Just as I lay down, I heard a soft knock at my door. Maggie stood there in her robe sporting a smug grin.

"Are you lost, young lady?" I asked with a wide yawn.

"Have you misplaced something?"

"You found my wayward dog I take it?"

I followed her into her bedroom. There lay Chance, on Maggie's bed, sound asleep.

"She looks comfy," I said with a touch of envy.

"She can stay here if you like," Maggie said and shivered a bit as she pulled her robe closer.

"If you like I can get a fire going for you. It is a little chilly in here," I said and looked at her small fireplace.

"Well, it's late," she whispered and shivered again.

"I can get one going in a minute and you'll be nice and toasty."

The small fire crackled as I stood gazing at the dancing flames. I looked over at Maggie. She was sitting on the edge of her bed, looking like a lost and frightened little girl.

"Okay, into bed," I ordered.

She smirked and crawled under the covers. "I am not a child, you know. You keep referring to me as if I were. It's rather annoying."

I stopped and thought about it. "I apologize. I don't mean to be insulting. You just look so young. Perhaps I'm just too old," I said, as I looked down at her.

She pulled the covers up her neck. "Too old for what?" she asked, in a soft voice.

Chance stirred then crawled up next to Maggie, put her head on her stomach, and closed her eyes.

"Well, she's yours for the night," I laughed, ignoring her question.

"You can sit by the fire for a while if you want. It's probably chilly in your room, too."

I looked at the huge chair. It did look inviting. "Well, maybe for a minute."

My body ached horribly. I sat down and a feeling of comfort engulfed me. I put my feet up on the ottoman and was in heaven. I stared at the fire, trying not to think about anything, but wound up thinking about everything.

"Kate, you need to stop thinking for a while and sleep."

"I will. Go to sleep. I'll sit here for a while," I yawned and lay my head back.

"That was pretty unusual wasn't it? I mean the hyacinth, but I wasn't scared, though," she said, sounding amazed at the idea.

"You weren't? Well I have to admit I was petrified. Teri is much better dealing with the supernatural than I am," I said, and closed my eyes.

"Well, you certainly don't show it. How do you remain so calm?" she asked, sleepily.

"Years of emotional detachment," I joked, amusing myself as usual. *Sad to say, I'm my best audience.*

"You know, I can't tell if you're joking or if you're being serious," she said while yawning.

"I'm at my most serious when I joke," I said quietly. "Go to sleep."

She let out an exasperated groan. "Good night, Kate."

"Good night, Maggie," I yawned and fell sound asleep.

I woke at six o'clock to the sounds of a peacefully snoring duet. I looked over at them. They both looked so comfortable. Maggie was on her back, with the covers all over the place, and Chance lay stretched out at her side with her head on Maggie's leg. As I got up, Chance raised her head. I gave her a stern, "Sshh!" and she yawned and closed her eyes, the lazy cur. I gently covered Maggie and slipped out of her room.

After a nice long shower, I put on my work clothes, as I called them, and got my camera equipment. I left the heavy equipment behind and took the smaller camera and a few extra rolls of film.

In a half-hour, it would be light. Hopefully, taking a few photos would help me think. As the coffee brewed, I went out on the deck.

The last of the evening stars were barely visible. The sky was clear and it was almost sunrise. I loved that time of day—just before sunrise, when the moonbeams still had their grasp on the sleepy world and the warm rays of the sun started a claim of their own. It was the beginning and the end all at once. I smiled and took a deep contented breath. I would die if I couldn't be outside. I didn't care what the weather.

However, there was a definite chill in the air so I guess I did care. I got my jacket and found a small thermos mug in the cabinet. I was ready for an adventure.

Usually Chance was with me, but the lazy thing looked too comfortable sleeping next to Maggie and I couldn't blame her. If I were sleeping all over Maggie, I'd... I stopped in mid thought.

Forget that thought entirely, Ryan. I left a note telling them where I'd be. Hell, they would still be asleep when I got back.

I walked into the morning air. There was a light fog hovering over the grounds. I crossed the yard and took the path that led into the woods and the lake. The sun was almost up and the wildlife had already begun sending out its wake-up call.

As I got to the lake, I saw a small gaggle of geese, which seemed to have forgotten which direction was south. They left a rippling wake as they lazily swam by. I continued to walk around the lake and came up to the sign as I did the day before. I took the rugged path that led to the Wildlife Refuge. It was about a quarter mile from the house, maybe a little less.

The refuge was on the other side of the lake. As I looked across now, I could barely see Maggie's house.

There was a five-foot shoreline, mostly rocks and boulders, and a path that continued around the lake, which I took. I tried to remember where I'd seen Miranda yesterday morning. I looked back across the lake and figured I was close. Then I saw the huge tree about thirty feet in front of me. I remembered when I took the picture, that tree was directly behind her. I walked over to it and looked around. I shivered, not sure if it was from the morning chill or something more menacing.

I walked around the area and noticed a very large hole in the ground, right behind the tree. I went up to it and it dawned on me— this was where Chance had been digging. I looked around the area for more signs. Then I saw it, a small swatch of burlap, and then another larger piece. I picked them up and put them in my camera case. I knelt and glanced around. I was right; my little mutt had been digging here, right where I saw Miranda. It was almost as if she was showing me where to look. Me? As I thought of Chance doing the scary dog thing, I realized Miranda was showing both of us. *God, don't go there, Kate, you're spooked enough as it is.* I heard something rustle in the woods. I got nervous and just knelt there, not moving.

"Are you praying?"

I jumped up and saw Maggie with Chance bounding along beside her.

"Jesus!" I exclaimed, "Don't do that!" With my hand covering my heart, I showed them what I'd found. "Maybe there's more around."

We combed the area pretty well. Although even Chance had her nose to the ground intent on her task, we found nothing further.

"Well, I'm not sure what I was looking for, anyway," I said. "There is so much crap going on here with your family, Maggie."

"I know. I'm not sure of anything," she said sadly, as she continued, "I take that back, I'm sure of one thing. I'm sure Uncle Nathan and mother had an affair and no one wants to come out and say it."

"I agree, completely, I'm afraid," I said, noticing the sad look in her eyes. "I'm afraid there's a great many secrets, Maggie, as Bedford said before he died."

"I only wish I knew what he was talking about," Maggie said, lightly kicking the ground. "It appears there is more buried than my mother's jewelry."

"Bedford is a puzzlement to me," I said and leaned against the tree. "I keep going back to what I overheard at the stable. He mentioned your grandfather, Alexander Winfield and Sarah sounded angry. If Bedford kept family secrets…" I stopped as I tried to keep up with my mind—not an easy thing for me to do.

"What Kate?" Maggie asked and watched me intently.

"Let's say during his time with your family, Bedford, overheard, oversaw, and watched as he did his job. I'm sure he'd seen plenty. He obviously saw too much. Now, if he had all this knowledge, what did he do with it?" I asked and Maggie's eyes widened.

"You think Bedford may have been blackmailing a member of my family?"

"I don't think so. If I was gonna blackmail someone and they're stinking, filthy rich—"

"Thank you."

"Sorry. If I'm blackmailing, I'm certainly not going to live on top of a garage for thirty years shoveling horse dung, washing cars and mowing the lawn," I said. "Nope. I think Bedford knew the family secrets but for some reason, kept them to himself."

"Why? Why would he do that?"

"Why not? He was alone, bored and your family, I'm sorry to say, seems to have a lot of material for Bedford to play with. The fact that, as he was dying, he told you there were so many secrets, told us right there, Maggie. Bedford knew something about someone and my gut says it was Sarah and Nathan."

"It's hard to believe that Bedford knew all this while he lived in a small garage apartment," Maggie said and shook her head.

The idea struck me. Why didn't I think of this sooner? "God, I'm an idiot. Maggie, do you have keys to Bedford's apartment?"

Maggie blinked in astonishment, but nodded slowly.

I looked around for Chance. She was on the other side of the lake running around like the insane dog she was. "Well, she's got the right idea, let's get back."

As we started back, we heard a noise in the woods and turned around to see a beautiful fawn coming out of the woods, toward the water. Ever so slowly, I reached into my bag and took out my camera. We were still behind the huge tree, hidden by the thick brush. I knelt on one knee to get a good angle and snapped off four or five shots. The little creature looked up right at us and stood perfectly still, its little brown-speckled body trembling. Her ear twitched and I snapped a few more. Then she scooted back into the woods.

"These woods are beautiful. How many people do you think come to this side of the lake?

"Since the murder, my guess is probably no one. These woods are pretty primitive. I can't remember every seeing anyone on this side."

"I think that's why he buried Miranda's jewelry here."

I heard the woods moving again. I whispered to Maggie in excitement, "It's probably another deer."

We slowly backed up into the brush and hid behind a huge boulder. I winked at her and put my fingers to my lips. She smiled and knelt. I knelt on one knee and steadied the camera. The brush was moving and rustling.

"It might be more than one," she whispered right in my ear and I shivered.

If I were a deer, my ear would be twitching. My heart raced and I could feel my face flush as I felt the lingering, soft breath. I glanced at Maggie who gave me an innocent look.

"Sorry," she whispered, with a smug grin as I narrowed my eyes.

"I don't think so," I challenged in a low whisper.

For some absurd reason, I was staring at her lips. I raised my gaze to those blue eyes that held a questioning, nervous gleam. Now I offered the smug grin.

Maggie now shivered. "Y-you'll miss your chance."

"I don't think so," I said, still holding her gaze. I gave my attention to my camera. "This could be a great shot," I whispered and looked through the lens.

I went cold and Maggie caught her breath.

It was Sarah coming out of the woods. She was alone and looked like hell. The early-morning fog lingered around her feet and her hair, usually pulled back and neat as a pin, was completely disheveled. I crept further behind the boulder, pulling Maggie with me.

Sarah was frantically looking at the ground, searching for something. I was petrified. I stupidly remembered two years ago when I was nearly in the same predicament in Wyoming , but back then there had been a wolf standing in Sarah's place. While I got a great shot, the wolf almost got me. This could be the same thing.

She was about thirty feet from us. *God, please don't let her come this way.*

She stood running both hands through her hair as if she was trying to pull it out. She looked like she was retracing her steps. She moved to the edge of the woods, walking closer to us.

Although it was cold, I was sweating profusely. I heard her mumbling; that scared me. People who mumble to themselves always bothered me. I know I talk to my dog, but I don't mumble. What in the hell was she doing?

As she came closer, Maggie had her hand on my shoulder, her nails digging into my flesh.

We heard Sarah say in a furiously low raspy voice, "Goddamned little bastard. Where is it?"

There was a rustling in the woods; it had to be a squirrel or chipmunk.

"Who's there?" she hissed in a low guttural voice.

I couldn't move even if I wanted to, I was so petrified. Sarah started walking our way until she was almost directly in front of us. The sweat was pouring down my back and I prayed to every saint that came to mind. Maggie held my arm in a vice grip.

Sarah looked around. "You don't scare me. You never did," she said defiantly, as though she was talking to the woods themselves.

Maggie and I looked at each other. Who in the hell was she talking to? A shiver ran down my spine as I realized who it was. We heard the rustling of the leaves and I slowly peeked out from behind the boulder.

Sarah took off like a bat out of hell and ran down the rugged path that led to her house. Oddly, the commercial *Coo-Coo for Cocoa Puffs* ran through my mind. I watched Sarah in stunned amazement, as she ran down the path and out of sight.

"You want to tell me what the hell that was?" Maggie asked.

I stared at the path. "I have no idea, but let's get the hell out of here."

As we started walking around the lake, I looked back every now and then. Maggie stumbled on the path and I grabbed her elbow. We continued, not talking but walking faster and faster. We got to the clearing and saw Maggie's house.

"Sanctuary," I said and we broke into a dead run, petrified to look back as we ran up to the porch, completely out of breath.

Mac and Teri were in the kitchen; both jumped when we made our entrance. I couldn't talk I was breathing so hard.

"What in the hell!" Teri ran over to me. "What happened to you two?"

I opened my mouth but nothing but a deep wheeze came out. I sounded like I had swallowed a harmonica.

"Come into the kitchen," Teri said frantically.

My legs were burning from running as I sat down. Teri took my camera case. Maggie sat across from me. She was in far better shape than I. She could talk. She took a deep breath and explained. Mac sat there amazed, looking from me to Maggie.

"You two are freezing," Teri said and put two cups of coffee down.

"Sarah?" Mac questioned. I nodded.

Hannah came into the kitchen. "Well, good morn—" she stopped abruptly as she looked from me to Maggie. "What in the world happened now?" she exclaimed.

I repeated the whole story. Hannah looked shocked but not as much as I thought she should, given the fact her sister-in-law had been running around as mad as a March hare. I looked at Teri. I could tell she agreed. I glanced at Maggie, who was had a curious look on her face as well.

"Christ, Kate, what the hell does this mean?" Teri asked.

It means Aunt Sarah's done a loop the loop. She's flying without a net and gone 'round the bend. In short, she's nuts! That's what it means. However, I graciously kept this to myself.

Maggie started again. "Well, it appeared she was looking for something."

"Okay, let's look at this logically," I said.

"After what we saw? Logic? Please," Maggie said sarcastically.

"I would have to say your aunt was looking for something that was not found by Chance. I think she knew what was buried out there." I finished and got up to get another cup of coffee.

Hannah and Maggie watched me. I looked at Teri, who gave me a sad kind of acknowledgment.

I hated what I was about to say, but I took a deep breath and continued slowly, "I think your Aunt Sarah knows something and is somehow, however obscurely, involved in this mess." I couldn't look at either Hannah or Maggie.

Hannah shifted uncomfortably in her chair. I didn't say anything about it, but Teri apparently noticed it, too.

"Given what I believe happened between Uncle Nathan and my mother I can see where her involvement would be logical," Maggie said.

"Well, she totally interrupted what Maggie and I started to do," I said and explained our conversation about Bedford and looking at his apartment.

Hannah shook her head. "What is happening to our family?" she asked sadly, as Maggie put her arm around her.

The Winfield family was unraveling before our eyes.

CHAPTER TWENTY

We took the steps up to the back entrance of the garage apartment, which was anything but small. It ran the length of the four-car garage. It was huge.

As Maggie put the key in, I was stunned to see the door was not locked.

"That's odd," Hannah said. "Bedford was very private and particular about his belongings. He had a thing about being neat. A place for everything and everything in its place. He would never have left this door unlocked."

I cautiously pushed the door opened and walked in.

"What are we looking for?" Hannah asked.

I glanced around and walked to the bedroom. "I'm not sure. I'm hoping Bedford wrote down whatever he knew, or left something else to give us a clue as to what he knew," I said and looked into his bedroom. "Bedford wasn't as neat as you thought, Hannah. Come and look at this."

Hannah and Maggie followed me into the room. The dresser drawers were slightly open with a few articles of clothing strewn about. I glanced at the small desk in the corner and again, the drawers were open.

"Either Bedford got dressed in a hurry, or somebody was looking for something, just as we are," I said.

"Kate, look at this," Maggie said. She was standing by the small desk looking at the floor.

There was a gold button lying on the floor. I picked up it and examined it. Maggie took it from me so she and Hannah could more closely examine it.

"It looks like a man's jacket button," Hannah said.

I opened the closet and saw no sports jackets or dinner jackets there, but he did have a nice selection of flannels. "Well, it's not from anything Bedford owns." I closed the closet door and took the button from Maggie.

"It has to be from someone," Maggie said and I agreed.

"Well, let's keep looking. I have a feeling there's something here," I said and held up the gold button. "And I have a feeling someone was already looking."

After going through every drawer, under the bed, through the closets and in every cabinet, we came up empty. "Crap," I said and flopped into the corner of the couch and sat back. I glanced to my right and saw a small bookcase holding about fifteen books. "Bedford read poetry?" I asked and reached for one of the books on the shelf.

As I took the book out, something fell into my lap. I looked down. It was a small composition book that looked very old. Like those we used to buy for English class. My heart raced as I cautiously opened the notebook.

"Uh, ladies, can you come over here please?" I asked.

Both were quickly at my side. "What is it?" Maggie asked.

"Some sort of notebook."

"Where did you find it?" Hannah asked.

"It, um, sort of fell in my lap," I said with a shrug. I nervously glanced around the room. Maggie and Hannah did the same. "You don't smell hyacinth, do you?" I asked. Both women shook their heads.

"Well, what's in it?" Maggie asked eagerly.

I opened the cover and leafed through the lined pages. "Well, let's start from the beginning. It says here: *New job seems good. Old man Alexander is an asshole. Not much money, but I get this place for nothing.* When did Bedford start working for you, Hannah?" I asked.

"Good heavens, I was a young woman, so it was nearly thirty years, as I said."

There was more scribbling, which looked like he was adding figures, probably his paychecks. I leafed through and stopped when I saw the name Sarah.

Settling into my job and getting to know the family. Old man Alexander still an asshole. Jonathon is asshole junior. I like Hannah, though. The youngest, Nathan, is a quiet guy married to the snake, Sarah.

"I don't think Bedford liked Alexander or Jonathon. Or Sarah for that matter," I said and read more pages of nonsense that contained nothing pertaining to family.

When I'd about given it up as being all about grocery lists and paychecks, I came upon an interesting passage that I read aloud.

Jonathon brought home a wife. What a beauty! Miranda is nice. What she's doing in this family?

I looked up at Hannah who sported an indignant look.

"But he liked you," I reassured her and Maggie laughed.

"Bedford liked horseracing," I said, leafing through the pages. "He scribbled about his bets. He mentioned Maggie being born— called you a cute kid. Called Charlie a bully."

"It's not like a journal. It's more like he's just writing down what he finds interesting," Maggie said. I had to agree.

"Hmm... listen to this. *Here's a corker—cleaning the limo, I found a pair of diamond earrings in the back seat. The old asshole took 'em and guess what? Snaky bitch Sarah had them on that night at a party at the house. Ohhh, Alexander...* Well, that might coincide with what I heard at the stable," I said. "I can't imagine Bedford talking about all this and not mentioning Miranda, though. It's got to be here."

I leafed through old, worn pages hoping to find something and I did. "Okay, here we go...*Big mess. Miranda found by the lake this morning. Somebody robbed and killed her. What a shame, nice lady. Little Maggie is so young, poor kid. Now she's left with an asshole father. I'll keep an eye out.*"

"The writing in this next passage looks shaky to me," I said and examined the handwriting. "It's not as neat as the earlier handwriting. However, listen to this: *Heard Jonathon and Sarah yelling—he's selling his old man's clinic. Nearly laughed my ass off—Sarah sounded like some crazy bitch ranting and raving. There goes her meal ticket!*"

"Here's the last entry. The handwriting is the same: *Can't wait to tell Maggie Sarah took off in her car this afternoon. Maggie's going to be pissed—can't wait to see the fireworks. Bet the old bitch is headed into the city with her cronies for some margaritas—it's Cinco de Mayo, ya know. What a bitch.*"

I leafed through the remaining pages. They were blank. Hannah reached out for it and I handed it to her. She carefully leafed through it, stopping to read from time to time. "All these years, Bedford kept this notebook. I can't believe it."

"I can't believe it literally dropped into my lap," I said as Maggie took the notebook and read it. "Let's get back to the house and call Steve. He might want to have a look at this and the button we found."

Mac and Teri were, of course, amazed at what we'd found in Bedford's apartment.

"I suppose there's still nothing we can do about the lost jewelry and glove," Teri said.

I thought about this for a moment. "Okay, with all that has happened, it can't be overlooked that Sarah and, possibly, Nathan are deeply involved with this mess. Now, we know someone took those baggies last night. Someone unlocked the door to the cellar. Someone tried to get *in* through the cellar last night, why? Let's retrace the evening. We were in the library with the evidence. Hannah came in to tell us Lily was looking for Tom and Steve. We all decided to talk later. We all left, but forget the bags—but do I remember Tom closing the door to the library. When we came out, Allison took Maggie for a walk. I, um, *we* got worried and left to look for Maggie."

"And you got *really* upset," Mac chimed in.

I grinned in spite of myself and looked over at Maggie, who was blushing horribly. "Yes, and I got really upset."

"So, what does this have to do with the evidence?" Mac looked confused.

"Okay, I hope my train doesn't derail here. What if taking Maggie out was a diversion to get us out of the house? Then whoever it was went into the library and took the evidence? Maybe they couldn't get it out of the house, though I haven't figured out why yet. So they slipped into the kitchen and down to the cellar and hid it there. Perhaps under the guise of getting more wine. Then they unlocked the cellar door and waited until after midnight to come back and take the bags. That is the only reason I can think of as to why there was someone trying to get back in last night."

"But Sarah and Doc checked the cellar last night," Maggie said.

"It's only a hunch," I said. "But let's go and check the cellar one more time to be sure."

Even in broad daylight, the cellar was dark, cold and damp. I hated cellars. I think I mentioned that.

"Okay, let's each take a section and see what we find," I said.

We all split up and looked under every box, chair, and old bicycle. Mac crawled behind any place he could get to and came up filthy. We checked behind the staircase. We opened boxes and checked every one. We even pulled out and checked behind every wine bottle. We all stood looking around the cellar, dusty and full of cobwebs.

"Well, at least the cellar is a little cleaner," Hannah said.

"Crap. I was sure," I said in a dejected tone. Maggie patted my shoulder.

"It was a good hunch."

I looked around and then I looked up. *No rafters or any place to hide something up there.* I looked at the wine rack and saw that the top almost reached the ceiling. Almost.

As I walked over to it, I noticed the stepladder. "Hey, guys," I said slowly.

I showed them the stepladder. There were footprints on the rungs and on the top of the ladder, covered with dust

"Geez, Kate," Teri said as her eyes widened.

I looked up to the top of the wine rack, it was at least seven, maybe eight, feet tall.

"Are you guys thinking what I'm thinking?" I asked.

"You bet," Mac said. He opened the ladder. I stood on the top of it and reached up.

"Be careful, dear," Hannah said.

"Really Kate," Maggie agreed.

"You all think I'm gonna fall off a stepladder? Geez," I said impatiently.

Mac laughed outright. "It wouldn't be the first time, Sherlock."

I couldn't see and had to feel my way around. "God, I hope there are no spiders up here, yeesh!" I shivered. I was serious. I hated spiders.

"Will you stop joking and be careful," Maggie said sternly as she held onto my leg.

Who's joking? Continuing the search, I felt something and pulled it down. I was shocked. I didn't think anything would be there; but there they were—both bags. I handed them down to Mac who was equally shocked.

Teri was beaming. "Sherlock strikes again!"

Maggie stared at the bags then looked at me. "Amazing!"

"Heavens Kate, you're a wonder," Hannah said, shaking her head.

"I'm a little pleased myself," I said happily.

We went up to sit at the kitchen table, as we were wont to do all weekend, and stared at the plastic bags, waiting for them to do something.

Teri suddenly jumped up. "Good grief, I forgot. Your editor friend dropped off the pictures while you were at Bedford's," she said and ran out of the kitchen.

"This should be interesting," I said as Teri came back and handed me the manila envelope. "Good thinking," I said about the magnifying lens she also handed me.

As I examined the pictures, I could see a faint milky white line by the tree.

"What is it?" Hannah asked and Maggie looked as well.

I looked at Teri and smiled. She bent down and looked through the lens. Then she stood up sporting an amazed look.

"I'll explain, if I can," I said. "I think this apparition, for lack of a better word, is Miranda. I think Miranda has been here, off and on, watching over you. Now, with all that's happening, she's here. I remember when my mother died. For an entire year, I had the feeling she was there. I came home on several occasions and thought for sure she was in the room. Teri had similar experiences. I don't know how it happens, but I believe Teri. For instance, the fragrance of hyacinth in this very room—Miranda was here. I have a friend who's a photographer. He's taken and developed hundreds of photos like these. People are sure they see their loved ones in the photo. In each case, once the photo is developed, there is only the milky-white shadow."

Maggie smiled in understanding. "There have been times when I thought the same thing. I never said anything, because I thought it was my imagination. But it's comforting in a way to think she might be here."

Hannah had tears in her eyes. "Every time I look at you, Maggie, Miranda is here." She reached up and touched Maggie's cheek.

"Well, let's get back to the other issue," I said. "I remember what Charlie said at the party about Allison losing a riding glove. We can't overlook Allison being somehow involved. To what extent I don't know. If you look at this logically, there are a few people we could consider because they all knew Miranda then and are still around now. Somebody knows something and I'm going to find out who and what, today," I said emphatically. "Okay, person-by-person. The glove implicates Allison. Next, Nathan. We are all on the same page in one respect: he loved Miranda and she him. That's a big motive especially if he wanted her and she said no. Then there's Jonathan. Same motive—love. Perhaps he found out and killed her in a jealous rage, but since he's dead now, how could he be responsible for the current turn of events involving Maggie?

"Next, we have Doc," I continued. "He knows something, I can smell it. What, I don't know. Although, I can't imagine him a murderer, but he surely knows something. Then we have Sarah. Her little psychotic trip through the woods today leads me to believe she knew where to locate Miranda's jewelry—and she was surely looking for something today.

"While mumbling to herself and talking to the woods are not points in her favor, it doesn't mean she murdered Miranda, but if she knew Nathan loved her then there's a motive there also. Now with Bedford's notebook, we know there was a good deal going on way back when with Sarah, Alexander and her fight with Jonathon over the Winfield Clinic. Who am I missing?" I looked at all of them.

"Tom Caldwell," Maggie said.

"Ah, Tom. Well, he admitted to gossiping about Nathan and Miranda. Maybe he loved her, maybe he told her he loved her and she refused him. Being the sheriff, he could possibly get away with it. Stretching it, I know, but why not. Why should he be left out?" I stopped and rubbed my forehead, I had a tremendous headache. I looked around the table, "Confusing, isn't it?" It was not a question.

"Completely," Hannah said. "How in the world are you going to find out?"

"Well, we have the jewelry and the murderer doesn't know this. That's a big advantage. Since we found the glove at the scene of Bedford's murder, once we have a suspect, we could possibly test any DNA on the glove and compare it to our suspect. That would surely help prove something." I got a cup of coffee and turned toward the table, they were all looking at me wide-eyed. I thought for a moment. "Common threads. Now, I've got a few, we just need to tie them together."

I stared at my coffee cup thinking of the evidence we had: The jewelry, the glove, and now the notebook and the jacket button. My mind raced. The button from the jacket. I whirled around to all of them.

"What? I can tell you have an idea, Kate," Teri said.

Maggie nodded. "I agree, I know you well enough, I can tell when the wheels are turning."

"There is one way to find out who is implicated or involved. We have the evidence." I thought for a moment. "Okay, first we need to make sure the evidence is safe, I mean really safe—literally—a safe."

I looked at Mac and Teri. "Can you take the evidence over to Steve and make sure he puts it in evidence lockup? Tell him everything and that I'll be in touch later this afternoon."

I watched them leave then looked at Hannah. "Call Doc and have him come over, please? I'm sorry Hannah, but he knows something and he's got to tell me."

"I'll call him." Without another word, she walked away.

Maggie looked at me. "What do you want me to do?" she asked tremulously. She knew what I was going to ask.

"Maggie, if you don't want to do this, I'll understand, but I need you to call Allison. This is the important part, Maggie: Tell her about the evidence, and that we found it. Tell her about the notebook. Then tell her I have a theory about this but I won't tell you. You and I had a fight over it. Tell her whatever, but see that she's here in an hour."

I saw the look of doubt.

"If you don't want to do this, please believe me, I understand. We'll do it another way," I said. "I know it looks like I'm playing with people's lives here, but there's a murderer out there and I've grown too fond of you to let anything happen."

"Yes, I can do it. You think Allison is going to tell Sarah, right?" she asked.

"I think she's already told Sarah a great deal. Now I want her to come here. I need to talk to her, Maggie. I hope I'm completely wrong about all of this, truly I do. However, we need to know who's implicated." I took a deep breath and regarded Maggie. "Sorry, Maggie, my gut tells me she'll tell Sarah and it will snowball from there. I don't want you to do anything you're uncomfortable with. I know how much you care about Allison. So please don't do anything you'll regret." I ran my fingers through my hair and Maggie gently touched my arm.

"I've been thinking about this since you found the locket. I'm not sure what it means, but I have to find out one way or the other. I can't live like this anymore: afraid of going out, afraid of thinking about the past and my mother. I've been alone and scared for a long time. I don't want to be alone and scared anymore."

"It'll be over soon, Maggie. I promise."

Once the phone calls were made, it was all set in motion.

Hannah returned, and put her hand on my shoulder. "Kate, this has to be finished one way or the other," she said. "I called Walt, he's on his way and I know he'll talk. Now, you two plan your attack. I have a kitchen to clean." She smiled and left.

Plan my attack? I hoped I knew what I was doing. I hoped for Maggie's sake most of all.

CHAPTER TWENTY-ONE

It turned cloudy and cold, and there was a rumble of thunder off in the distance as Maggie and I stood on the deck waiting for Allison and Doc.

I noticed Maggie deep in thought. When she caught my inquisitive glance, she smiled. "I've been thinking about Aunt Sarah. I remembered when I was little she used to tell me to stay out of the woods because it was where they found my mother. I became afraid of them, and I started dreaming. My father got frustrated and sent me away to school for a couple of years. Kate, there is so much I am remembering this weekend that I never thought of before." She stared at the woods.

"I remember when we were younger, Allison and Charlie used to tease me about my dreams and my fear of the woods. I used to cry myself to sleep sometimes, missing my mother and feeling alone. Then my father had Aunt Hannah come and live with us. I-I had to come home from school. I was asked to leave," she said sheepishly.

"Asked to leave? Now, why would a sweet little girl like you be asked to leave?"

"I have no idea. It was only a little fire," she said, looking down at the deck.

I was shocked. "You started a fire? Where and why?" I was completely intrigued.

"In the chemistry lab, I put magnesium chips in a test tube and held it over a Bunsen burner and kablooee! They extinguished it quickly though. As to why? I wanted my father's attention, I guess. I was lonely and scared," she said with a shrug and looked at me apologetically.

"Hmm, burning down a chemistry lab? I can see you as a kid, freckle faced and full of the devil," I said, laughing. "How old were you?"

She struck a thoughtful pose. "God, it was nineteen years ago! I was fifteen." I did the math.

"Yes, I'm thirty-four," she said sarcastically and I felt the color rush to my face. "You great detective, you," she added, with a grin. "By the way you talk, you must be at least fifty."

I laughed out loud at that one then abruptly stopped and frowned.

"I'm not fifty," I said, quite seriously, as if she needed reassurance. Perhaps I was the one who needed it.

She laughed then. "It doesn't make any difference to me," she assured me.

We looked at each other for a moment, then the thunder cracked overhead and she jumped.

"Christ," she laughed nervously as Hannah came to the door.

"Walt just pulled up," Hannah said.

The moment, whatever it was, was gone.

"Sorry Doc, but I could use your help." I told him everything I knew, and he was visibly shaken. "Doc, if you know anything, please tell me." I almost begged him.

Doc looked old and tired and I saw Hannah give him a sad but affectionate glance.

"Walt, I know we promised each other long ago, but now this changes everything," Hannah said to him.

Maggie had come into the room and we gaped at each other. I flopped into a chair.

"What changes what?" I asked, completely dumfounded.

Doc let out a deep sigh. "I have no idea where to start. If you hadn't brought Sarah's name into it I would never be telling you this."

"Understood," I said. "I don't want any of this either Doc, but Christ, somebody killed Bedford and they have been trying to do the same to Maggie. If Sarah can help in anyway, don't you think we should take that chance?" My patience, which I lacked horribly as it was, was running short.

He nodded and continued. "After Nathan married Sarah and brought her home she started having headaches. Nathan told me about them. We tested her, she was fine—no tumors, nothing. I thought it was migraines. It went on for a few years. She and Nathan have always had problems. I often wondered why in the world he married her."

"I know why," Hannah said. "Nathan is a gentle soul. He's weak and he saw strength in Sarah. That's what he told me, at least. When I first met Sarah, I too saw her strength of will and purpose. When my father started the clinic, she was tireless in her efforts. She was very good at fundraising, getting influential people to donate money. Father admired her for that. I believe that's why he gave her so much authority."

"I agree with you there. There was a spark between Alexander and Sarah. They worked well together," Doc said.

Maggie and I exchanged glances. *I'll bet.*

"Later on, I found out Sarah was seeing a psychiatrist who was medicating her for severe manic depression and paranoia," Doc said. "I found out quite by accident. I never told a soul but Hannah. We've never spoken of it since the day I told her. But, Nathan would call me at all hours, and I could hear Sarah in the background, screaming. I would go over there and she would be livid, claiming Nathan was cheating on her, everybody hated her and the like. Poor little Charlie was always on the stairs, looking like a scared rabbit. She'd run up to him and cradle him, saying no one would ever take him away from her, whatever that meant. It wore Nathan out. Even when she was taking her medication, she was still a very nasty person, which I don't think had anything to do with her illness." Doc stopped for a moment and drank his coffee. "It nearly cost them their marriage."

Maggie leaned forward. "Instead, Uncle Nathan and Mom had an affair." It was not a question.

Hannah again had tears in her eyes. "Yes, Margaret. I'm sorry, I know of one occasion. Before you were born. I am almost sure of it a few years after that, I'm sorry. After Miranda was killed, I didn't think it would serve anyone to say anything." She looked apologetically at Maggie, who covered her aunt's hand with her own. Maggie looked at Doc.

"I always suspected but never knew," Doc said. "When Miranda was a volunteer, I would see them at the clinic. She was always there when Nathan was on duty."

"Doc," I said, "we found a notebook in Bedford's apartment, tucked away next to a book of poetry. In it, Bedford talked about

Alexander Winfield and Sarah. The other day at the stable, I overheard Bedford and Sarah talking. Alexander's name was brought up again. You said they worked well together. I'm wondering how well? Do you know anything about that? Hannah?"

They exchanged glances and I knew then that they did.

"What do you know?" Maggie asked.

"I can prove nothing," Doc said. "However, I felt certain that Sarah and Alexander, at some point were..." his voice trailed off.

Hannah merely nodded.

"Perhaps that was one reason Sarah got on the Board of Directors at the clinic," I said.

Doc looked uncomfortable for a moment, shifting in his seat. "A great deal went on in the Winfield family back then. That's why I decided to get my own practice and get out for a while. Hannah and Nathan were the only ones worth anything. Though they were father and son, Alexander and Jonathan didn't like each other. Poor Hannah and Nathan were on the Board because they were family.

"Before he died, Alexander wanted Miranda on the board. Sarah was livid. She felt she had done a great deal for the clinic. Believe me, she was always right there, helping to keep the place running— that was the only good thing she ever did. As I told you the other night, she kept that clinic afloat and got the State's Medical Board to approve it. I don't think she wanted to share the limelight with Miranda, who didn't want it, but Jonathan granted his father's wish. He was a hard man, Jonathan. So was Alexander." Doc looked at Hannah, who nodded, so he continued to Maggie. "Sarah stopped at nothing. I'm sorry, Maggie, but your father was a stinker; a philanderer, I guess, is the proper word. Why he cheated on your mother, I will never know. But he did, from the onset. Miranda would come to see me and cry like a baby. This went on for years, long before you were even born. She would get phone calls from these women boldly asking for Jonathan. She confronted him on several occasions but to no avail. Jonathan wasn't the man any of us thought he was. The honeymoon was over quickly once he brought Miranda home. I think this is what drove her to Nathan." He put his hand on Maggie's shoulder. "Sorry, sweetie."

"It's okay, Doc. I never could get close to him, either. Believe me, I tried. I just felt he never liked me. I thought it was because I reminded him of mother." She stared sadly out the window.

Well this truly sucks. "So what stops did Sarah pull?"

"She threatened to expose Jonathan for what he was, thus scandalizing his beloved reputation in the business world and the community," Doc said. "Then, as if that didn't do it, she promptly stated that Alexander Winfield seduced her and she would expose the entire situation. I personally can't imagine Alexander doing that. But, now that you have Bedford's notebook, it makes sense."

"Do you think Sarah knew about Miranda's affair with Nathan?" I asked.

"Yes, I think she did."

"Do you think she or Nathan is capable of being involved in Miranda's murder?" I asked.

His eyes widened a bit, I could feel Maggie tense and heard Hannah gasp. He appeared to think for a minute. Nobody moved or said anything further. Boy, patience might be a virtue, but I don't have it. I tried to remain quiet, even though I wanted to scream.

Finally he said, "Yes. I think she could be in some way involved. I'm not sure about Nathan though." We all looked at each other.

I fished the button out of my jean's pocket and held it up. "Maggie found this in Bedford's apartment. His room looked as if someone had gone through his dresser and desk, obviously looking for something that might be incriminating. Bedford had no suits or jackets in his closet. By the way, where is Nathan? Is he still in Dubuque on what was it? An emergency surgery?" I looked at Doc as I toyed with the gold button.

"So, now what?" he asked.

I glanced at the clock, almost one. Allison would be there soon.

"I think Allison is in some way involved with Sarah. Sarah mentioned a couple of things to me last night that she could only have known through Allison. I also overheard her conversation with Maggie last night by the lake. Sarah thinks I'm to blame for the recent problems. Allison cares for Maggie and believes Sarah."

"What are you planning?" Doc asked curiously.

"I'm hoping Allison is only an innocent dupe, not a dope, and that she'll help us. Then I'm planning on finding the jacket that belongs to this button."

And that was my plan. It had sounded so good a moment ago, when it was a mere thought.

Kate Sweeney

CHAPTER TWENTY-TWO

Maggie shot me an angry look. "Oh, you are so *not* going to do that."

I stared at her for a moment. "Is that a double negative?" I asked curiously, trying not to grin while she glared at me. I was getting used to that expression. I rather looked forward to it now, in some perverse way.

"Steve should be here. He's the sheriff," Hannah said.

"No. If Allison sees Steve, she won't cooperate."

"And you think she'll cooperate seeing you?" Maggie asked.

"I hope so," I said. "Maggie, I'm planning on getting into your aunt's and uncle's house. I'm thinking Steve would frown upon breaking and entering."

"Kate, this is no game. Do you realize how many times you've been hurt this weekend? First, someone throws you through the door, then you're almost killed in the fire. I think you are accident-prone. I will not have you hurt anymore, that's it. If you go through with this hare-brained scheme, then I go with you," Maggie finished firmly with a challenging look.

"Me, too!" Hannah announced.

I glanced at Doc who stood and put on his coat. "I'm leaving. I feel the Winfield stubbornness coming. I'll be at the clinic if anyone needs me or if anything happens." He looked at me. "I don't want to see you there again." He kissed Hannah and Maggie then left.

I'm used to being on my own—no ties, no worries. I live a simple, easy life and I hate complications. I looked at the object of my complication and shook my head.

"Maggie, do you understand that I don't want you or anyone involved or getting hurt?" I asked, trying to make her understand.

"Kate, do you understand that I *am* involved, and I don't want you or anyone to get hurt anymore?" she asked with equal simplicity and determination.

I had to admit—good point. *I hate when that happens.*

"Jesus, you're stubborn," I said, ignoring my own stubbornness. "Why don't we announce it over a P.A. system as we pull into your aunt's driveway?"

"There's no reason to be sarcastic," Maggie said.

"Oh, I beg to differ," I snapped back. Inwardly, I was beginning to enjoy the strolls down Sarcasm Lane with this feisty woman.

I was about to continue our debate when the doorbell rang. Maggie was still glaring at me as she walked away. I could hear Allison's dulcet tones all the way in the den.

"God, sweetie, you look awful," we heard Allison say. "We need to talk."

"We need to talk to you, too, Al," Maggie said as they came into the den.

Allison was shocked to see me "What's going on here?" she asked.

"Allison, we need your help," I said quickly.

She sneered at me. "You need my help? I doubt that."

"Al, please, sit down," Maggie said. Allison sat on the couch as Maggie sat on the ottoman facing her.

"Allison, we know you told Aunt Sarah about the glove and the possible DNA testing," Maggie started.

"What makes you think I told her that?" she asked.

"Because you knew about it all," I said. "Sarah didn't. You knew about the glove, Sarah didn't. You knew about the possibility of reopening the case, she didn't. When she talked to me about it all, I realized there was only one way she could have known and that's from you," I said evenly.

"All of this started happening when you got here," Allison yelled at me. "You ran Maggie over, you're the only one who saw the intruder, you were with Maggie when she got thrown from the horse. Maggie might think you're charming—"

"Oh, charming my ass!" I said vehemently. *Charming?* "You told Sarah, right or wrong?" I asked, not looking at Maggie.

"Yes, I told Sarah, she's onto you as well." Allison now stood over me.

I tried to get up, but Maggie stepped between us.

"Allison, you told Sarah? Why?" Hannah asked.

Allison said nothing, but her shoulders sagged. She looked at Maggie and she softened, but still she said nothing.

I knew why. I said quietly, "Because Allison cares a great deal for Maggie and Sarah used Allison to find out what I knew. She told Allison I was the cause for all this and I shouldn't be trusted. Allison seized the opportunity to protect Maggie and get me out of the way, any way she could. So she listened to Sarah, thinking she was doing the right thing."

I looked at Allison, who sat down and stared at the ceiling. "That's absolutely right," was all she said.

Maggie sat back on the ottoman and took Allison's hands and held them. Allison looked at Maggie with tears in her eyes.

"Someone tried to kill Kate," Maggie said. "They broke into my house. They killed Bedford. Al, what do you know? We need your help."

"I thought I was protecting you," Allison said in a small voice.

I felt bad for her. She had no clue what she had done.

"I know. Now you can help. Tell us what you know," Maggie pleaded with her.

Allison took a deep breath. "Sarah asked me to stay close, and if I overheard anything, I was to tell her. She said she was trying to figure this thing out as well, and we shouldn't trust a stranger. So I agreed. That's all. She never confided in me. Although..." She trailed off.

"Although, what?" Maggie asked. "Please, Allison."

I said nothing, letting Maggie handle this one.

"Sarah told me that if I helped her solve this, she would make sure I was compensated," Allison said and stopped.

Okay, Maggie, please ask her...

"How would Aunt Sarah compensate you, Al?"

I could see the color rise in Allison's beautiful long neck. "Money. She promised to help me with my antique shop. Y-you know I'm having difficulties."

"Al, you could have come to me. I would have helped you," Maggie said and I heard the sincerity in her voice.

"Mags, we're not seeing each other anymore. How can I ask you for money?" Allison questioned in a quiet voice.

"Aunt Sarah, I'm afraid, is somehow involved in all this, Al," Maggie said. "We found a notebook in Bedford's apartment that really implicates her. We need your help now, to determine how deeply she's involved. It could even be that Uncle Nathan is involved as well."

Allison's head shot up at the statement. She looked from me to Maggie. "How can that be?"

Maggie looked over at me.

"There's a great deal going on here, Allison," I said. "Too much to go into now. You'll have to trust Maggie, and help her, not for me, but for Maggie's sake. Someone is trying to kill her."

"Allison, dear. For the sake of all of us and for all the years we've known each other, please listen to Kate," Hannah implored.

Allison sat back against the cushions of the couch and stared at nothing in particular. "What do you want me to do?"

"I need you to get Sarah out of her house for at least an hour this afternoon," I said.

Allison gave me a curious look. "Okay, I can call her and take her to lunch."

"Tell her Maggie told you that I found more evidence. That should do it," I said confidently. "Look, Allison, I know you and I got off on the wrong foot, but do you believe what we've said?" I asked.

"Yes, Kate I do. I-I'm sorry, I wasn't thinking. I can't believe I've been so blind," she looked at Maggie and smiled sadly.

"I would suggest that you go on as normally as possible. Tell Sarah what you think she needs to hear, but please be careful. One person is dead, and three others have been tossed around. So, please, don't take any chances with her. If she says or does anything strange, tell Maggie or Steve right away."

Allison agreed and took out her phone.

With Allison gone to get Sarah out of the way, we planned our mission. Mac and Teri returned from town. Steve had the evidence in the evidence locker at the police station.

"Well, let's put together a plan of attack," I said. "We'll get to the house and then, Hannah, you lead us to the right closets. We check out the rooms and we're gone. That's it. In and out as quick as we can." I looked at Hannah. "Right?"

She nodded. "R-right."

We all gave her a suspicious look. "Hannah, right?" I asked.

"Yes, yes. I said it would be fine. Don't make me nervous."

"Crap, this is going to be a nightmare. Okay, let's go. I suggest we walk, just in case."

The day was dark, gloomy and depressing. Although it had stopped raining, the thunder still rolled in the distance.

"Okay, please, let's all be careful not to disrupt anything. In and out," I urged as we walked down the path. I tried not to feel like as if I was leading a funeral procession.

They all agreed.

"No worries, we'll be fine. As long as they don't come back early," Mac said and I nodded.

We came to the clearing as Allison's car pulled away—perfect timing. We slowly walked up to the house and Hannah pulled out her keys. She turned with a gleeful smile.

"I feel like I'm, what is it called? Breaking and entering?"

"Don't kid yourself, that's exactly what we're doing. Even though you have the keys, Aunt Sarah would be highly aggravated right now if she saw us," Maggie said dryly. "So Aunt Hannah, please just let us in."

"Heavens, which key is it?" Hannah sighed and fumbled with the keys.

I felt ridiculous as the five of us stood crammed at the door.

"Hannah, may I?" I asked and took the keys from her. She pointed to the right key.

We slowly walked in and looked around. "Okay, Hannah, which room is Sarah's and Nathan's?" I asked.

Hannah looked up the stairs and hesitated. "Well, I think…" she started.

"You think? Aunt Hannah, don't you know?"

Hannah rang her hands. "Well, I thought I did. Don't make me nervous, Margaret," she said.

I rubbed my forehead. "Okay, okay, let's split up. Mac and Teri take the closets on the first floor. We'll go upstairs."

Teri and Mac nodded and went to the closet in the foyer. Upstairs, there were three bedrooms. "Okay, we each take one. Be careful," I said.

As we split up, Hannah and I started for the same bedroom, nearly bumping into each other. I gave her a helpless look.

"Sorry, dear," she mumbled and headed for the next room.

I quickly checked out the closet, searching every article of clothing. There were men's clothes but no jackets or coats. Actually, it looked like a spare room that wasn't actually used. There was a bed and dresser but nothing else of a personal nature.

From the hall, I heard Hannah exclaim. I dashed out to see her holding a silk scarf.

"I knew I gave this to Sarah!" she announced triumphantly.

I hung my head and Maggie patted my shoulder.

"Aunt Hannah, dear, please, we don't have time," Maggie said. "Now put that back exactly where you found it."

Hannah gave me a sheepish smile, which I acknowledged with a patient smile. She turned back into the room.

Maggie laughed and walked back to her room.

In a few minutes, Maggie called me. *This better not be a borrowed pair of earrings.*

Maggie held a man's jacket. I was exhilarated. Mac and Teri came up the stairs. Maggie was staring at us, amazed. Hannah came in behind us.

On the front of the double-breasted jacket were two rows of gold buttons; the top button, however, was missing. I was shocked. I hadn't expected to find anything.

"Where did you find this jacket?" I asked Maggie.

"It was thrown on the chair in the corner. I just picked it up," she said, stupefied.

I took the jacket and checked the pockets, then checked the lining. There were initials embroidered on the lining of the inside breast pocket: NAW in script.

"Nathan Alexander," Hannah supplied. "Oh, dear."

"Well, that answers that," I said.

"Okay, let's get out of here," Maggie said, shivering.

"We'll have to tell Steve. Leave the jacket; let's put it back the way you found it," I said and handed the jacket back to Maggie. "*Exactly* as you found it."

"Can't we take the jacket?" Teri asked.

"No. If we take it, they'll know we were here. We need an advantage and if they think they still have the upper hand, that's our advantage."

CHAPTER TWENTY-THREE

M aggie and I drove into Cedar Lake later that afternoon to fill Steve in on what was happening. He sat there holding the gold button.

"Nathan?" he asked, sounding incredulous.

I had to agree, this whole mess was incredulous. "I haven't seen Nathan since the party. He was called away for some emergency," I said.

"I know. I saw Sarah this morning," he said. "She told me he was still in Dubuque, but he'd be back tonight. I suppose I'll take a run over there and have a chat with him when he gets home." He picked up the phone and called Sarah. After a brief discussion, he hung up. "Sarah says he's still not home, but thought maybe he should be by now. I'll check later. I don't like this."

"I don't like this either, Steve," Maggie said and I heard the weary tone in her voice.

"You still have all the other evidence in the safe," I said.

Steve motioned behind his desk, "Yep, all secured." He picked up Bedford's notebook. "I read this little thing. Not much evidence, but it does tell us about the family. Your grandfather and Sarah? Shit. And what's this about taking your car, Maggie?"

"I have no idea why Bedford would write that. He was right, though. I was angry with Aunt Sarah for taking my car and not saying anything. I don't remember why she took it."

I picked up the book and found the page. "Cinco de Mayo. That would have made it what? The fifth of May, right? If my Spanish serves me correctly, which it usually doesn't. That reminds me of a great Mexican restaurant in Chicago…" I looked at Maggie who grabbed the notebook and stared at the page. Her complexion had turned ashen. "Maggie, what's wrong?"

She said nothing and looked from Steve to me. "Dad died on the fifth of May, six months ago."

Steve sat forward and took the notebook. I sat there, stunned. "Sarah borrowed your car on the same day your father died in a hit-and-run in Chicago. And the driver was never found."

Steve whirled around to the file cabinet and plucked out a manila folder. "Jonathon Winfield. DOA at Northwestern University Hospital in Chicago, on May 5, 2006. Hit-and-run. Blah, blah, no driver found, no witnesses. Time of death, approximately 2 a.m...." Steve skimmed through the other pages. He looked up. "Well, I suppose I'll have to talk to not only Nathan, but Sarah. This doesn't prove anything. I'm sure she has an alibi. She could have been anywhere with your car. Okay, so why don't you two go home, and I'll call you later? Don't talk to anyone about this. Of course, tell Hannah but stay put until you hear from me. I can't believe we found this out. It's amazing."

The king of all understatements.

We all sat in the kitchen, once again trying to cram five people around the table. No one had much of an appetite as we picked at our food.

I told all about our meeting with Steve. Hannah was visibly shaken. Maggie sat next to her and put he arm around her. Mac and Teri were equally stunned.

"This doesn't look good for Sarah, but Steve is right," I said. "She could have been anywhere and I hope she has an alibi. And I'm worried about Nathan, that button from his coat found at Bedford's doesn't help him at all either. Let's think of Sarah and all that we have seen so far. She broke into the house—I know it was her. She argued with Bedford. She ran around in the woods like a crazy person. According to Bedford's notes, she had something going on with Alexander and had a screaming match with Jonathon. You know, come to think of it, Bedford's handwriting—I said it looked shaky in the passages about Jonathon and the Maggie's car."

"What do you mean?" Teri asked.

"Shaky like an elderly man was writing it, which could mean that the argument would have precipitated Sarah taking the car on May 5th. Maybe the two are connected, maybe not. I hope Steve finds out. It's in his ballpark now. It's a police matter."

"Well, I for one can't believe the turn of events in the past few days. My God, what will happen now?" Hannah asked sadly.

None of us could answer that. I only hoped I was right and Steve could take it from there. It was late, and the mood was somber. We all decided to try and get some rest. We had no idea what tomorrow would bring.

A nice hot bath, I thought and when I eased myself into the hot water, I felt instantly relaxed. I laid my head back and closed my eyes as my mind wandered, and I thought about the week's events. Now I really had a headache.

There was a knock on the door. "Kate?" Teri whispered.

"Hmm, c'mon in," I sighed dreamily.

She poked her head in. "You've been in here a long time. Maggie wanted me to check on you."

"I'm fine Teri, I'm fine. I…" I laid my head back and put the hot cloth on my face.

"I know. You're not used to the attention. Well, I think it's…" she started again and I interrupted her.

"Oh, can I please take a bath by myself?"

I lie there for a while longer and almost fell asleep right in the tub. I was extremely stiff when I lay down on the bed and Chance jumped up. "Hey, you mutt, where've you been?"

Again, there was a knock at my door. "C'mon in, Teri, the door's open," I said with my eyes closed. "You can tell Dr. Winfield I'm fine and I didn't drown."

"Well, she'll be relieved. She was told you were accident prone," Maggie said and I opened my eyes.

"I thought it was Teri," I said and started to sit up.

She waved me back. "Don't get up. How do you feel?"

"I'm fine," I said. I noticed she had her doctor bag.

She followed my gaze and smiled. "It occurred to me I haven't checked your shoulder," she said as she came over and sat on the edge of the bed.

"I'm fine," I repeated. She opened her bag and took out a tiny flashlight.

"I know. I want to check out your head, see if there's anything there," she said frankly. "Lie back please," she said professionally, as she shined the light in my eyes. "Now, look straight ahead."

I did. She put her finger up. "Follow my finger," she said professionally and I did. *If she says, look at my thumb…*

"Mm-hmm," she said and turned off the light. I hate that doctor thing they do.

"Whatta ya mean, 'Mm-hmm'?"

"It's just as I suspected," she said, shaking her head. "You have a definite independent streak. I'm afraid it's inoperable." She gave me a smug grin.

I let out a hearty laugh. "Okay, I had that one coming."

"Go to sleep and no getting up to wander in the woods in the morning," she ordered.

"Okay, okay, you bossy thing," I said. Chance jumped up and lay at my side.

Maggie ruffled her ears. "You, too, go to sleep," she said as she kissed her head. Chance was in heaven; her tail was wagging so fast I thought she'd take off.

Then, unexpectedly, Maggie leaned over and gently kissed my forehead then my cheek. "I wouldn't want you to feel left out. Good night," she said tenderly as she walked out.

My heart was racing as she left me staring at the door like an idiot. I was doing that a lot this week. However, I knew how Chance felt. If I had a tail...

I woke at six-thirty, sat on the side of the bed and flexed my neck. I heard a noise behind me and turned. Maggie was standing there half-asleep. She looked tired, worn and, God help me, adorable.

"Kate, what are you doing? It's only six-thirty," she said, with a yawn.

"Waiting for a bus. Go back to bed," I said.

She was leaning against the door as I walked up to her.

"I can tell you're not a morning person," I said softly and for a moment, she grinned and leaned into me. I could feel her warm body close to mine. I swallowed with difficulty and didn't trust my voice at that moment. She was like a zombie as I guided her back to her room.

"In you go," I said.

"Mornings are not my best time," she whispered and crawled back into bed.

As I pulled the covers over her, she looked up through sleepy eyes. "No going out. Stay in the house." She yawned and snuggled into the covers.

"Yes, doctor, now go back to sleep," I said.

As I turned away, she reached for my hand.

"I do appreciate all you're doing. Truly I do," she whispered tiredly.

I looked down at her sleepy face. She looked so young and so peaceful. Before I knew what I was doing, I bent down and gently kissed her forehead. As I pulled back, she sighed and pulled the covers up to her neck. Yes, I noticed the slight grin as she cuddled the blanket to her.

"Go back to sleep," I whispered and gently tucked the covers around her, desperately trying to ignore my racing heartbeat.

Mac was in the kitchen reading the paper and drinking coffee. He looked up and smiled. "Good morning. Teri's still sleeping. How are you feeling?"

I poured a cup and sat across from him. "Fine and good morning. I don't suppose Steve called?"

"Nope, not yet. He will."

"Mac, he's got to solve this soon. I feel like we're so close."

"I know. I thought for sure he would have called already. Well, it's early."

I was making breakfast, again, when Hannah came into the kitchen.

"Good morning all," she said in a quiet voice. She looked a bit haggard.

"Sit, Hannah, I'm making breakfast," I said.

Hannah sat next to Mac. I poured coffee for all of us. They both talked absently and I tried unsuccessfully to not think about Sarah.

Mac nudged me and I looked up. "Okay Sherlock, what's on your mind?"

"I was thinking about Sarah. What was she arguing about with Jonathon? The notes said the Winfield Clinic. What was the big deal? It's a clinic. But Bedford said, 'there goes her meal ticket.' Okay, then it's a big deal. If it was Sarah and Nathan's meal ticket and Jonathon was taking away the meal, that's a motive. And you did say they were running through money like shi… well, they were running through money. Right, Hannah?"

"Yes, they are," she said sounding very tired. "Sarah loves to spend."

I thought of Allison's comment yesterday about her compensation. "How was Sarah going to compensate Allison for being a dupe if she had no excess money?"

"I don't know, dear," Hannah said.

"I missed that yesterday. What is Allison's deal?" Mac asked.

"Well, it appears Sarah was telling her I was the one who was causing all the problems and she wanted Allison to stay close to Maggie to protect her," I said and thought about it. "Once again, we're back to Maggie, dammit. This is annoying."

I looked out the kitchen window. It was a cold and rainy, blustering fall day. "Maggie," I said, thoughtfully. "What did she have to do with that clinic? She had no money invested in it. She doesn't work there. Because she was family, and Jonathan died, she was now on the Board of Directors. Big deal."

"It's not only the seat on the Board, dear. Once Jonathon's will is out of probate, she'll have controlling ownership of the Winfield Clinic."

I looked at Hannah and, for the first time, like an idiot, thought about Maggie's inheritance. "What about his company? Who gets that?"

"Well, Charlie works there, I think he's in there somewhere, but Maggie is his sole heir. But it has always been that way. And of course, she has her own money from Alexander, so Margaret doesn't need the Clinic or Jonathon's company. I'm not quite sure what she's planning. With all this, we've never even talked about it."

My mind raced as I thought of a possibility. "Hannah, what happens if something happens to Maggie? What happens to the company and the clinic?"

Hannah thought for a moment. "Because of the complexity of the family business and the clinic, I believe it would be as it was with my father. The bulk of his estate went to Jonathon, who in turn would leave it to his heir. It as my understanding if anything happened to Margaret, who is without an heir, it would revert to the next surviving male heir..." her voice trailed off as she frowned in contemplation.

"And that would be Nathan," I said.

We sat in silence for a moment.

"I never realized how wealthy Maggie is. Wow, so she's loaded," I said jokingly, trying to lighten the sudden dark turn this was taking.

Hannah gave me a superior look. "No wonder Allison needs Margaret so desperately," she said with more than a trace of sarcasm. "What Margaret needs is someone to love." She was still sporting a superior look as she smiled sweetly.

Maggie came into the kitchen. "Good morning." She apparently tried to sound cheery though she looked exhausted.

"G'morning," I said and noticed her sad eyes.

She sat at the table and said nothing. Mac nudged her. "You okay?" he asked and she nodded.

I poured a cup of coffee and put it in front of her. She looked up and smiled. "Thanks."

"Margaret, what's wrong? You look terrible, dear," her aunt asked.

Maggie took a deep breath. "I had a horrible dream. Like the dreams I had when I was young, about being chased through the woods, but I couldn't see a face. I just kept running." She stopped and put her hands over her face.

I pulled up a chair and sat next to her. "Maggie," I whispered and put my hand on her shoulder.

She sobbed and, suddenly, she threw her arms around my neck. I was shocked at first and didn't know what to do. She cried mournfully into my neck and I put my arms around her and held her tight.

"Hey, Maggie, it's okay," I said. "It was only a dream. Don't worry, we'll get this thing solved and you won't have bad dreams anymore. I promise." My hand found its way to her soft wavy hair. I gently smoothed it back off her face.

She clung to me for a moment then pulled away, completely embarrassed. "I am *so* sorry." I handed her a napkin. She smiled and dried her eyes.

"Don't apologize," I said. "I'm glad I had a shoulder." I smiled and gave her an encouraging hug.

With breakfast finished, we sat in the den not knowing what to do next. Then the phone rang and Maggie nearly flew to it. Thankfully, it was Steve. Maggie handed me the phone.

"Good morning, Kate. I haven't been able to locate Sarah, but I did talk to Nathan. He's still in Dubuque. He's coming back tomorrow."

"Did you tell him about Sarah, and Bedford's notebook?" I asked and leaned against the desk. It was then I noticed Allison standing in the doorway talking to Maggie. Where did she come from?

"I did not. I didn't want to tell him over the phone. He has no idea where Sarah is. I tried to call her this morning and left a message. My deputy has been patrolling the estate and he's calling in periodically. So far, all is normal. Last night, the lights were on, but that doesn't mean she was home."

"Why don't you go get her?" I asked and suddenly had a nervous feeling in the pit of my stomach.

"I drove by and she wasn't there. Kate, I hear the impatient tone in your voice. Sarah, until proven one way or the other, is a very prominent figure in this community. I can't go around harassing her."

"Steve, you're not harassing her. You're questioning her. And as for prominent figures, doesn't Maggie count as one of those? I mean the poor woman has been scared to death on more than one occasion. Bedford's dead and now we're talking about Miranda *and* Jonathon having been killed." I stole a glance at Allison, who, with Maggie, was listening intently to my side of the conversation.

"Kate, I know what you're saying. Please let me do my job and I'll call you when I've contacted Sarah."

He was so calm and he sounded so like the hospital psychiatrist, I wanted to strangle him, too. "Okay, I'm sorry. I'm a little impatient. We'll wait for your call." I hung up the phone, calmly.

Allison sat on the couch with Maggie. "I take it he didn't talk to Aunt Sarah," Maggie said.

"No, he'll talk to her today. He *did* talk to your uncle. He'll be back tomorrow." I looked at Allison and wondered what she was telling Sarah, if anything. "You haven't seen Sarah, have you?" I admit I had an accusatory tone.

She glared slightly. "No, Kate. I have not seen her at all."

"My advice is for you to go home and, if she calls, tell Steve. He's looking for her to answer a few questions." I was hesitant because I still didn't trust her not to alert Sarah.

"Well, I can't go home. I have a business to run and it's my busy time of year," she said in a challenging tone. I could tell she still considered me a threat to Maggie. "So, on that note," she said and stood, "I'll get back to the shop."

Maggie put her hand on Allison's arm. "Al, this is serious. We don't know what's going to happen. Please, just listen to Kate, promise me."

Allison walked over to her and affectionately cupped her face in her hands. "I like you worrying about me, Mags." She caressed her cheek and then kissed her on the lips.

It didn't appear to me as if Dr. Winfield minded in the least.

CHAPTER TWENTY-FOUR

Maggie had gone up to her room. The rest of us sat by the fire. I stared at the flames. "This waiting is killing me. I feel helpless," I said and ran my fingers through my hair, letting out a groan.

"It's okay. You've come up with quite a bit. We just have to figure out why someone wants Maggie out of the way." Teri smiled hopefully.

"Is that all?" I asked. "Well, I don't think I could've gotten *this* far without you," I said, meaning every word.

"We'll bill you later," Mac said with a wink. "Better yet, we get to use your cabin for a month."

"Mac, I couldn't love you more if you were my own brother." Then I stopped dead in my tracks. *My own brother.* "I'll be a sonofabitch!"

They both gave me a worried look. "Okay, stay with me. All this time we've been hearing how Nathan's picture was in Miranda's locket. No one wanted to come out and say Nathan and Miranda were having an affair. If they couldn't say that, then they'd never be able to face the obvious conclusion."

I retrieved the photo album and handed it to Mac. "Mac, pick out who you think is Maggie's father." Teri stared at me.

"Okay." He started to leaf through the photos of aunts, uncles, relatives and friends. There were a lot of men from which to choose. He looked for five minutes and shook his head. "I couldn't even guess. Maggie doesn't look like any of them. Well, maybe this guy." He turned the album around. There was an old black and white photo of a skinny young man, perhaps in his twenties.

"We must not have seen that one. I wonder who it is." I gently took the photo out of its place and turned it over. I was shocked. I thought I might be right, but never believed it. I handed it to Teri who looked like someone socked her in the gut. She handed it to Mac.

He stared at the writing on the back and said slowly, "Nathan's 21st birthday, July 1961."

We all sat and stared at the photo. In the distance, I heard the phone ring. My stomach flipped. I hoped it was Steve.

"Kate, do you know what this means?" Teri whispered.

I merely nodded. I put the photo back and closed the album. "I'll be a sonofabitch."

Hannah came back into the room and sat down. "Where the heck did you disappear to?" I asked. "I heard the phone. Was it Steve?"

"No, dear. It was Allison. She—"

Maggie walked in just then, looking a little worn. "Look, I'm going to go out for a while. Don't worry I'll be back in an hour or so."

Hannah said nothing as I looked at her, then Maggie. "Whoa. We need to talk. I don't think it's a good idea for you to go off alone right now. Where are you going?"

"Can't I even go out by myself? Do I need your permission? Christ, I don't need a chaperone. I'm just going out for an hour and I'll be right back for Christ's sake," she said with a caustic bite.

I stared at her with my mouth open. "Hey, hey, don't get snotty with me. I just asked. Have you forgotten what's happening around here?" I started sarcastically then stopped. "Look, you do whatever you want. You're going to anyway," I said and threw up my hands in resignation.

"You—" she growled. "I will be back in an hour," she said angrily and stormed out.

We heard the front door slam and the car engine rev. The tires screamed as she pulled away.

I stood staring at the front door. "Want to tell me what in the hell just happened?" I asked.

Mac and Teri sat dumfounded.

Hannah played with her ring. She said, not looking at me, "She went to Allison." She coughed nervously, and said, "I, uh, listened on the extension."

Teri put her hand to her mouth. Mac smothered a grin. I gave her a shocked look.

"You what? Hannah! Shame on you," I said in a stern voice.

We all sat there for a moment.

Finally, I looked at her. "Well, where did she go?" I asked casually.

"Allison's antique shop," she said.

"She could have told us that. I don't care where she goes; it's none of my business. I just didn't want her going off by herself, that's all. She said she'd be back in an hour," I said and looked at my watch, "Okay, it's three-thirty."

I got up, poured myself another cup of coffee and sat down. "I mean it's none of my business where she goes. I don't care."

"You already said that," Mac said.

"I know what I said," I said quickly. "Do I look like I don't know what I'm saying?"

"No, no, not at all," Teri said.

"Well, then, let's forget it shall we? What the hell was I saying anyway?" I asked.

"Nathan and Miranda," Mac said.

"Okay, right."

I looked at Hannah and told her what I was thinking and what happened with the photo of Nathan. She listened, amazed, and looked at all three of us.

"Let me see that picture," Hannah said urgently.

Mac handed it to her.

She stared at it with tears in her eyes. "This was right before he and Walt went to med school. I remember taking this picture." She looked up at me. "Kate, can this be possible?"

"Hannah, it makes perfect sense. If what Doc said was true, and Jonathon had a wandering eye like your father, then he was not home very much. And when he was, he was not very attentive to Miranda. It's very possible Maggie is Nathan's daughter. Don't you see the possibility?"

Hannah nodded slowly. "Yes, I do, and honestly, I've thought of the possibility many times. It's just something you don't discuss. Miranda never confided in me about anything like that. Neither would Nathan. So I suppose it is possible."

"But if it were true, why would Nathan want to kill Miranda?" Mac asked.

"As we said, perhaps he wanted her and she refused him, or he wanted to continue the affair, and she refused him," I said. "Or maybe Jonathon found out and couldn't bear it."

"I can't imagine Nathan involved in this. I just can't," Hannah whispered.

"Maybe he's protecting Sarah. She's very unstable, Hannah, you know that. Unfortunately, we have a woman intruder but a button belonging to Nathan's jacket in Bedford's apartment," Teri said. "This is confusing."

"Just because the button was from Nathan's coat does not mean he was wearing it. Remember, I initially thought the intruder was a man. It turned out to be Sarah, I'm sure of that. So, if we all agree Nathan wouldn't do anything to Maggie and doesn't have the stomach for murder, then the alternative is Sarah. Sarah who threatened Bedford, and fought with Jonathon and used Allison. And let's not forget her romp in the woods." I was sure of what I was saying. "My only other issue is the fight Bedford overheard with Jonathon about the clinic. And we have to face the facts: If we're looking at everything honestly, the clinic is Sarah's life. I'd love to know what happened there because the next entry in Bedford's little notebook is Sarah taking Maggie's car the same day Jonathon was killed in a hit-and-run. Coincidence? No such thing." I got up and stoked the fire absently. Then I walked over to the doors and looked out at the woods. "Miranda, if ever Maggie needed you, she needs you now."

Hannah looked right at me. "Well, are you going to go bring her back?" she asked.

I looked at all of them and sighed. "Look, she's a grown woman, with a definite mind of her own. She's got ten minutes."

I picked up a magazine and started leafing through it. "The hell with ten minutes," I said, angrily. "Okay, I'm going. I don't like this at all. Boy, she'd better be in trouble, that's all I have to say. If I'm not back or haven't called in half an hour, call Steve," I said.

They gave me a worried look. "Kate, don't go off," Mac started.

"Mac, do you think Maggie would do this and not at least call?"

"Take Mac with you," Hannah pleaded.

I shook my head. "I'm probably over reacting, so I'll feel like a big idiot. However, I'd rather feel like an idiot all alone, thank you," I said seriously. I looked at Mac and Teri. "Half an hour."

"Be careful," Teri called after me as I left.

"Geez, don't say that," I said, helplessly, and closed the door.

Kate Sweeney

CHAPTER TWENTY-FIVE

I parked a few stores down from Allison's and turned off the engine. I sat there for a moment and watched as someone turned the sign in the door to "Closed" and shut off the lights. I felt a little foolish. *Shit Ryan, the woman is in love, and scared to death. Wouldn't you want to be with the woman you loved? If you had any idea what that is like, that is.* I was about ready to tell myself to shut up and start the car when I thought I saw a flashlight scanning the inside of the store.

I got out and walked across the dark street. With all the other shops closed, no one was around. I walked down the alley behind the shop and tried the back door. Surprisingly, it was unlocked. As I walked in, I smelled a pungent odor.

My blood ran cold as I realized it was gasoline. I cautiously shut the door and walked around the shop. Careful not to knock anything over, I strained my eyes against the darkness to see anything, or anyone.

Then I heard a muffled noise. I slowly turned and, in the far corner, I noticed a railing and staircase that led, more than likely, to Allison's storage area downstairs. I looked around for something to use to protect myself, like a cane or baseball bat, and found nothing—nothing I could lift anyway. *What was this junk?*

I looked over the railing and could see a faint light. The odor of gasoline was everywhere. I got panicky and slowly descended the stairs.

To my horror, I saw Maggie and Allison sitting in chairs, bound and gagged. I ran over to Maggie, she had a horrified look on her face as she frantically shook her head.

I knelt and took her gag off.

"Kate behind you!" she screamed.

I turned and jumped at the same time.

Something hit me and I went flying into a bunch of boxes that came showering down on me. I was stunned but still able to kick the boxes away. As I struggled to get to my feet, preparing for another attack, I saw Sarah, wild eyed and smiling wickedly.

I made a move toward her then abruptly stopped when I saw she had a small handgun pointed at my midsection. It was a definite equalizer. I straightened and stood perfectly still.

"Good girl, Miss Ryan, though you're not as stupid as I hoped. Now, step over there, into the light." She motioned with the gun.

I slowly made my way toward the desk and stood by the desk lamp.

Maggie and Allison sat right in the line of fire. As Sarah moved forward, I noticed a kerosene lamp on another desk. She saw me looking at it.

"Be careful, scarecrow," she said, pointing to the gasoline can. "You are tenacious. I'll give you that. I thought you'd give up," she said sweetly.

"When, Sarah? When you broke into the house the other night and left that sick note on Maggie's pillow?"

She gave me an approving look. "Very good! You figured it out. What gave me away? I thought the disguise went well. I love disguises. I do so *love* Halloween," she said maniacally.

My mouth was completely dry as I tried to swallow. This woman was nuts. "Your perfume," I said. "I thought you were wearing it at Hannah's party as well. You were, weren't you?"

"Yes, yes, I was. You're very good. That was stupid of me." She laughed then stopped abruptly. "You know I have to kill you now."

"Please, Aunt Sarah, you don't want to do this," Maggie pleaded.

Sarah raised her eyebrows. "Oh, but I do, dear. You have *no* idea how much," she said and pointed the gun at her.

I took a step and Sarah turned the gun on me and said playfully, "Ah, ah, ah. No sudden movements or I'll blow your meddling head right off."

She turned back to Maggie. "Do you have any idea how much trouble you've caused? Between you, your whore of a mother and the whole Winfield family, it's been quite an exasperating twenty years, I must tell you," she said, shaking her head.

She walked over to Allison and took the gag off. "Well, what do you have to say for yourself?" she asked flatly. "You are a grave disappointment to me, Allison. I had such hopes for you," she said, almost sadly as she stared off into the distance.

"Sarah, please don't do this," Allison pleaded.

"Shut up, you useless cow," Sarah said then sighed with mock exasperation.

We all were silent for a moment; I could hear my heart beating in my ears. I cautiously looked around for something—anything.

Then the crazed woman blinked. "Where was I? Oh, yes, Maggie dear," and she stared off again, but this time she had the gun pointed at Maggie.

"Sarah, why did you kill Miranda?" I asked quickly.

I noticed Maggie and Allison were completely shocked. It was all clear to me now. All the pieces fit. A little late, but...

Sarah whirled around to me and stiffened. Her face looked pained and white.

"So, you figured that out, too. My, my, you have been a busy bee."

She gave Maggie a disgusted look. "Did you know your whore of a mother was sleeping with your Uncle Nathan—*my* husband?" she asked. "And—"

Maggie interrupted her. "Yes, I did."

Sarah screamed at her. "Don't interrupt me again!"

Spittle flew from her mouth, making her look like a rabid animal. I instinctively took a step then stopped.

"Good thinking," Sarah said viciously without looking at me.

Clearly, this woman hated interruptions.

She took a deep breath and put a hand to her hair to straighten it. "Did you also know that your uncle is also your father?" she asked, laughing helplessly. "Oh, the trouble you've caused."

I looked at Maggie. She was ashen. Sarah looked from Maggie to Alison.

"I'll take your vapid looks as a no," she said, obviously very satisfied with herself. She looked at me. "How about you? I bet you knew."

I watched Maggie who looked sad and confused. She undoubtedly was thinking about her life.

I gave Sarah a hateful look. "I had an idea," I said, with disgust. "It seemed a plausible conclusion from Nathan's affair with Miranda and from the pictures in her locket. I'm sure a paternity test would eliminate any doubt. However, I have a bigger question: Why did you fight Jonathon over something as stupid as the clinic?"

It was then I realized my mistake. Never say stupid to an insane woman with a gun. Especially when it's pointed at you.

"Stupid? That clinic was my life, Miss Ryan. It was mine, all mine. The only thing in my life that was my own. Except for Charlie. Alexander fucked me and then took it and gave it to Jon, who was going to fuck me and sell it to a big medical group in Chicago. And you know I *simply* couldn't let that happen."

"So, you took Maggie's car and went to Chicago," I asked. It was all becoming clear to me.

"How did you...?" She stopped and took a deep, angry breath. "Bedford. I *hate* that guy. He was the rat in the Winfield woodpile. Allison tells me you found a notebook."

Maggie shot a look at Allison, who hung her head. What a dupe. "Don't blame Allison," Sarah said. "She can't keep her trap shut. What Charlie saw in you, I will never know."

Sarah leaned against the desk. I stole glance at Maggie and Allison: Both looked petrified.

"We found a man's coat button in Bedford's apartment. That was you?" I asked.

"Yep. I was looking for the same thing you were, earlier that morning. I thought if I dropped Nathan's coat button, someone would find it. Allison told me you thought the intruder was a female, so I needed to throw you off the track. Clever?" she asked, giggling.

It was then I noticed her hand was shaking. I figured it was not a good time to aggravate her any more. "Yes, it was very clever."

"Thank you," she said and curtsied politely.

She was just plain nuts and I was running out of time.

"Okay, enough talking," she said tiredly. "You bore me."

She picked up a gasoline can from behind her. She began to pour it all over the floor and on the boxes.

"Now, Miss Ryan, come over here please. Come, come, don't be shy," she motioned with the gun.

I glanced at Maggie; she had tears in her eyes.

"Katie, no," she pleaded, quietly.

"Very touching," Sarah said impatiently.

"Why Sarah?" I asked again, looking for time. "Was it so horrible that Maggie would have control of the clinic now that Jonathan was dead?"

She glared at me and I thought for sure she was going to shoot me right then and there.

"Yes, it was!" she spat out angrily. "Do you have any idea what I've done for that clinic? I gave my life, and deserved to have it, but no, that old fop Winfield had to give it Jon, who had to give it to Maggie, who will now, *give-it-back-to-me*," she said emphatically, then sighed. "They all talked about me behind my back, you know," she said with psychotic frankness. "They did. They thought I couldn't hear them, but I heard them. I heard them all the time, plotting to get Miranda-the-Lovely in. Miranda-the-Lovely, Miranda-the-Whore. I even heard them in my sleep. But I got them in the end," she said, glaring at me.

I was petrified and my heart beat like a drum. *Okay, Steve, anytime.*

Sarah continued, wiping the saliva from her mouth. "Well, I hated her," she said. "I hated her so much I wanted her dead! Do you understand me, dead! But I got the old fool and Jonathan to get me on the Board. I deserved it. Then Nathan had to whore around and get Miranda pregnant. They were ruining everything, all my plans. Everything was fine until a few months ago," she said vehemently. "Jon was a greedy man, just like his father."

She was now pacing like a caged lion. She then stopped and looked at me.

"I wanted it all. I wouldn't let them destroy what I planned." She gave me a quizzical look. "Did you know I seduced Maggie's grandfather? He thought he could discard me, so did Jonathan. Well, I proved all of them wrong.

"Maggie is the only stumbling block, and soon she'll be out of the way. She'd already be dead if you hadn't come along last Thursday, you and your stinking dog. That put a crimp in the weekend festivities," she said and looked at Maggie. "You were supposed to die on Halloween, like your mother. But no! Nature girl had to show up. But no matter."

"Why did you kill my mother?" Maggie asked.

"Why did you kill my mother?" Sarah repeated in a whiny voice. "God, you are such a little sap," she said, appearing completely

exasperated. "You *are* like your father." She looked at me. "Go ahead, you tell her," she said and rolled her eyes in a psychotically comical fashion, waving her gun in the air. "No, let me, we're running out of time. Quite simply, Nathan was going to leave me, and that could not happen. And she came so willingly," she said almost reverently.

"Why did she come so willingly?" I asked. The question bugged me this entire week.

Sarah looked down, raised her eyebrows and smiled like a child. "Well, I told you I liked Halloween. I left her a note on her pillow, too, as if it were from Nathan, saying that he loved her and needed desperately to talk to her. I put on Nathan's clothes and the stupid idiot thought I was Nathan and came to me with open arms," she said, chuckling in disbelief. I was terrified.

"So you buried the jewelry?" I asked. She was nuts enough to answer all my questions. I was biding time until the cavalry got here.

She laughed. "Yep. Tried to get your little cur, but, boy, that dog is fast." She shook her head in amazement.

"She knows crazy when she sees it. Up your meds, Aunt Sarah," Maggie said sarcastically. Sarah glared at her and took a step.

Dammit Maggie.

"Now, Maggie," I said evenly and Sarah stopped and cocked her head in my direction. "This took a lot of planning," I said with admiration, I hope.

Sarah curtsied again. "Thank you, again. I still have to kill you, but at least you appreciate me."

She walked over to Maggie and slapped her across the face, it sounded like a whip cracking. Maggie's head snapped to one side and I flinched, but stood still. "That's for not appreciating me," she said sweetly and turned away.

"Continue, Miss Ryan. I love to hear my exploits," she leaned against the desk, but kept the gun pointed directly at me.

I swallowed and continued. "You took the evidence didn't you? Got us out of the house by duping Allison. She took Maggie for a walk and I'll bet you even suggested the lake. When we all went to look for her, you grabbed the bags—but why hide them in the cellar?" I asked another nagging question.

She looked at Maggie. "Out of all the Winfields, I truly like Hannah, but she was a fly in my ointment that night. She followed me everywhere. Chattering away, blah, blah-blah, blah-blah. I swear if I had a gun, as I do now, I'd have shot her. So, when I had a moment to myself I tried to leave but there she was again, and got me in the kitchen. When she asked me to go get a bottle of wine, that's when I had the idea. Clever, Miss Ryan?"

"Yes, very clever. You hid it on top of the wine rack then unlocked the cellar door. That's why you offered to check the cellar, to make sure no one else would go down there. It was you who came back that night, am I right?"

She glared at me. "Yes, and you screwed that up for me as well. You are beginning to annoy me as much as Maggie." She lifted the gun.

"Sarah, why kill Bedford?" Allison asked quickly.

Sarah glared at her, and then looked at me. "Continue, continue. It's all right so far. Not that it matters, you're all dead," her voice was void of any emotion.

"Because he knew and threatened to expose you. I bet that's what he was telling you after he fixed your horse that morning by the stable. Did you argue that night? So, you took a shovel, bashed in his skull and dragged him over to Thunder's stall. It was supposed look like another accident," I said.

"And why didn't it look like an accident?" she asked and waited for an answer.

"Because—" I started to explain.

Sarah interrupted me and screamed in my direction. "Because you are a meddling *bitch!*"

I flinched and took a step back. Who was I to argue? I'd been called worse, but never from someone this insane.

She closed her eyes, took a deep breath and said calmly, "Okay. Now, Miss Ryan, as I said before, come over here." I didn't move. "Fine. I'll just shoot your beloved Maggie and be done with it." She pointed the gun at Maggie.

"Okay, Sarah, okay," I said quickly and started to move in her direction.

I purposely walked around both Maggie and Allison and walked away from them, to get them out of the line of fire, if there was going to be any. I noticed there was a sheet or tablecloth of some sort covering one of the boxes next to Sarah. If I could only fling it at her, maybe...

As I made my way over to her, we heard a noise. Someone was knocking and banging at the door upstairs. Sarah flinched for a second, which gave me just enough time.

I lunged for her and she fired in my direction, then quickly took the lantern and threw it past me. It crashed into the boxes, which immediately burst into flames. I tackled her and grabbed for the gun. We struggled and I was amazed at her strength. She was grunting and whining, trying to get the upper hand, as she did when we tangled before. Mercifully, the gun flew out of her hands.

By now, there was smoke everywhere, and the flames were engulfing everything in sight. I reared back and punched her dead in the face. She screamed and folded onto the floor.

I could barely see anything as I ran to Maggie and Allison. I fumbled with Maggie's ropes and finally got her free. She threw her arms around my neck and I hugged her for dear life, then pulled away.

In the distance, I could hear someone coming down the stairs. From behind me, I heard a growl and then a scream. I threw Maggie out of the way and I heard a gun go off.

I turned and stared at Sarah, who was standing in front of me with a bewildered look on her face.

Then, all at once, blood oozed out of her mouth and she dropped face down on the floor. I watched for a stunned second, then ran over to Maggie, who was not moving. With all the confusion, I thought Maggie was shot by Sarah.

Steve was at Allison's chair untying her, before he quickly guided her through the smoke and up the stairs.

I picked up Maggie and carried her to the stairs. Coughing uncontrollably, I couldn't see a thing. I blindly climbed the stairs behind Steve, who had picked up Allison and now carried her.

Once outside, Mac met me and grabbed Maggie as I fell to my knees. Teri had her arm around my shoulders as I coughed.

"Are you all right?" Teri asked urgently.

I nodded but couldn't say anything. I looked over at Maggie. She started coughing. Breathing a sigh of relief, I knelt next to her.

"Maggie," I exclaimed as I put my hand under her head, lifted her and held her close. She opened her eyes, and coughed again.

"Why did you push me?" she demanded in a raspy voice. *Why the little...*

"Push you? You little idiot, I saved your ungrateful hide," I said staring down at her.

My arms were around her and I never thought I'd be this content to argue with her once again.

Kate Sweeney

CHAPTER TWENTY-SIX

Hey, Maggie, you okay?" Steve called out. He looked awful, coughing and wheezing as he ran up to us.

"Yes, thanks," she said coughing as we stood.

I looked around to see the Fire Department soaking Allison's building. They moved us back to a safer distance as we stood watching the flames.

Then Allison ran over to Maggie and hugged her. "Maggie, are you all right, sweetie? Please tell me you're fine."

"I'm fine, how about you?" Maggie asked as her hands roamed over Alison's body looking for signs of injury.

I looked at them then walked away. Looking back at the burning building, I saw a fireman come out with Sarah's lifeless body. Mac and Teri were talking to Steve as I turned away once more. I heard Teri calling me and saw another ambulance with its lights flashing. A paramedic came over to me and guided me toward the ambulance.

"What the hell are you doing?" I asked pulling myself free.

"Ma'am, you're bleeding," he said and put his gloved hand on my ribs.

I looked down at the blood on my side.

Mac and Teri came running over. "What in the hell?" Teri said looking at me.

"I don't know. I feel fine," I said.

As I sat down on the back of the ambulance, the paramedic looked under my shirt.

"Well, it looks like you got nicked," he said.

"I don't feel like I've been nicked," I said. "Nicked by what?"

He gave me a worried look. "Well, I'm no expert, but I'd say by a bullet."

Mac was shocked. "Kate, get in the ambulance!"

I got in and then I felt something. Funny how you don't feel sick until someone tells you—you look sick.

Teri got in and looked at Mac, "Go tell Steve and Maggie." He kissed her and was gone.

"You two are so corny."

"Shut up," my wonderful sister said as the door of the ambulance closed and we took off.

I smiled ruefully at Teri. She smiled and patted my hand. "When we get back you have to tell me what the hell happened," she said.

"You'll never believe it."

The paramedic had opened my shirt and put a huge gauze pad on my side. "I've never been shot before." *I'm sure he cares.*

"First time for everything," he smiled and patted my shoulder.

The clinic—my favorite place next to the kitchen table.

Once again, the small emergency room greeted me. Doc was standing there smiling sadly. "Okay, I think I've seen about enough of you," he said and put his hand on my forehead. "Had a full day?"

I explained the ordeal as he worked on me. Several times, he stopped and stared at me in amazement. When he was done, he sat back.

"Well, either you live right, or you're the luckiest SOB I've ever met," he said, shaking his head. "It was definitely—" he started as Maggie burst into the room.

She stood there breathing heavily for a moment, then rushed over to the bedside. "You can't be left alone for a minute," she said, and grabbed my hand.

"I've been nicked," I said stupidly, enjoying the concerned look in her blue eyes.

Maggie looked at Doc, who nodded and said, "Well, she's right. I was about to say, it was definitely a bullet. It grazed your side, doesn't even need a stitch. Just keep it clean."

He smiled sadly. "I'll stop by and we can get this sorted out." He kissed Maggie and patted my shoulder. "And you, I think you're accident prone," he said and left the room.

"How do you feel?" she asked softly and put her hand on my brow.

"I'm fine. Let's get out of here." I stood and buttoned my shirt.

She tried to help but I waved her off as my wall formed brick by brick. She gave me a bewildered look and stepped back as I walked out ahead of her looking for that safe, detached loop I had misplaced a few days ago.

Amazingly, we all sat in the living room. I retold the story from beginning to frightening end as they all sat in stunned silence.

"Sarah wanted to see the new antiques I got in. We went back to my shop and that's when she started," Allison said and put her hand to her forehead. Maggie put her hand on her shoulder. "She told me that I was useless. She ranted and raved. I was petrified and didn't know what to do. Then she pulled the gun and told me to call Maggie; if I didn't, she'd kill Maggie and me. I didn't know what to do." She looked sick and I felt bad for her.

"I don't blame you, Allison; she scared the life out of me as well," I said.

"Then Sarah slapped me across the face and I blacked out. When I came to, I was in a chair and so was Maggie," Allison said and looked right at me. "Maggie said you would come, and you did. Thank you," she said, looking at her hands.

"Well, it's over. Have you gotten in touch with Nathan or Charlie?" I asked Hannah and Maggie.

"Nathan is on his away back as we speak," Hannah said. "This is going to devastate him. I can't believe Sarah did all this." She sighed. "And Charlie, I have no idea how he's going to react. He's in New York. I've already called him. I'm sure he'll be calling soon."

Maggie shook her head. "I can't believe it. Uncle Nathan is my real father. Do you think he knows?"

"My guess is he *might* have suspected, but I don't think so," I said.

Steve tiredly rubbed his face. "I can't believe this. I can't believe in five days you broke open and solved a twenty-year-old murder. I'm impressed."

"Well, I wish there wasn't such heartache attached." I took a deep breath and winced.

Teri frowned. "I can't believe how many times you've been tossed around this weekend."

"I know. I can't either. Good thing this isn't my full-time job anymore."

"What difference does that make?" Mac said. "Remember when you fell off that ledge, taking that picture?"

"Okay, okay. I get it," I said chuckling.

We all laughed for a moment then the laughter faded.

"I can't believe how close we came to being killed," Allison said and shivered as she grabbed Maggie's hand. I tried not to notice that.

"Kate, you saved a family. I feel like a tremendous weight has been taken off my shoulders," Hannah said as she took my hand and cried softly.

"I'm glad for both of you, Hannah."

Tears now filled my eyes and I blinked them back. I was exhausted.

"So you called Steve?" I asked both Teri and Mac.

"Exactly a half-hour after you left. We met him at the shop. We tried the front door, then Steve and I smelled the gasoline. We ran around back and the door was open."

Steve nodded. "I went down the stairs and saw someone. I thought it was Sarah, coming after you holding something over her head. I didn't know what it was but I fired," he said, staring at the table.

I reached over and touched his arm. "Steve, she was crazy, and I do mean crazy. Thank you."

"I know. I just never shot anyone before," he said sadly.

"Wyatt, thank goodness your aim is good," I said, very relieved.

Steve, who had already gotten full statements from all of us, left.

I looked at my watch: nine o'clock. I was tired and my side ached. Maggie and Allison had left the living room. Not that it mattered to me at all.

"Well, I think I might go to bed," I said tiredly.

"Where in the world is Margaret?" Hannah asked, looking around.

"She's where she should be, Hannah," I said getting up and feeling very old.

"I can't believe you did this. I can't believe you got shot," Teri said sniffling. "Dad would be so proud of you."

Mac put his arm around her and agreed. "Maybe you should try it again? Private investigating worked once."

I cringed, feeling the back of my neck. "Forget it. I can't wait to get back to the mundane, everyday life of photography. We leave tomorrow." I sighed heavily and ran my fingers through my hair.

"Go to bed. Tomorrow is another day," Teri said philosophically. Mac and I stared at her.

"Oh, I wish I'd have said that," Mac said, disappointed. Teri slapped his shoulder playfully.

"Good night, children," I said and waved them off.

Sprawled out on the bed was my dog. I looked down at her. "Boy, you missed everything, you lazy mutt."

I went into the bathroom and looked at myself in the mirror. "Well, Kate, you did it. Almost got killed, but you did it."

A few minutes later, lying there in my bed, staring at the ceiling, I felt relieved. I also felt a bittersweet happiness. Sarah was the cause of all of this, true, but she was still someone's wife, someone else's mother, and now she was dead.

So many lives involved, so many people hurt. I put my hands over my face and started to cry; Christ I was emotionally drained. I lay there alone, crying like a fool.

Chance, apparently feeling my sorrow, jumped up on the bed and laid next to me, putting her head on my chest. I looked down at her.

"Well, Chance," I sniffed, "it's just you and me, mutt."

I took a deep breath and realized I had a tremendous headache to match everything else. Well, Maggie was finally over this mess. She could now finish her internship and continue her life. I was glad for that. She loved Allison I could see that. I only hoped it would be good for her.

I thought about Miranda, and smiled. Now, perhaps she could rest. Perhaps now all of them could be at peace.

It was my last thought, as I faded off to sleep.

I was half-asleep when I thought I heard my door open. Then I felt a hand on my forehead and I leapt up.

"Sorry," Maggie whispered, sitting on the edge of my bed.

"Geez, you scared the hell out of me," I whispered then got panicky. "What's wrong?"

"Nothing. Everything is fine, now. Go back to sleep. I was just checking in," she said softly.

I closed my eyes and sighed openly as I felt her warm hand on my brow.

"What time is it?"

"It's very early, four-thirty," she whispered as her fingers lightly caressed my forehead.

I blinked, trying to open my eyes. "In the morning? Why are you dressed?" Then I realized she had been with Allison. "Oh, never mind," I said and closed my eyes.

"Go back to sleep. I'll tell you all about it in the morning," she whispered and left the room.

I woke up tired and achy. Mac and Teri were in the kitchen with Hannah, who was, of course, cooking. I smelled bacon and coffee and was ravenous. Hannah greeted me when I walked into the kitchen.

"Well sleepy head. How do you feel?" She kissed my cheek.

"Fine, thanks." I looked at the clock, nine-thirty. Christ, I slept for almost eleven hours.

"You still looked pooped," Mac said affectionately and Teri concurred.

I sat down and Hannah put a cup of coffee in front of me and patted my shoulder.

"Thanks, Hannah," I said quietly. *I'm going to miss her.*

Maggie came into the kitchen. She looked rested but still had tiny circles under her eyes.

"Good morning," she said smiling and kissed Hannah on the cheek. She poured herself a cup of coffee and asked if anyone needed a refill, then sat down next to Mac. He nudged her playfully.

"How're ya feeling?"

"Actually, I feel pretty good." She looked at me. "How do you feel this morning?"

"Fine, I slept like a rock."

"You still look exhausted," she said, frowning.

"Well, I guess I need a north woods fix. A month of solitude at my cabin should do me just fine," I said a little coolly. Maggie stopped drinking her coffee and looked at me.

"Oh, please, you spend too much time up there alone as it is," Teri said.

"It's where I belong," I said, drinking my coffee.

"Well, Maggie, have you talked to your uncle?" Mac asked, and realized what he said.

Maggie patted his arm. "It's okay. This will take some getting used to. I'm not sure I can call him Father yet, but yes, I talked to him. Charlie flew in as soon as he got Aunt Hannah's call. He and I talked about with Doc and Aunt Hannah. Poor Uncle Nathan was as devastated as Charlie. God, he's my brother. Now *that* will take some getting used to," she said sarcastically and laughed. "It was sad to see them so brokenhearted, but is does make sense now— how I've always felt closer to Uncle Nathan than to my father."

I got up to get the coffeepot, Maggie offered to get it and I waved off her help.

"I can get it," I said. She gave me a troubled look and didn't argue. I came back to the table and poured myself a cup.

Maggie continued. "Uncle Nathan was shocked as I was. He suspected I was his daughter, but when Mother never admitted it, he never questioned her again, out of respect for her. He loved her. He knew Aunt Sarah was sick, but never expected anything like this. We stayed up till four talking about it all."

As I poured Mac a cup of coffee, I looked at her. "Is that where you were all night?" I asked.

I missed Mac's cup entirely and poured the coffee all over the table.

"Jesus, Katie!" Mac yelped and jumped up, wiping his pants.

"Christ, Mac. I'm so sorry," I said, putting the pot down and handing him a napkin. He left the kitchen, mumbling to himself.

"Yes. Where did you think I was?" she asked, apparently confused.

I turned a little red. "I thought perhaps you were with..." I couldn't finish my statement.

She gave me a shocked look. "You thought I was with Allison?"

Hannah and Teri bumped into each other trying to hurry out of the kitchen. I watched their bumbling retreat.

"Well, it's not that far fetched," I said in an irritated tone and not knowing why.

"Kate," she started. "I can't believe how much you've done. I will never be able to repay you."

Repay me, so that's what she feels.

"Look, you owe me nothing. I will not have you feeling obligated to me," I said as I tripped over my pride.

"Obligated? What in the...?" she started and stopped. "Christ you're infuriating."

"Me?" I said and leaned forward. "Me?" I repeated.

"Yes, you!" She stormed out of the kitchen.

I'd had it. I struggled trying to get out the chair while holding my side. *Christ what an ordeal.*

I followed her into the living room. Mac, Teri and Hannah were sitting by the fire. They all turned to us when we made our noisy entrance. I grabbed Maggie's arm and turned her around.

"Talk about infuriating. You go running off again with that woman, right in the midst of all this, and you call me infuriating? You're lucky Hannah was listening on the extension, or you'd be dead right now. You stubborn, little..." I raised my voice. "If I had half a brain, I would have yanked you right out of that car!"

"Why didn't you?" she asked. "And keep your voice down!" she said just as loud.

"Why shouldn't everyone hear me? Arguing is what you and I seem to do best," I said angrily then stopped. "Why didn't I what?" I asked stupidly.

She took a deep breath. "Why didn't you stop me?" she asked and looked right at me. Then she turned and went out onto the deck.

I stood there gaping at her.

Hannah got up, walked past me, came back with our jackets and helped me into mine before handing me the other.

"Good heavens, get this straightened out," she ordered affectionately as she pushed me toward the door.

EPILOGUE

I took a deep breath and walked onto the deck. It was a cold, dark November day and the sun was trying its best to peek through the clouds. Maggie was standing with her arms folded across her chest, shivering.

"You'd stand out here and freeze, wouldn't you?" I declared as I held her jacket for her.

"Well, so would you." She slid into it and avoided looking at me. Then she turned and faced me, I took an instinctive step back. "I was with Allison last night, but only to take her home and explain how I felt," she started. I opened my mouth to say something, but she said, "Will you please keep quiet and let me finish?"

I closed my mouth and leaned against the railing.

"She didn't need much of an explanation. She knew there wasn't much left between us. She is however, someone I will always care about," she finished and looked out at the woods. "For the first time since my mother died, I really feel happy and content. I know she was here this weekend and I know she helped. I feel so at peace now and I know she is, too. I have you to thank for that, Kate. You came into my life and I don't think I'll ever be the same," she said with tears in her eyes.

I pulled out a hanky and handed it to her.

She laughed quietly and took it from me. "You and your hankies."

I held her hand and studied it for a moment. Such small hands, I thought stupidly.

"Maggie, you've been through so much. I'm glad I was able to help and I think I can speak for Mac and Teri, that they feel the same way." I smiled and held her at arm's length. "This is a great time for you, Maggie. You can concentrate on finishing your internship, become a good doctor and be happy. That will be a wonderful testament to your mother." I took the hanky out of her hand and gently wiped her cheeks. "So enough tears. Honestly, I've never seen a woman cry as much as you."

She took my hand away and held it. "Thank you, Kate Ryan. I don't know what I would have done without you. Once I finish my internship, I have a feeling you'll be a steady patient of mine," she said and I couldn't help but notice her blue eyes dancing wickedly.

"Possibly, but you won't charge me," I said and felt myself grinning wildly. *How long has that been?*

"We'll just have to see. I think there should be some type of payment plan," she countered with a wicked grin.

Then something caught my eye behind her in the garden next to the deck. I strained to see what it was.

Maggie followed my curious look and turned around to the garden. I stood behind her, with my hands on her shoulders. She reached back and put her hand on mine.

"Oh, Mom," she sighed and took a deep quivering breath.

We looked in quiet amazement at the end of the deck at the small garden—the garden that she and Miranda planted so many years ago.

Amid the scattered, lifeless autumn leaves, there was a sign of life, of hope.

A small purple hyacinth stood blooming alone. Although it was a cold dreary November day, a warm summer-like breeze softly blew and the hyacinth danced and joyfully gave up its heavenly fragrance.

I felt Maggie lean into me as she let out a contented, quivering sigh. I couldn't help but think about Miranda.

She waits all these years. Waits and protects her daughter as best she can. And now she waits no longer.

As I held tightly onto Maggie's hand, I could almost hear Miranda's lilting laughter fading with the warm, gentle breeze.

-The End -

ABOUT THE AUTHOR

In her debut novel, *She Waits*, Kate Sweeney introduces Kate Ryan, the reluctant heroine of the Kate Ryan Mysteries series. Kate also has a collection of short stories and novellas that run the gamut from funny to sad, erotic to romantic, and anything else in between. She invites you to read them on her website at www.kateryanmysteries.com and drop a line at mks@kateryanmysteries.com. Born in Chicago, Kate currently resides in Villa Park, Illinois.

Other Intaglio Publications Titles

Accidental Love, by B. L. Miller, ISBN:1-933113-11-1, Price:$18.15
What happens when love is based on deception? Can it survive discovering the truth?

Assignment Sunrise, by I Christie, ISBN:978-1-933113-40-1, Price:$16.95
The disappearance of three women in the FBI witness protection program leads FBI Special Agent Adison to a small artsy town in Northern California. Her mission—go undercover, and collect evidence on two suspected gangs.

Code Blue, by KatLyn, ISBN:1-933113-09-X, Price:$16.95
Thrown headlong into one of the most puzzling murder investigations in the Burgh's history, Logan McGregor finds that politics, corruption, money and greed aren't the only barriers she must break through in order to find the truth.

Counterfeit World, by Judith K. Parker, ISBN:1-933113-32-4, Price:$15.25
The U.S. government has been privatized, religion has only recently been decriminalized, the World Government keeps the peace on Earth—when it chooses—and multi-world corporations vie for control of planets, moons, asteroids, and orbits for their space stations.

Crystal's Heart, by B. L. Miller & Verda Foster, ISBN:1-933113-24-3, Price:$18.50 - Two women who have absolutely nothing in common, and yet when they become improbable housemates, are amazed to find they can actually live with each other. And not only live...

Define Destiny, by J. M. Dragon, ISBN:1-933113-56-1, Price:$16.95
Catherine Warriorson is a woman without any hope. All she wanted was to be left alone with her own demons to live her life as a recluse. When Jace Bardley's job brings her to New Zealand, little does she know that the experiences of the world good and bad were literally going to begin right here…

Gloria's Inn, by Robin Alexander, ISBN:1-933113-01-4, Price:$14.95 - Hayden Tate suddenly found herself in a world unlike any other, when she inherited half of an inn nestled away on Cat Island in the Bahamas.

Graceful Waters, by B. L. Miller & Verda Foster, ISBN:1-933113-08-1, Price:$17.25 - Joanna Carey, senior instructor at Sapling Hill wasn't looking for anything more than completing one more year at the facility and getting that much closer to her private dream, a small cabin on a quiet lake. She was tough, smart and she had a plan for her life.

Halls Of Temptation, by Katie P. Moore, ISBN:978-1-933113-42-5, Price:$15.50 – A heartfelt romance that traces the lives of two young women from their teenage years into adulthood, through the struggles of maturity, conflict and love.

I Already Know The Silence Of The Storms, by N. M. Hill, ISBN:1-933113-07-3, Price:$15.25 - I Already Know the Silence of the Storms is a map of a questor's journey as she traverses the tempestuous landscapes of heart, mind, body, and soul. Tossed onto paths of origins and destinations unbeknownst to her, she is enjoined by the ancients to cross chartless regions beset with want and need and desire to find the truth within.

Incommunicado, by N. M. Hill & J. P. Mercer, ISBN:1-933113-10-3, Price:$15.25 - Incommunicado is a world of lies, deceit, and death along the U.S/Mexico border. Set within the panoramic beauty of the unforgiving Sonoran Desert, it is the story of two strong, independent women: Cara Vittore Cipriano, a lawyer who was born to rule the prestigious Cipriano Vineyards; and Jaquelyn "Jake" Biscayne, an FBI forensic pathologist who has made her work her life.

Infinite Pleasures, Stacia Seaman & Nann Dunne (Eds.), ISBN:1-933113-00-6, Price:$18.99 - Hot, edgy, beyond-the-envelope erotica from over thirty of the best lesbian authors writing today. This no-holds barred, tell it like you wish it could be collection is guaranteed to rocket your senses into overload and ratchet your body up to high-burn.

Journey's Of Discoveries, by Ellis Paris Ramsay, ISBN:978-1-933113-43-2, Price:$16.95 Caitlyn (Cat) Craig is in an eleven year relationship with her partner Theo Gray when their lives are changed forever after a weekend in Napier, New Zealand. As a result of a motor car accident, Theo's life hangs in the balance. When Detective Sarah Adams, with her charming Irish brogue, gets involved, Cat's past life is about to catch up with her.

Josie & Rebecca: The Western Chronicles, by Vada Foster & BL Miller, ISBN:1-933113-38-3, Price:$18.99 - At the center of this story are two women; one a deadly gunslinger bitter from the injustices of her past, the other a gentle dreamer trying to escape the horrors of the present. Their destinies come together one fateful afternoon when the feared outlaw makes the choice to rescue a young woman in trouble. For her part, Josie Hunter considers the brief encounter at an end once the girl is safe, but Rebecca Cameron has other ideas....

Misplaced People, by C. G. Devize, ISBN:1-933113-30-8, Price:$17.99 - On duty at a London hospital, American loner Striker West is drawn to an unknown woman, who, after being savagely attacked, is on the verge of death. Moved by a compassion she cannot explain, Striker spends her off time at the bedside of the comatose patient, reading and willing her to recover. Still trying to conquer her own demons which have taken her so far from home, Striker is drawn deeper into the web of intrigue that surrounds this woman.

Murky Waters, by Robin Alexander, ISBN:1-933113-33-2, Price:$15.25 - Claire Murray thought she was leaving her problems behind when she accepted a new position within Suarez Travel and relocated to Baton Rouge. Her excitement quickly diminishes when her mysterious stalker makes it known that there is no place Claire can hide. She is instantly attracted to the enigmatic Tristan Delacroix, who becomes more of a mystery to her every time they meet. Claire is thrust into a world of fear, confusion, and passion that will ultimately shake the foundations of all she once believed.

None So Blind, by LJ Maas, ISBN:978-1-933113-44-9, Price:$16.50 - Torrey Gray hasn't seen the woman she fell in love with in college for 15 years. Taylor Kent, now a celebrated artist, has spent the years trying to forget, albeit unsuccessfully, the young woman who walked out of Taylor's life...

Picking Up The Pace, by Kimberly LaFontaine, ISBN:1-933113-41-3, Price:$15.50 - Who would have thought a 25-year-old budding journalist could stumble across a story worth dying for in quiet Fort Worth, Texas? Angie Mitchell certainly doesn't and neither do her bosses. While following an investigative lead for the Tribune, she heads into the seediest part of the city to discover why homeless people are showing up dead with no suspects for the police to chase.

Private Dancer, by T. J. Vertigo, ISBN:978-1-933113-58-6, Price:$16.95
Reece Corbett grew up on the mean streets of New York City.
Faith Ashford grew up wealthy with all the creature comforts that money provides. Faith wasn't like the other spoiled rich girls and had no desire to follow those rather shallow footsteps. Instead, the aspiring actress follows her dreams and finds a tall drink of water by the name of Reece Corbett who in turn had been looking for "this woman" all her life.

Southern Hearts, by Katie P Moore, ISBN:1-933113-28-6, Price:$16.95 - For the first time since her father's passing three years prior, Kari Bossier returns to the south, to her family's stately home on the emerald banks of the bayou Teche, and to a mother she yearns to understand.

Storm Surge, by KatLyn, ISBN:1-933113-06-5, Price:$16.95 - FBI Special Agent Alex Montgomery would have given her life in the line of duty, but she lost something far more precious when she became the target of ruthless drug traffickers. Recalled to Jacksonville to aid the local authorities in infiltrating the same deadly drug ring, she has a secret agenda--revenge. Despite her unexpected involvement with Conner Harris, a tough, streetwise detective who has dedicated her life to her job at the cost of her own personal happiness, Alex vows to let nothing--and no one--stand in the way of exacting vengeance on those who took from her everything that mattered.

These Dreams, by Verda Foster, ISBN:1-933113-12-X, Price:$15.75 - Haunted from childhood by visions of a mysterious woman she calls, Blue Eyes, artist Samantha McBride is thrilled when a friend informs her that she's seen a woman who bears the beautiful face she has immortalized on canvas and dreamed about for so long. Thrilled by the possibility that Blue Eyes might be a flesh and blood person, Samantha sets out to find her, certain the woman must be her destiny.

The Chosen, by Verda H Foster, ISBN:978-1-933113-25-8, Price:$15.25 - animals. That's the way it's always been. But the slaves are waiting for the coming of The Chosen One, the prophesied leader who will take them out of their bondage.

The Cost Of Commitment, by Lynn Ames, ISBN:1-933113-02-2, Price:$16.95 - Kate and Jay want nothing more than to focus on their love. But as Kate settles in to a new profession, she and Jay become caught up in the middle of a deadly scheme—pawns in a larger game in which the stakes are nothing less than control of the country.

The Gift, by Verda Foster, ISBN:1-933113-03-0, Price:$15.35 - Detective Rachel Todd doesn't believe in Lindsay Ryan's visions of danger, even when the horrifying events Lindsay predicted come true. That mistake could cost more than one life before this rollercoaster ride is over. Verda Foster's The Gift is just that – a well-paced, passionate saga of suspense, romance, and the amazing bounty of family, friends, and second chances. From the first breathless page to the last, a winner.

The Illusionist, by Fran Heckrotte, ISBN:978-1-933113-31-9, Price:$16.95 - Dakota Devereaus, an investigative journalist, is on a mission to uncover the secrets of Yemaya, The Illusionist. However, in her quest for an expose on this mysterious woman, she uncovers more than she bargained for. Dakota is targeted by a power hungry CEO, determined to learn The Illusionist's secret--at all costs-- and a madman intent on fulfilling his perverted fantasies.

The Last Train Home, by Blayne Cooper, ISBN:1-933113-26-X, Price:$17.75 - One cold winter's night in Manhattan's Lower East side, tragedy strikes the Chisholm family. Thrown together by fate and disaster, Virginia "Ginny" Chisholm meets Lindsay Killian, a street-smart drifter who spends her days picking pockets and riding the rails. Together, the young women embark on a desperate journey that spans from the slums of New York City to the Western Frontier, as Ginny tries to reunite her family, regardless of the cost.

The Price of Fame, by Lynn Ames, ISBN:1-933113-04-9, Price:$16.75 - When local television news anchor Katherine Kyle is thrust into the national spotlight, it sets in motion a chain of events that will change her life forever. Jamison "Jay" Parker is an intensely career-driven Time magazine reporter; she has experienced love once, from afar, and given up on finding it again...That is, until circumstance and an assignment bring her into contact with her past.

The Taking of Eden, by Robin Alexander, ISBN:978-1-933113-53-1, Price:$15.95 - Frustrated with life and death situations that she can't control, Jamie Spencer takes a new job at a mental health facility, where she believes she can make a difference in her patients' lives. The difference she makes in Eden Carlton's life turns her world upside down and out of control. A spur-of-the-moment decision sets in motion a turn of events that she is powerless to stop and changes her life and everyone around her forever.

The Value of Valor, by Lynn Ames, ISBN:1-933113-04-9, Price:$16.75
Katherine Kyle is the press secretary to the president of the United States. Her lover, Jamison Parker, is a respected writer for Time magazine. Separated by unthinkable tragedy, the two must struggle to survive against impossible odds...

The War between The Hearts, by Nann Dunne, ISBN:1-933113-27-8, Price:$16.95 - Intent on serving the Union Army as a spy, Sarah-Bren Coulter disguises herself as a man and becomes a courier-scout for the Confederate Army. Soon the savagery of war shakes her to the core. She stifles her emotions so she can bear the guilt of sending men, and sometimes boys, into paths of destruction.

With Every Breath, by Alex Alexander, ISBN:1-933113-39-1, Price:$15.25
Abigail Dunnigan wakes to a phone call telling her of the brutal murder of her former lover and dear friend. A return to her hometown for the funeral soon becomes a run for her life, not only from the murderer but also from the truth about her own well-concealed act of killing to survive during a war. As the story unfolds, Abby confesses her experiences in Desert Storm and becomes haunted with the past as the bizarre connection between then and now reveals itself. While the FBI works to protect her and apprehend the murderer, the murderer works to push Abby over the mental edge with their secret correspondence.